Ladies Who Lunch & Love

A NOVEL

Nathan Hale Williams

WHyN Press
NEW YORK/LOS ANGELES

ISBN: 0692488227

ISBN 13: 9780692488225

Library of Congress Control Number: 2015946652

WHyN Press, Los Angeles, CA

Ms. Wenequtt

Thank you for the

blessing that is your son!.

Hope you enjoy my ladies

Love,

Nadine Hale

"You come to love not by finding the perfect person,
but by seeing an imperfect person perfectly." – Sam Keen

Dedicated to my first lady who lunches –
Marcia "Momma J" Williams

Ladies Who Lunch & Love

Chapter One

Love & The City

Love is singularly the one thing we all pursue. We all have known it, and we all have lost it. It is ever changing and ever so confusing. Love (and its beguiling ways) is what makes us tick. It is the foundation of life and the core of our existence. Anyone professing to completely understand love is a liar. So I'll just say that I am its student. Whitney Houston was singing about it as I stepped in front of the mahogany floor-length mirror beside my matching bed. According to the song, she found out what she'd been missing, and it was love. Thankfully, just in time to be rescued, she discovered a lover who gave her good love. Good for her. For me, my love for the new leather blazer my parents sent would have to do for now. Love comes in many forms.

It was the occasion of my thirty-ninth birthday, and I'd screeched up to the edge of forty. Not sure what it is about the big 4-0 that perplexes the minds of men and women, but I was certainly not immune to its vexations. It is universally the age where you take full stock of everything you have done - and everything you have not. I was usually ecstatic about celebrating my special day, but the tolling bell made me less so.

Sure, there was plenty of love in my life. And yes, there was also a lot to be grateful for, and I am. I get to do what I love to do for a living. I also have a loving family rooted deeply in Chicago's south side. A bevy of dear friends who have become family. Oh, and we can't forget that one of the biggest loves of my life, New York City, is the place that I call home.

I was seven years old when I first visited the enormous metropolis that is New York, and I was instantly seduced. It felt so different from Chi-town. The smells, the rhythm of the city - intoxicating. From the moment my father opened the taxi door in front of my cousin's apartment building in the West Village neighborhood of Manhattan, I knew I had met my match. There was so much noise. So much going on. And the people! The people were all beautiful and dressed like in the movies. Everyone seemed to be going somewhere important to do important things. At seven years old, I knew this city would be my destiny. Don't know how I knew, but I did.

With every subsequent visit, I grew surer that no other city understood me quite like New York did. She was the one that made me feel normal, and so my love blossomed. As with any great lover, I knew that I had to make my move when the time was right, so I stayed just north of Chicago for college. At Northwestern University's Medill School of Journalism, I sharpened my wit, toughened my spirit, and for four years prepared to take on one of my biggest challenges. I wasn't afraid. I was ready. And so, I accepted an offer from *Time* magazine and, six days after graduation, took the plunge. The short, anxiety-filled plane ride required two vodkas on ice to soothe the energy brewing inside. The memory of stepping out of LaGuardia Airport into the summer air and inhaling the uniqueness that is the city of big dreams and challenges remains fresh. The summertime smell of New York is overwhelming for most. For me, it is perfume. Still, when I finally arrived at the apartment building on the Upper West Side where I had rented a small room from an older friend, I began to cry. At that moment, it finally dawned on me that I had realized my dream. I had proposed to my lifelong lover, and she had said, "Yes."

Now, as I walked in the brisk March air down Broadway to my birthday celebration, I smiled at the wonderful memories and big accomplishments. But, to be honest, New York and I had been through some rough times, too. She is the type of lover that can be abusive in a way that makes you like it. Makes you think the abuse is for your own good. And in many respects, she is right. Because eighteen years later, I was much wiser and stronger than I ever imagined I could be. She did that to me and required that of me. I had been broken down by her love and built up so many times that I believed that it was the way it was supposed to be.

Until today. As I peered over the cliff of middle age, I felt like something was missing. Or maybe what was missing had become more apparent. The uneasiness could stem from the major movie deal that fell through months ago. The work for a producer in New York is not a very deep well, and with the failure of that project my well had run dry. So I had made the decision to bite the bullet and leave. I was headed for the City of Angels armed with the belief that the abundance of opportunities in show business there would resurge my career and make things all right again.

The fact that I was leaving was a secret and I'd decided to make my big reveal tonight. Usually my birthdays are like a national holiday for me, a spectacle. But this year, I had surprised everyone by requesting an intimate cocktail and dinner situation with my dearest sister-friends and their partners. Sister-friends. I wish I could credit the term as an invention, but truthfully it was co-opted from the late and great Dr. Maya Angelou. It perfectly embodies the fullness of the relationship I have with five women who add sparkle and wonder to my life.

With each of them, the relationship is complex and simple at the same time, if that's possible to understand. I definitely have a male energy with them all that is paternal, chauvinistic, and downright obstinate. They quietly like the masculine thing with me, especially when it comes to those gentlemanly graces I've taught them all to expect from all men. My sister-friends pause at doors when a man is around. That's from me. My sister-friends expect a man to handle his responsibilities. Me. More importantly, my sister-friends expect the men in their lives to show up, be present, and be men. Yep, that's me, too. OK, I'm probably taking a little more credit than I deserve, but since I'm telling the story, we'll go with it.

Our closeness is partly attributable to the fact that sex is not a part of the equation. As a gay man, they are safe with me. Although I've been guilty of being an equal opportunity flirt, I'm not trying to sleep with them. Intimacy, yes. Sex, never. We cuddle. We hug and kiss. Not quite like brother and sister, but certainly not like lovers either. It's just special and wonderful and freshly loving. And, not your (stereo)typical gay best friend relationship either. Number one: I hate to shop (although thanks to them I know way more about designers and fashion than I care to admit). Can't do your hair or your makeup. I have never worn a pair of high heels. And please do not call me when the game is on (they ignore this all too often). No, these relationships fit no formula, and I like it like that. As much as I love New York, the real difficulty would be leaving them.

Just as I got sad contemplating how much I would miss them, a cat-sized rat ran in front of me, jumped his fat ass over a mountain of snow in a single bound and scurried down the sewer in the street. After letting out a shriek in stereo, I got over myself and picked up the pace. Love or not, it was time to get the hell out of New York.

The good news was that the Time Warner Center was only a couple more blocks away. I had convened this celebration at Stone Rose, one of my favorite bars. Great drinks, a killer view of Columbus Circle and Central Park, and its eclectic mix of people from the cool to the corporate made it so. One of my sister-friends, Rebecca, actually had an apartment upstairs so we were always able to get my favorite table by the window. Just like that and thanks to the rat, I had snapped out of the lamenting that was racing around in my mind, and I got excited. If for no other reason than the fact that these girls knew how to party and would not stop until I had enjoyed my birthday to the fullest.

"Happy birthday!" yelled Vikki from across the room, her usual exuberant self. The black knit dress she wore kissed the racetrack curves of her figure. She pranced toward me in sky-high stilettos, not caring that the entire room was watching. In fact, that was the point. A joy rushed over my spirit, and suddenly I was so happy to be exactly where I was. I didn't waste any time stopping at the hostess, weaving through the dimly lit room toward the oversized picture window where the rest of my sister-friends were sitting.

Vikki met me halfway with a warm, tight-gripped hug and a smooch on the cheek. Like a proud momma, she looked me up and down with a toothy smile that made me feel the love she had for me.

"Sweetie, you are serving me in that coat. Is it new?" she asked.

"Why thank you, and yes it is. Though I'm still mad that I'm wearing a coat and blazer three days into spring. Plus, I got attacked by a damn rat."

"In Columbus Circle?"

"It's New York. Rats are everywhere."

"Look on the bright side. You have a fabulous new coat to wear on your birthday!"

We continued our trail over to the rest of the group who had been standing waiting for our arrival. They let Vikki have her moment alone, as there was a silent hierarchy in the friendship that was understood, but without resentment. She was my best friend amongst best friends. She knew it. I knew it. They knew it. No shade, just reality.

"Happy birthday, dear! You look great," said Rebecca as she stepped up to hug me. She looked amazing too in an expensive-looking purple pantsuit that cinched at the waist of the jacket giving her a great shape. Undoubtedly, she'd worn my favorite color on purpose. Rebecca was that thoughtful. With her flawless caramel, wrinkle-free skin, you'd never know that, at forty-two, she was the oldest of the group. She still looked every bit of thirty with her brown, highlighted tresses up in a youthful ponytail. Rebecca always looked like money in whatever she wore. She should. She had a ton of it.

"Wait until I take off the coat! My mom and dad sent me that leather blazer I wanted."

"You are so spoiled," said Rebecca. "Mommy and Daddy still sending you gifts."

"Don't hate because my parents love me."

"Spoiled."

"You do look fabulous," said Lauren as she stepped up to hug me next. She flipped her blonde ringlets back, which made her blue eyes sparkle even more. At 5'10", she was my only sister-friend who would be caught alive in a pair of flat shoes. Never one for makeup, she maintained a freshness that made her seem naïve, but that would be a bad assumption if ever made. She was a nature girl, a modern-day hippie with an understated elegance that erred on the side of comfort and ease. Yet, it was her spirit that made her one of the best dressed in the room.

"Happy birthday, sir," added Josh, Lauren's handsome husband. He shook my hand and gave me a manly embrace. As we got close, I could tell he had started the party without me. But, that's what birthdays are all about - a celebration to be had by all.

I felt like royalty with such a grand entrance and an extended receiving line. Now it was time to join Josh and get the party started. On perfect cue, a slinky waitress in a short black skirt and a tight-fitting tank top draped by an apron approached as I began to peel off my outerwear.

"What can I get you?" she asked with a husky, Kathleen Turner-esque voice that immediately set my mind to work. Inspiration for new shows and films came from the most unexpected places. A leaf falling; a car screeching, and, this time, a voice. A blessing and a curse all in the same gift. If only producing all of those blossoming ideas were as simple as discovering them. That thought erased the inspiration just as quickly as it had come.

"He'll have a Grey Goose gimlet," proclaimed Vikki. I guess I'd taken too long to respond, still hanging on the tenor of the waitress's voice.

"What if I wanted something else?"

"Sweetie, you order one of two things. For twenty years. It's either a vodka gimlet or tequila on the rocks. Brands might have changed. Order hasn't."

"Well, that's not entirely true. We went through a French martini phase." The familiar voice corrected Vikki from behind me. It was Ruby, who was always fashionably late to everything. Her tardiness was so predictable that when meeting her one-on-one, I would either tell her the wrong time or purposely arrive late to avoid being irritated by sitting alone for thirty minutes or more. You have to meet your friends where they are, not where you want them to be. She also always came with a flair that was worthy of a post time arrival. Today was no exception. She was dressed to the nines - a chic, sexy Léger dress and a floor-length sandy fur coat that made her olive-toned skin shimmer and her auburn hair pop. The hair color was natural (hence the name), and today it was swept in an intentionally loose chignon (a term learned from early episodes of a secret, guilty pleasure - *Top Model*). People always questioned her ethnicity, and she rarely disabused them of their uncertainty. It allowed her to play in many circles, and Ruby manipulated the exotic ambiguity masterfully.

"Yes, we did. From 2006 to 2009, I believe."

"Happy birthday, babes! Glad I'm not too late."

"Depends on your definition of *too*, considering you arrived after the birthday boy." The snide remark came from Vikki, who was not the biggest fan of that precious stone.

"Vikki, always with the quick wit," quipped Ruby.

"Oh Ruby, I'm just joking. Lighten up."

"I'm ligh…"

"Ruby, I swear you never gain weight. How's that possible?" Lauren's interruption was timed perfectly to avoid the gladiator showdown that was brewing.

Rebecca stood up as an additional intervening force, "She'll never tell her secrets." I have to admit I was a little bummed that they didn't let it continue. Vikki and Ruby's exchanges are the thing of which legends are made. As the kids say, a vintage read. For the most part, my sister-friends got along, but there was something about Ruby that made her take a seat outside. To me, she was everything that was fabulous - over the top, gorgeous, sexy, sexual, and a fighter. St. Louis had spawned killer edges. New York had camouflaged those edges in Prada and Lanvin. Thinking about the many head-to-heads by these two made me wonder where was Krissy, the only other person who enjoyed the battles as much as I did. She, unlike Ruby, was never late, especially for my birthday party (or any party), which made me worry.

"Did anyone talk to Krissy? And what happened to Gerand, Rebecca?" I asked.

"Gerand is still working, as usual. He's going to drop by to say hi, though a bit later. Haven't spoken to Krissy in about a week."

"I saw her last night at an event at the Studio Museum. She said she would see me here, so I know she's coming," added Lauren. "You know Krissy wouldn't miss this. Something obviously came up with work."

"Why don't you call her, sweetie," suggested Rebecca. "We all know you won't rest until all of your angels are here, Charlie."

Without delay, I pulled out my phone and said, "Call Krissy mobile." Modern technology has rendered me dumb when it comes to remembering telephone numbers, even those of my best friends. Just as the phone was "Calling Krissy mobile" I felt a tap on my shoulder. Seeing the smile on Lauren's face, I knew it was my ride-or-die chick. I quickly turned around. "Krissy!!!"

"Yasss, she has arrived hunty! Now, the party can begin," said Krissy in the way only she could. I really do believe there is a gay man trapped in that full-figured body. If you took away the breasts, the ass, and well, everything else that definitely made Krissy a woman, left over would be some man named Percy or 'Twan. "Chile, I'm so sorry I'm late. I was trying to leave the office, and I think there's an alarm that goes off when I put on my coat. I was like, don't you see me tryna' go. You know how it is, though. I got here as fast as a bitch could in 5-inch Choos hunty."

"Just so happy to see you. Happy to see all of you! I was a bit down earlier about this birthday, but now it's all good."

"Why?" quizzed Rebecca as we sat down and the waitress brought over my gimlet.

"Next year is the big one, that's why."

"Oh, for goodness sake, forty came and went. I barely noticed. You'll be fine. You're handsome. Successful. You have the most wonderful friends a guy could wish for. If I may say so myself," joked Rebecca as she patted her chest with a faux arrogance.

"I know, I know. I am truly blessed, but..."

"Um, aren't you the one that always says blessings don't have a but?" reminded Lauren. I hate it when my words come back to bite me in the ass.

"I think we need some shots," proclaimed Krissy as she stood and motioned the waitress over. That was the signal that it was about to go down. Whenever someone orders the first round of shots, we all know they won't stop until the job is done. The good news is the older I got; the faster the job got done. The bad news is the recovery time was much longer. None of that mattered now. It was time to get the party started.

"It's my birthday!!!!!" I was genuinely happy about it in the way that I had been happy about this day for the previous thirty-eight years. I was grateful to be celebrating another year, especially with the family that surrounded me. My family by love.

"Let me offer a toast to my best friend, trusted adviser, and most dependable person I know. We love you. Happy birthday!" said Vikki.

A chorus of "Cheers" made the entire room look at our table. "Thank you guys for helping me celebrate. I appreciate you so much. And I have some news to share." I took a long deep breath and then downed the extra shot on the table. A little liquid courage wouldn't hurt. "I'm moving to Los Angeles." I was expecting a reaction but not the dead silence I received. In a flicker, the party went from joyous celebration to funereal pall. I looked around at all of their crooked faces trying to fix themselves without much success. "Well, that went over well," I muttered while taking a sip of my gimlet.

"How'd you expect it to go? We're here celebrating your damn birthday, and your ass springs that you're moving across the fucking country during the toast," Krissy always kept it real.

"Let's not turn this into something it doesn't need to be. We're just shocked, love. It was kind of awkward timing," reasoned Lauren.

"I just wanted to get it over with. You know it's been rough lately. And for years people have been telling me that things would happen easier in LA. I love New York, and I love you guys. But I gotta keep it moving."

"That's understandable. But it is a bit sudden, dear...for us. That's all," said Rebecca sadly.

"I'm not moving tomorrow. It'll take me some time to get everything in order."

"I must say I'm shocked that this is the first time I'm hearing about this," Vikki said in a way that made me know she was more than shocked, she was upset. She did have a point. I should have told Vikki I was even contemplating such a big change. I shared most things with her and couldn't think of a reason why I hadn't shared this except that I was scared that she would talk me out of it. There was certainly still time for her to do just that, and I would be lying if part of me didn't want her to do it. Being in one place so long makes you feel slightly incapable of making an adjustment to a completely new city with a very different vibe and culture. So yes, part of me wanted Vikki and the rest of them to talk me out of it. It would make it so much easier. Yet, I knew none of them would.

"Look y'all, I didn't mean this to come off like bad news. You all have your lives, your families, your careers all set. I'm still hustling hard and clearly not getting any younger. It's now or never."

"I say fuck it, do what you have to do for you," came from Ruby, of course. Vikki shot daggers in Ruby's direction and took a long sip of her drink.

"So, when are you planning to move?" asked Lauren.

"Not sure yet. Like I said, it's going to take some planning. I've been here for eighteen years, so it's not like I can just jump up and leave. But, I promise, I will keep you all in the loop." Vikki had a look of doubt on her face. "I promise."

"You know we support you no matter what. Let us know if we can help." Lauren was always considerate.

"Yeah, good luck, bro. You know I'm always there anyway, so I'll get to see you probably even more," said Josh with his blue eyes getting a hazier shade of red by the minute.

"Of course, dear, anything you need. We're here," added Rebecca.

"Chile, you know I got your back. At least I'm gonna have a place to stay in L.A. now," joked Krissy.

All eyes shifted to Vikki who was still pouting. "I don't like it. Not one bit, and I'm going to be a twelve-year-old for a minute. But, you know good and well..." Her smile was forced, but I knew there was sincerity underneath. "It's a good thing we're all going on vacation to Miami because I certainly need it now."

"Stop being so dramatic."

"I know you're not calling me dramatic, mister 'hey y'all, I'm headed to LA, deuces.'"

"Oop! I'm with her, boo! I think this calls for some more shots," and then Krissy stood up and motioned for the waitress. It was time to resume the party.

Chapter Two

Miami Heat

"Meet you by the pool. I'm going to work on my tan," declared Vikki as she flung a bright, floppy sun hat on her head and sashayed out of the door. She was as good at exits as she was at entrances. Two weeks later, Krissy, Lauren, Rebecca, and I had collected ourselves at Vikki's Miami beachfront pied-à-terre (although there was nothing 'pied' about it) for some rejuvenation and reconnection.

Vikki was the master coordinator and hostess, always rallying the troops to pull it together, adjust schedules, and make each year happen. It was our springtime ritual and always right on time because the weather in New York in April can be fickle and the snowstorm that happened three days before we left was proof and encouragement to leave. Initially, the trip was labeled a "girl's weekend," until I protested the entire first time, and since then it had become a much-anticipated prelude to summer fun. It was now called "our weekend," and the trips over the years had yielded some classic times, unforgettable memories, and countless vows of secrecy. South Beach with my sister-friends is a perfectly situated vacation. Sun. Great food. Great nightlife. Great people watching.

It didn't hurt that Vikki's condo in the Fountainbleu was über fabulous with wraparound balconies and a 180-degree view of the beach and downtown Miami in the distance. A prize from her first divorce from Mark, the basketball player who liked to play with more than basket…balls. They met while she was getting her master's from Georgetown and he was playing for Washington. Mark treated Vikki very well, and they seemed like the ideal jet-set couple. She was an intelligent bombshell basketball wife, and he was a star in the league. After they were married, I remember saying to her, "Girl, you're rich!" Her reply was innocently matter of fact, "I know." Vikki was the first truly rich friend I ever had, and Mark's and her extreme generosity also allowed for their families and close friends to enjoy it, too. Not excessively because Vikki was always great with money and Mark trusted her to manage theirs for them, but they certainly didn't let the Benjamins collect too much dust.

After Vikki finished her degree, they made New York their permanent residence even though Mark still played in Washington. Vikki commuted between their apartment in New York and their house in the nation's capitol. To some, the setup was odd. But if you knew Vikki and her free spirit, it was perfect. Until the night Vikki surprised Mark and dropped in on their DC home unexpectedly. The surprise turned out to be on her when she walked in on Mark getting an extra "coaching" session from the team's assistant coach. Shocked but not devastated, Vikki and Mark settled things quickly to avoid any media attention, and the settlement made Vikki a very rich but single woman. It always concerned me how nonchalantly she dealt with it all. At first, I admired her strength to accept things as they were, but later I worried that she had failed to deal with the shocking way her marriage ended. I think that she had her suspicions all along, which is why she wasn't as surprised as the rest of us were when it happened. But she didn't want to talk about it. One thing about Vikki is that you don't question her when she says something. My job was to help her find a new (straight) man. It has been said, "The best way to get over an old lover is to get under a new one." So I put her through gaydar boot camp. It was like I was training her for the Olympics, making her jump and leap as we encountered various men. He's straight. He's not. He ain't sure. Hell no. Making a joke out of it all made it easier for her. She might not have gotten to the box of wine, terrycloth robe, and Oreos phase of heartbreak, but she was human. No matter if she wanted to talk about it or not. So we made her search for a new man a game.

In truth, finding a man was no hard task for Vikki. Her unfortunate fate always came during the selection process. Invariably, she picked men, who ultimately weren't looking for her. Had her name been Victor, she would've been perfect for Mark. Had she been a high-paid prostitute, she would've been just right for Paul, her second husband. Such a fantastic human being deserved to find love, and it often bummed me out that she'd been so unlucky. Something was wrong, and I couldn't quite understand it. Still, to her credit, Vikki never gave up trying. She could've easily resolved to be bitter and single. Instead, she chose to keep getting back in the saddle every time she got knocked off. Determined, she was going to find her M.R. — Mister Right.

By the time the rest of us descended on the pool at the posh hotel/condo complex, Vikki had ordered a round of drinks and was flanked by two gorgeous men in our private cabana. Vikki doesn't waste time.

"Jack and Bobby, meet my wonderful friends," Vikki shouted as we neared the cabana. The guys stood up and began to greet the ladies first. I picked up the rear. I couldn't help but notice the perfection of their chiseled, tanned physiques. No one could ever say that Vikki didn't have good taste.

"Sweetie, Jack and Bobby are team players, and it's for yours," whispered Vikki to me through a slanted grin as she took a sip of a frothy frozen cocktail.

"President...Senator," I joked as I shook both of their hands. I could tell the joke went over their heads, but my sister-friends laughed. Beauty plus brains is a rare package. It didn't matter, Miami is about eye candy, and the "Kennedys" were satisfying to any sweet tooth.

"I took the liberty of ordering a round of cocktails," said Vikki.

"Looks like that's not all you ordered," chimed in Krissy, who was also taking in the confections.

"Well, you know how I do. Nothing but the best for my friends, sweetie." We all laughed as the boys stood there looking perfect and clueless. Conversation is overrated anyway. Plus, I had my girls for mental stimulation.

"What do you all want to do for dinner tonight?" asked Vikki.

"Let's do Prime 112," suggested Krissy.

Rebecca jumped in, "Oh no. You know Prime 112 equals gluttony, and I refuse to walk around South Beach with my stomach poking out. I've been working hard in the gym, and I plan to show it off. We can save that for the last day."

"I agree. Let's do Lario's on Ocean. Love the drinks, and the food is decent," I offered as a compromise.

"OK, I'll have the concierge make a reservation. Now that's settled. Time for a little Vikki update of her own."

"Y'all and these updates. You're moving, too," Krissy questioned sarcastically.

"Oh, hell no! New York is where I will die."

"When you have condos around the world, what's the point of moving," I joked.

"Stop it. Now listen, I'm not moving. It is important, though." We all settled into our lounge chairs and prepared ourselves. With Vikki, you never could be sure what the latest was. Of all my sister-friends, her life was the most dynamic. She'd lived all over the world, was involved in a million things, and knew everyone there was to know. She definitely lived the fabulous life.

"I met a boy!"

"A boy or a man?" quizzed Lauren.

"A man, but slightly younger. Not cougar town, but definitely fresher than the guys I've dated in the past."

"Ain't nothing wrong with a virile young man tuning up your engine. I say, get it if you can, when you can, and as often as you can," said Krissy. She and Rebecca clicked glasses.

"Believe it or not, no tuning has gone on." Everyone took a pause and just stared at Vikki.

I asked the questioned, "Well, how long have you been seeing, um...?"

"Dax. His name is Dax. And it's been about nine months."

"Wait, didn't I just get lambasted on my birthday for keeping secrets. You've been dating someone for nine months and didn't tell me? The nerve, you little cradle- robbing hussy," I chided as Rebecca and I burst into laughter.

Krissy was still stuck on Vikki's other statement, "You've been dating for nine months, and you haven't hit it?"

"Nope. We're waiting. Girl, you know sex will screw shit up. If it's good. Flashlights, hoodies, and drive-bys. If it's bad, forget about it. The finest man can get ugly real quick."

A chorus of Amens.

Vikki continued, "And for the record, I kept it to myself because I get tired of introducing guys to the group and then it doesn't work out. I wanted to see where it was going first."

Immediately, my mind went to Vikki's track record, and with a name like Dax I was skeptical. What warm-blooded, heterosexual man would wait nine months before expecting a little playtime?

"I'm sure you've done other things. Girl, I know you," said Krissy.

"Nope. Just kissing and a bit of foreplay. Don't get it twisted, Momma's checked out the equipment and it's all good...and then some."

"You could give me an electric drill, but please don't ask me to build something with it," preached Krissy as she sat back with her arms folded. Not hearing the chorus she said, "I guess y'all don't hear me."

"Naw, you're right!" Every good congregation knows its cues. "Say that!"

"Wow! Viks, tell us more about this freak of nature," I said while continuing to sip on one of the most delicious gimlets I'd ever been served.

"We met at a friend's art showing in London. I was there doing my obligatory three weeks for the magazine, and he was there on vacation. He founded an e-commerce site with some friends from MIT, it went public and made him a multimillionaire by age thirty. Since then, he's been working on a new company and just traveling. We were both tired of the hot, two-week flings, so we decided to wait and get to know each other first."

"Yes, you are definitely the Queen of the quick-and-burn," I added. Rebecca cut her eyes at me. It was the truth.

"No, he's right. It's no secret that I haven't had the best time in the love department. Well, that's not true. I've had a great time," Vikki laughed, as did we all. "But so far, so good."

"Do things differently for a different result. Get it. I just can't believe no sex," I said.

"Sweetie, I learned how to take care of me a long time ago."

"OK," exclaimed Krissy as she high-fived Vikki.

"Jack and Bobby, do you mind getting us all another round of cocktails. Tell them it's on my account," purred Vikki to the two statues I'd forgotten were even there. My memory returned as they stood up, revealing again their perfection. Certainly, they had the "don't speak, just be pretty" thing down. We all enjoyed watching them walk away and then Vikki dropped a bomb, "He's asked me to marry him."

I almost spit out the last swallow of my gimlet. Almost. A professional never wastes good liquor. "And what did you say?" I asked after swallowing.

"I told him that I'd think about it. But I'm going to say yes...I think."

"Really? Without giving it a test drive?"

Vikki nodded. "I can't describe how this man makes me feel. It's unlike any man I've met before."

"But you've only known him for..."

"Nine months, I know. But, I feel as if I've known him for a lifetime. It's beyond crazy, which is why I told him I'd have to think about it. Still, it's the good kind of crazy and, yeah, I love him."

"I say fuck it! Go for it. What's the worst that can happen? You get a divorce. You've been there, done that," chimed in Krissy.

"I don't know. I mean, I haven't even met him yet," I said.

"Didn't you meet the other two? Look what good that did," added Krissy. I snarled at her comment, albeit a valid one. Who was I to make myself the arbiter of Vikki's love life?

"But he'll be in New York in three weeks. You can meet him then."

I took a moment to take in my gorgeous sister-friend. She was aglow with the excitement of love. It's what we all want to feel and what we want for our friends. I chilled my skepticism and looked forward to meeting Mr. Dax in the Big Apple.

"Only one thing to do," Krissy said with the most excited and devilish expression. "Bachelorette party begins tonight!!!!"

Vikki stood up with both hands in the air to proclaim, "I'm in Miami, bitch!"

◆ ◆ ◆

I had to retract my statement about Lario's food being decent because our meal was delicious. The time since I had been there last made me forget that it was a great place. For some reason, there was always some anticipation that I would see Gloria Estefan in the restaurant that she owned. In my many visits, it never came to pass. We still had an exceptional time at dinner. We also had an exceptional number of mojitos. As we strolled along Ocean Drive taking in the activity, the bodies, and the too-many-already folks, we didn't feel much pain either. Miami is a fun place to be when it's not a major weekend or event. Too many drunken college kids and old folks acting like college kids stumbling and fumbling about to really enjoy it. Although my girls were mature, none of them were matronly. So it was a hassle dealing with the "Hey, babies," "Where you goin', girls," and my all-time favorite, "Yo', shorty." Other places, a man could tell these were not the kind of women that would respond to the primitive advances no matter how chiseled a face and body he had. Miami, during a holiday weekend, they didn't seem to care.

It was perfect now because the weather was great. There was an energy that Miami owns that was present. And I didn't have to worry about dragging out the south side of Chicago to defend one of my girl's honor after she let some drunken boy know that he was being disrespectful.

"I want to go to a gay club tonight," declared Vikki.

"Nahhh, let's do the W rooftop. The gay clubs here are not fun...even for me," I protested.

"It's her bachelorette party she gets to choose." Lauren's diplomacy seemingly knows no limit. It was racking my nerves, though, right now, and it wasn't really her bachelorette party. The last place I wanted to be was some thirsty and dingy club when there were so many beautiful spaces to keep the party going in the MIA. I knew I was ultimately going to get outnumbered because my sister-friends liked going to the club with the guys who told them they were beautiful, bought them drinks, and didn't act like predators searching for their next prey. They could let down their hair and be appreciated for their fabulousness without much worry. In Miami, a couple of them had been known to make out with a guy or two all the while insisting that it didn't count because he really wasn't interested. Then the rest of us would be pinky-sworn to secrecy during our sober recollections the next morning.

Just as I was coming around to the idea, a slightly plump guy in "Daisy Dukes" and a tight tank top from Baby Gap with two gorgeous women stopped in front of us. I recognized them all but couldn't place from where.

"Vikki girl, when did you get back to Miami? You didn't call me," said the man in the Dukes. The two girls he was with immediately pulled out their cell phones and took four steps away from us. Clearly, they didn't want to be bothered. That's cool.

"We just got here, Tony. You know I was going to call you tomorrow. I can't go too long without getting this wig fixed."

"You better not let anyone else touch that head. I have people watching, girl."

"Never." The rest of us just stood there waiting for an introduction. The fact that one hadn't been given made me presume it was intentional on Vikki's part.

"What y'all doing tonight?" asked Tony Dukes.

"Awwh, we just had a great dinner. We're going to head back home and chill out. It's been a long day." The lack of introduction was definitely intentional. Two minutes ago she was talking about getting it turned up with the boys.

"Oh, alright then. We're going to the club."

"You kids have fun. I'll call you tomorrow," said Vikki.

"OK, chica. Nice to meet you guys," said Tony, although we all knew we hadn't met. The two cell phones walked off in front of him, and he followed quickly as I noticed he had on kitten heel sandals to match the Daisy Dukes.

We kept walking along Ocean collectively waiting for them to be out of earshot. As soon as they were I asked, "Who is he?"

"Sweetie, that's Ms. Tony from that show *The Ladies of Miami*. He does my hair when I'm here."

"He's not one of the ladies, is he?" asked Lauren genuinely.

"He thinks so. No, the two deaf mutes were on the show until they got kicked off for fighting."

"Isn't that the point?" It was the lawyer's turn to ask as the encounter left so many questions for us all. Krissy may be round the way, but she is a round the way high-powered attorney who would never be caught on a reality show — showing out.

"No judgment. I have watched my fair share. I always feel guilty after I do, though using work as my excuse," I said.

Lauren was confused, "You wouldn't produce a show like that, would you?"

"Shit. If the money is right." Lauren looked surprised while Krissy and Vikki laughed. "I'm just kidding. Calm down. It's a messed-up portrayal of women, particularly women of color. Personally, my biggest issue is the way all of those shows portray black gay men. We all don't rock Daisy Dukes, carry purses, or wear high heels. Not knocking those that do, but if that's all you see, I have a problem."

"You should write about that for the magazine. I was thinking about a piece about how straight women have co-opted so much of the language, mannerisms, etc. of gay men. I wonder if that makes us more or less lady-like or appealing to straight men," said the always working and thinking Vikki. "Let's talk about it when we get back to New York. It'll be a tight deadline. The issue closes in less than three weeks."

"I haven't written a piece for a magazine in years. The creative juices haven't been flowing much either lately. Actually in a very long time."

"I will pay you as a feature."

"Deal." The money was right.

Chapter Three

Hedging Her Bets

The unique click-clack of six-inch stilettos walking up the steps of my apartment hallway got louder and louder. It was undeniably the signature sound of Krissy. It was the signal that a good time was in store. Krissy is always a popped Champagne bottle bursting with life. She's the number dialed when it's time to shake the world off. If fun had a college, Krissy would be the dean.

"I'm not coming back to your place until you get an elevator," she puffed through her fire-engine red lips. I don't know why she'd opted for such a bold lip color. Her lips were loud and clear without any lipstick. But that was Krissy. We hadn't seen each other since Miami, so we'd planned a night of catch up and fun.

"It's three damn flights!" I closed the door behind her and motioned for her to take off her stilts.

"Don't worry, boo, I brought my slippers. You and these damn floors." Yes, I don't want my floors scuffed so I make people take off their shoes. One of the perks of living in a brownstone in Harlem is having gorgeous hardwood floors. Plus, luck had been on my side when I found this floor-through apartment in a renovated building in SoHa. To be clear, I don't mean SoHo, which is the area in Manhattan that is "South of Houston" Street. No, I live in SoHa, a gentrified area in Harlem that is south of 125th Street. More "non-natives" live here. The rent and mortgages are higher because of it.

Friends who live in Brooklyn tease me about Harlem still being the ghetto. Depending on the season, time of day, and block they might be right, but you get so much more for your money than any other place in Manhattan. Well, at least that used to be the case. Never mind, the point is that I still live in Manhattan and don't have to take an airplane to Brooklyn every day. My address says, "New York, NY!" Enough said.

A Harlem native, Krissy always shuts the argument down with her ode to the virtues of being from "Harlem, USA." It's not even a separate city, but don't say that to a real Harlemite, Krissy included. She is arguably the queen of Harlem. Stylish to a trendy fault. Outspoken with a distinctively uptown accent. Can walk into any restaurant, bar, liquor store, and Popeye's chicken in Harlem and get "hooked up." Krissy is synonymous with Harlem. But she *lives* on the Upper West Side. "I didn't have to live in Harlem all of my life to love it. I earned my George-and-Weezy moment, and I've moved on up."

Full of all her brilliant contradictions, my most brash sister-friend plopped her curvy frame on my sofa, grabbed a pillow and asked, "What's for dinner?" Once a month we took turns cooking, watched trash TV, gossiped and talked about our love lives. I loved when it was her turn because Krissy is an exceptional cook. Truth be told, Krissy is exceptional at everything she does, except dating. Upwardly mobile though she was, Krissy had a penchant for downwardly spiraling guys. Black guys, white guys, Latino guys, (and one Korean) it didn't matter. If you were down and out, a deadbeat, good for nothing, "waiting on a big settlement check," you name it...you were the man for Krissy.

"I'm taking you out to the Red Rooster instead!" Krissy looked at me and rolled her eyes. You would've thought I killed someone given the epic pause she took.

"Nope. Not gonna do it. You will not drag me down to that sadiddy ass place with all of those old people. Nope. Not happening tonight, bruh."

"It's not like that, and you need to try some places other than the Shrine and Moca. We have options these days. After what just went down with Carlos, you need a nice banker or lawyer."

"I don't want a nice banker or lawyer." The last three words in a mocking tone.

"Oh so you'd rather keep having to bail your boyfriends out of jail every other week."

"I let his ass stay there last time, remember. Anyway, bail money here or there is better than some prissy, controlling, narcissistic, arrogant, overcompensating, little dick metrosexual. I deal with their asses at work every day. I certainly don't need to be fucking one. Nope. I'll go home and order in. You go to the Rooster and hobnob. I'm tired and not feeling that situation. At all!"

This was going to take some of my reserve mojo to get her to go. "After dinner, they're having an ole' skool hip hop party, and we're on the VIP list." She didn't budge and instead sat there with her red lips tightly pursed.

"DJ Poison Ivy is spinning." Her favorite DJ had been hired for the night when my good friend, the general manager, called in a panic about a canceled DJ. I saw it as an opportunity and recommended Poison Ivy. Still, she didn't move. "OK, damn! If you go and you don't like it, I will go with you to the Shrine."

"What!? You at the Shrine? I might walk hot coals to see that. I know I'm not going to like it, so I'm down. I want it on record that I'm going under extreme protest. Let me run home real quick and change."

"I got you boo," I returned the mocking favor. "You have at least four outfits in my closet from times we've passed out here. I had them cleaned. And they all match your pumps." Krissy gave me that "you such and such" look. "Exactly. You're not going to get home and call back saying you're tired. Or not call at all and pretend like you "accidentally" fell asleep. I know your moves, hookah!"

"I hate your ass," she exclaimed while pulling out makeup from an enormous Chloé duffel bag! Krissy never went anywhere without a full-on makeup kit. She was always Boy Scout-prepared to kick it. "I'm telling you the minute some geriatric Don Juan comes up to me, we are out! So get your slow whine ready 'mon! We'll be at the Shrine in no time. Bwoh bwoh!"

"I thought the Shrine only played Fela's music like the Broadway show?" Krissy just shook her head at me and walked into the bedroom to change.

◆ ◆ ◆

When we walked into the brimming Rooster, my friend whisked us to our table. Since it opened, the restaurant had been overflowing with the who's who. Famed Swedish (by way of Ethiopia) chef Marcus Samuelsson struck gold when he decided to merge upscale dining and soul food right on the top edge of SoHa. Downtown elite flocked for the buzz and cool points, Harlem's elite flocked for the convenience and people watching. Before the Rooster landed, we hadn't had an "it" place in Harlem in a while, and it quickly became the place to be seen. Even President Obama made a well-noted visit when it first opened.

We were seated at one of the tables in the bustling bar, which I had specifically requested. I was here on a mission to introduce my sister-friend to some truly eligible bachelors. Ones without maxed-out credit cards and multiple baby mamas. A guy who was sincerely interested in more than a casual relationship. She wouldn't admit it to you, but I knew Krissy could hear that clicking Timex in her womb. Oh wait. We're talking about Krissy, so it would be a diamond and gold Rolex. Either way, I knew she wanted kids, so it was time to stop playing around.

As we settled in, I could see her face crinkling up. A defense mechanism.

"Stop it," I whispered. A chic group of three sat next to us at the communal table. Krissy glanced at her bedazzled watch. "And why are you looking at your watch? We just got here?"

"I'm making sure I have enough time to catch the DJ at the Shrine." Pursed lips poking out as she continued to survey the room disapprovingly. Frankly, I'm not sure what she was sneering at because the bar was brimming with gorgeous, sophisticated people having a good time. With some places, I agree, they can be a pretentious snooze. It's why I spend little time on the Upper East Side. The Rooster though, was elite, not elitist. Big difference.

"My dear, so good to see you!" A friendly meow at our side revealed one of Harlem's mainstays and resident divas, Tina Jones. "A hot mocha-chocolatta," was her self-given, appropriate handle as she always percolated with a graceful sex appeal that turned everyone on. And I mean everyone. Perfect timing because she and Krissy had been friends for years. Maybe Krissy would lighten up a little bit.

"Tina girl, I was just thinking about you," said Krissy as she hopped down and exchanged air kisses with the buxom diva. Tina was what they called a brick house back in the day. She wasn't full-figured like Krissy, but her old school Coca-Cola bottle body was definitely stacked. It would be easy to imagine Tina on the cover of one of those men's magazines back in the day. Still, in her mid-forties she was very well maintained.

"Chile please, I've been trying to cocktail with you for weeks. Another invitation, and I'd start to think I was trying to get in your panties. But, I can't be mad when you bring such wonderful eye candy for Ms. Tina to devour like this beast right here." Tina slithered up to me in the way only a true siren could and pushed her perfect breasts firmly against my chest.

"You know how to make a man smile. Tina, you look fab as always. And don't feel bad. I practically had to offer her my first born to get her here." I stood up and gave her a tight, suggestive squeeze and was treated to a whiff of the most intoxicating perfume. Tina, if nothing else, was an expert at presentation.

Krissy jumped back in, "Girl, you know how I am. Save the snobbery and foolishness for someone else. I like my bars and men hood."

"But, it's not '99, we're grown-ups now. Even Jay-Z wears suits for goodness sake. You're way too educated and successful to be holding onto that Boyz N Da Hood fantasy. It's so passé!" Tina has a way of doing and saying things that on someone else's tongue would be offensive. Her air, though, was digestible as a result of its authenticity.

"Thank you, Tina. I've been trying to tell her that," I said, affirming the validity of my mission.

"Look, you both can suck it. I like what I like, end of story. Now, all I care about is the fact that I'm thirsty."

"Well, by all means, I never stand in the way of a cocktail." A tall European- looking man walked up and grabbed Tina by her waist. Without turning around, she began to smile. "I know the strength of those hands. It can be no one else, but Fredrik." Tina turned around and melted in the handsome man's arms. He embraced her with all his might. Another one of Tina's multi-million dollar conquests, no doubt. Never married, but she knew how to pull them rich and fine. She'd once said that marriage bored her, and she thought it bored every man that she'd met. She liked the freedom of being able to go when she was ready. Keeping it cute and casual. That was ten years ago, though. I wondered to myself if she still felt the same.

"As you can see my knight in shining has arrived, so we must ride off." And then, Tina did just that without introducing us. Again, that was the way she rolled. I would've thought it rude of anyone else, but I know Tina and she never intends to be rude. She just didn't want to waste our time and his time with introductions that would ultimately not matter. She'd be riding another thoroughbred very soon.

The manager sent over some drinks to the table as well as a sampling of Samuelsson's delish appetizers. In New York City, knowing people is essential to survival. I was hungry and Krissy was clearly thirsty because that Long Island traveled down her throat like a bullet train. She was motioning to the waiter for another before I had even taken a sip of my gimlet.

"I hope you'll let me buy the next one for you," said a distinguished, deep voice behind me. I turned slightly, but before I could see who it was, Krissy jumped on it.

"No, thank you. I can buy my own drinks. And how do you know I'm not on a date already. Rude." Just as Krissy was putting him in his place, I got a full view of my friend, Edmond.

"'Cause he knows we're not on a date, Evilene. Edmond, wassup man? How've you been?" I stood up to give him a handshake and shoulder bump.

"Life's good, but it would be much better if you stop hiding all your fine friends from us. I know where all the women are. They're with you." We both laughed, but Edmond did have a point. Most of my sister-friends had it going on, and so did Edmond He was a man's man handsome. The kind my mother's generation found irresistible. A Denzel-like swagger, but lighter and much younger. Maybe twenty-five, he still had a regal carriage that belied his real age but complimented his good looks. He was definitely cheetah hunting with Krissy. As Miss Celie says, in my favorite film, *The Color Purple*, "I was waiting to see what color the wall gon' be."

"So can I buy your next round of drinks, or are you gonna continue to put up a fight?" Edmond directed his attention back to Krissy. His eyes tightly and seductively fixed on her face. He was good. Damn good. Wasn't sure how this one was going to turn out. Rocky versus Tyson. Two heavyweights engaged in the ring.

"If I say yes, then you'll think that's an invitation to interrupt my night. If I say no, you'll think I'm a bitch and leave us alone. You seem quick, you figure out which option I'm going with." Krissy then got up from the table and went to the bar and ordered another Long Island. It was going to be a long night.

Edmond shook it off, gave me a fist pound and laughed at Krissy as he walked away. I guess Tyson kicked Rocky's ass tonight. It was a speechless transaction. There was nothing left to be said after Krissy had hammered that, period. I sat there stunned, waiting for her return.

As Tyson pumped back to the table, I could tell she was proud of herself because she was pumping extra hard sipping on her drink. She eased back onto the stool, crossed her legs and sat up erect, daring me to scold her. I didn't oblige the provocation. She knew what she had done, and I wasn't going to dignify it by responding to it. She was a grown woman, and she knew better. I heard so many women complain so much about men; the lack of good prospects, how they're approached, how they're treated, and then a nice guy like Edmond steps up and Krissy acts a fool. I was done. I decided it was time to abort my mission to upgrade her. If she wanted to stay exactly where she was, I was going to let her.

Defeated and annoyed, I said, "We can head over to the Shrine. Let me just pay the bill." Sensing my frustration, Krissy's proud chest deflated a bit, and she put down her glass. In silence, she looked around the bar. I could tell it was the first time she was seeing them without the lens of judgment. Everyone was enjoying the night and could care less about Krissy's presumptuous attitude. She relaxed even more.

"I thought you said they had good greens here," she said by way of an apology. I knew it was the most she could muster, so I took it as such. I motioned to the cocktail waiter who was standing by the bar. A short Latino guy with a goatee and ear-length curly hair approached the table with a smile. I couldn't tell if he was smiling so hard at Krissy or at me. I was happy that she'd decided to calm down that it didn't matter. I ordered some greens and another gimlet for me.

And then we began to do what we do best—have some fun. We gossiped, laughed, drank more, and encouraged each other. One of the things I loved most about Krissy is that when it comes to work, she is beyond focused. She has Ferrari-like drive and an unrelenting will to succeed. When you walk along the road less traveled, you need other people in your life that push you to be your best and sympathize when you've been beaten up and are struggling. Despite all of her brashness, Krissy did that for me.

"Can you believe that I bailed him out of jail...twice?"

"He bought you a Teddy Ruxpin for your birthday."

"It was a Build-A-Bear, thank you. It was cute."

"If you were two. Not thirty-two."

"It was the thought that counted. Right?"

I just looked at her.

"Damn, I'm a mess."

"You are not a mess. Romantically challenged, yes. Far from a mess."

"Shit, my mother calls me every other week to borrow money, so I guess I'm just used to it. We won't even start on my daddy. He only texts met at New Year's and on my mother's birthday wishing me a happy birth-day. WTF?"

"We all got issues. All of us. Just different. In most things, you're great; so don't be too hard on my girl. We just need to work on the fellas."

"You know I don't think I've ever been in love."

"Really?" As I asked the question it dawned on me that I had never heard Krissy utter the words, "I'm in love." I hadn't thought about it deeply because as long as I'd known her she hadn't been with anyone worthy of her love. I wondered how many people would say that they'd never been in love by their thirties. It seemed a shame, especially for a wonderful woman like Krissy.

"I liked some dudes a lot. Unless you count high school. But who counts high school? Even people who marry their high school sweet-hearts don't count high school."

"True."

"It ain't easy trying to change your course. Chicks like Lauren have time to fall in love. I have time to get these bills paid."

"Do you think that it's harder in New York?"

"Think? My friends my age in other cities are all married."

"Our friends are married here."

"No, you have married friends. Other than your crew, girls I know in New York that are professional and educated are not married. It's fucked up."

"I never thought about it like that."

"The women you roll with aren't the norm, boo."

"Present company included. But I do think that they are more normal than people would think. A lot of stuff and titles don't make you immune from life."

By then the Rooster was crowing with people, and the mood was high. We'd finished our cocktails and appetizers. Now it was time to party. Not wanting to push my luck, I asked, "Any interest in going down to Ginny's to hear Poison Ivy?" By this point, it didn't make a difference to me either way as Krissy had been a trooper and opened her spirit to this new experience. The least I could do was return the favor and slow whine at the Shrine.

"No, let's stay. I'm having fun. Plus, your friend keeps hooking us up with drinks and you know a sistah loves a hook-up," she laughed as she jumped off the barstool.

We walked downstairs bobbing our heads to Heavy D's, "Now That We Found Love." One of the great things about the Rooster's parties was they played music from the '80s and '90s in addition to the Top 40 you hear on repeat at most clubs. Always took me back to high school and college when people actually danced and named their dances: the wop, the Reebok, the Running Man and, everyone's favorite, the Cabbage Patch. Those were the days. At least, those were my days.

Krissy and I ate the tile off the floor dancing (as I was a bit tipsy, and she was a bit drunk). Drenched in sweat, we were the energizers of the dance floor. No complaints about hair or feet. People were cheering us on as if we were a dance team. Our routines did look choreographed. Many nights of practice breeds synchronicity.

Practice or not, age was a real thing. At least for me. I was getting tired and, although Krissy was used to these late nights more than me, I could tell she was looking for an out as well. "Let's get another drink," I said. Krissy silently responded with a nod of agreement. People high-fived us as we walked off the dance floor like we'd just debuted on *Soul Train*. It felt good, though. You want to be appreciated for the work you do, and we had put in some serious work.

The bar was crowded with the Harlem sophisticates and women who were not interested in sweating out their hair. The ones with hurting feet had commandeered the small section of tables in the back. You could tell their feet were hurting by the occasional self-massage coupled with a grimace. It was a fun party, though; no one was leaving anytime soon, especially not the "I don't get out much" gang. You know, husbands, wives, kids, etc.

"I just love when they take it back. Ms. Tina enjoys getting her groove on! Come on gorgeous, join me. Don't let Krissy have all the fun," Tina grabbed my waist in a gyrating motion to lead me to the dance floor.

"You know I would, Gorgina, but we just finished. I need a drink. Plus, I'm tired."

"Don't be a bore. C'mon!"

"Where's Lancelot?"

"The package may be stellar, but the rhythm remains challenged. Have my drink, it's a fresh gimlet." Tina was always prepared to get what she wanted. I gave Krissy a look for approval, silently hoping she would deny Tina's request. Instead, she waved me off with a limp-handed "go." It was Tina so, ultimately, I didn't mind and joined her on the dance floor.

The good news is that being a sex siren, Tina didn't move very much. A remarkable change from the frenetic popping and locking that Krissy and I had engaged in just moments before...a relief. Instead, we did the sophisticate's version of the slow whine, which ultimately developed into a slow grind. The steam was definitely rising until the "shining armor" arrived to whisk Tina away. Now, a flirty hand flapped me goodbye as she smiled, excited by his bit of jealous energy. Still love that I can get guys jealous with the girls.

As I walked back to the bar, I saw Krissy doing the pretty girl hair twirl. You know the action all girls with long hair (natural or with receipts) do when they're talking to a guy they like. I got closer and saw her talking to this drop-dead gorgeous guy with dreads, an untucked but tailored shirt with a simple design, some jeans and some spanking-new retro Jordan's. "Typical Krissy," I thought. Only she would come to the Rooster and find the one broke B-boy. Not too bad, though, because he was drop-dead. Can't be mad at her for that.

"I see you didn't miss me at all," I said to Krissy over his shoulder. He turned around, and I got the full look. Typical, yes, but again, not mad.

"Justin, this is one of my best friends. He's gay," she said quickly. Death-look straight at her—that's not an introduction.

"What's up, man?" I tried to give him a fist pound, but he reached out to shake my hand. Surprised, I gave him the firm handshake my grandfather taught me to have when meeting someone, and he did the same. Did I mention I was not mad? At all. Still, I knew she'd be crying over how he'd embarrassed her in front of colleagues or slept with one of her friends, in short order. But it might be worth it.

"A pleasure to meet you. Krissy has talked about you the entire time you were getting your groove on the dance floor. I was starting to get jealous." His voice was like a soothing boom, deep and inviting at the same time. He had the Casanova act down. Most heartbreak hotels know how to stay occupied. I wasn't falling for it. My mission was to find Krissy a good man with a mortgage.

"Yeah. Sorry to interrupt, but I'm tired and ready to go home."

"You can't take her away from me now. We were just getting to the good parts."

"I can imagine."

"Seriously, Justin is very fascinating, and we were just talking about work." Translation: You told him what you do, he saw a gold mine; and he told you about the altar in his True Religions. Same script, different cast.

Sarcastically, I went in for the kill, "Well, what do you do, Justin?" Usually, I hate that question when first meeting someone. It was customary in New York, but I hated it nonetheless. As if someone could sum you up merely by what you did or did not do. With that said, I was sure this "model/actor/origami sculptor" or "I'm in between gigs, man" was just another one of Krissy's deadbeat notches. Drop-dead or not.

"I manage a biotech hedge fund. It's small, and we just started, but I love it." I was trying to motion the woman walking past us so she wouldn't step on my face that was on the floor.

"Oh!" Couldn't manage much more. Highly embarrassed by the assumptions I'd made about the cover of this book. Slightly excited that I'd been wrong.

"But I understand that you want to roll out, brother. So, hopefully, Krissy will take my number and we can continue our conversation over dinner." Wait! You're not going to tell me that you'll "take care of her and bring her 'home'?" Points won. I looked at him again as if he were an apparition. Something has to be wrong with him. I mind-slapped my own hand again. I should be celebrating. Not hating because in fact this was my mission, and it had been accomplished.

"Well, that's up to Krissy, bro. What I will do is meet her upstairs and let you all finish in private. Nice to meet you, Justin. Treat my girl like the treasure she is."

"On my word, brother. On my word." With that, I left Krissy blushing and hair-twirling, talking to the drop-dead who runs a hedge. Fifteen minutes later, she came upstairs, elevated from a great conversation with a guy who I hoped proved to be a great man for Krissy.

Chapter Four

Home Run Out The Park

The signal went up like Batman's. "Let's lunch...Arte Café at one...my treat," was the text I received from Ruby. We were due to meet to discuss our plans for the Literacy Gala, which we were co-chairing, but this was about more than reading books. We only hit Arte Café when there were sorrows to be drained. I'd hatched my own relationship breakup there, and I was all set to hatch Ruby's.

I hopped into a gypsy cab knowing that unlike some regular taxi or Über drivers, the driver was surely going to disobey every ideal of good driving to get me there on time. I walked in the door and slowed down when I saw strands of tossed long auburn hair falling face down over a Blackberry. I knew I had to prepare myself for this afternoon. I hoped whoever was making drinks had a heavy hand.

Krissy jokingly called Ruby a "handsome woman." She must have accepted her masculine features because she often questioned whether people thought she was a drag queen in pictures. To me, she was gorgeous. But then again, I'm also attracted to men. So, there you go. Nonetheless, she was my sister-friend and, though I saw many shortcomings in her spirit, my view was a perfect one.

"Hey gorgeous! I got here as soon as I could. I was sure I'd still beat you here, though. You know how you do," I joked as Ruby lifted her face to me. She forced a smile, and if I didn't know any better I would say she was named after the color of her eyes, not her hair. Normally, an icy grey color there was always a distance behind them. But this time distance moved over for distress.

She was in pain, and I hadn't quite seen it this bad.

"I'm done with that motherfucker!"

I sat down and prepared myself for the tale. Good thing I had sensed something was awry from the shortness of the text. The tempting "my treat" was her way of begging me to come and not leaving any room for objection. I wouldn't have objected anyway to a call of distress.

"At Jacque's party, some bitch comes up to me and says she'd just fucked Steve in the bathroom," she stammered a bit through tears. All of the typical faux-confidence gone. Now, just raw from the hurt. Imitating the skeezer, she said, "It was good. I see why you stick around...although I'm not sure how you put up with that girly whimper." She began to sob a bit uncontrollably, causing the waitress who was en route to turn around and check on a neighboring party of three. It was a good thing for Ruby's sake that the restaurant was slow that afternoon.

Ruby was definitely one of the ladies who lunch. She'd worked her way up through New York society, disavowing her modest roots in St. Louis (actually Kinloch, Missouri) and stepping into the glamorous life. Sheila E. might not have known Ruby, but she knew a Ruby. Everyone in New York does.

Around me, Ruby was just a regular girl from right outside of St. Louis that could keep it one hundred percent real and still wear a hundred thousand dollar gown. I admired her ability to code switch. She could hang with the billionaires and the street ballers. The princes and the pimps. Truly, I believed if she showed more of those midwestern roots more people would genuinely like her. Instead, I think many people saw through her or thought they did.

I just saw her heart, which was generally good and clearly hurting at that moment. Problems with Steve's infidelity weren't anything new. It was an every three-to-four month occurrence. Her brother repeatedly chastised her about always going back for more. I agreed with him. By forgiving him and taking him back each time, she was inadvertently condoning it. I wondered if this would be the nail in the platinum coffin.

"Did you confront him about it?" I asked.

"When we got home. I didn't want to make a scene at the party."

Poise is one thing. Crazy is another. I couldn't believe that she'd gone through an entire dinner party surrounded by all of New York, knowing her man had just hit a Derek Jeter home run in the bathroom. "Has she lost her mind?" I wondered.

Well, what did he say?"

"That I was paranoid. That I shouldn't keep listening to jealous women who make up things. That I caused most of our issues by entertaining such "nonsense" and to drop it before he got upset."

My internal dialogue went on a rampage. Thoughts of the women in my family permeated my brain. Steve had picked the right one. Because had he been dating any woman in my family, this conversation would be happening on a two-way phone with us separated by bulletproof glass being recorded by the officer in the next room. The women in my family don't play that. At all. I recalled a time when my dad told me that he was afraid of my mother and overhearing him she yelled out, "You should be." The dynamic in my family was that although the men wore the pants, the women definitely owned all the belts and suspenders. There was a balance that existed that if scrutinized might seem to be problematic, but it worked and is still working in most cases.

Imagine sitting across from a highly attractive (masculine features or not), educated woman and hearing these words come out of her mouth. Knowing she'd done just what he demanded and dropped it. Déjà vu becomes far too frequent when insanity comes into the picture. Einstein's definition of insanity – doing the same thing over and over again and expecting a different result – came to mind. He must have contemplated Ruby's relationship with Steve when coming up with that one. Ruby may not have been insane, yet the way she acquiesced to Steve's treatment of her and their relationship was undoubtedly crazy. Still, I was there for support and not to further denigrate her.

And, although I knew the answer I asked, "So, what did you do?"

The floodgates opened again, this time broken by the shame and cowardice. I didn't need her to answer, as my suspicions were correct.

She'd cried herself to sleep lying next to him in his California King Bed in the biggest bedroom in Westchester in the biggest house in a 20-mile radius. That was the hook.

Four years ago, Ruby had found herself facing eviction from her rented Riverside Drive duplex overlooking the Hudson River. Other than the ridiculous monthly rent she paid, she had nothing to show for herself except a closet full of expensive gowns from Bergdorf's, a stack of invitations to galas to which she could not afford to buy a ticket and an image that was neither authentic nor well regarded. She'd been the belle of the ball while married to New York's top lawyer and heir to the Minkoff fortune – Alex.

Alex left Ruby with a nice settlement and portfolio, which she quickly wasted on summer rentals in the Vineyard and month long vacations to Fiji. With no children, she had no security and no steady source of income. I had tried to bring her in on a couple of projects to get her earning again, but diva antics and laziness quickly ended that charity. With all of this, I did feel sorry for her because her circumstances had led her here. She truly didn't know how or what else to do – having married Alex straight out of Barnard. Certainly, she couldn't go back to St. Louis, let alone Kinloch. At least not beaten by the city and defeated by her own failures.

Enter stage left one of New York's most eligible bachelors, Steve Sommers. Steve is a top music executive who has discovered some of the industry's top talents. He'd also made some great deals at the beginning of his career, which made him a multimillionaire hundreds of times over. Like Ruby, he'd grown up on the wrong side of the tracks in rural Texas, but he'd used the tools of education and charm to buy the railroad. At the core, it was why they got along and understood each other. The difference was that Steve held all the power. Ruby had no stock except her beauty, or at least she believed. Steve was used to having the upper hand in all situations, which made a woman like Ruby vulnerable to his game. Even in music, if you wanted to make it you had to pass by Steve's desk. And, somehow, when the rest of the business was taking a hit, Steve was still making money. At a young forty-six, his well-maintained, affable looks were elevated by his sizable bank account.

That kind of rags-to-riches success also lends itself to a sizable ego, and Steve's was incomparable. Still, to most people he was a good guy. Well-liked and philanthropic, if you didn't cross him he used his power for good and spread his money around to the many charitable causes that fuel New York's high society scene. If you had a fundraiser, you wanted Steve Somers there, and for the past four years that meant having Ruby there, too. She was great arm candy, and he always made sure she was draped in the best cloth Europe exported.

Since divorcing his first wife, Maris, Steve had had a string of Ruby types – Jessica, Sarah, Lydia and Beth – all extremely intelligent, beautiful women who escorted him to the Met, the ballet, and dinner at Daniel. But each woman only got four to five years. Steve had publicly vowed never to remarry – a self-proclaimed and proud eternal bachelor. Maris, the reported love of his life, had taken his heart and bank account to the cleaners. Then, she shipped their two kids off to boarding school and set out on a victory tour around the world, spending Steve's money on boys and booze. Ivana Trump took notes from Maris's playbook.

As I watched my sister-friend decompose across from me, I couldn't help thinking that maybe her expiration date had come, too. It had been four years, and although indiscretion on his part wasn't new, it had never been this crudely blatant. Steve was definitely a party boy on the not so low, but never to this point of complete disrespect. It signaled to me that Steve was over it and no longer cared about Ruby's feelings. When and if that time ever comes in a relationship, it is usually time to go. I hoped Ruby was going to be strong and finally have the courage to move on.

"Have you spoken about it since that night?"

"No, I haven't returned his calls or texts. I wanted to talk to you first."

"Well sweets, you already know what I'm going to say. Been saying it for the last year. How much more of this are you going to put up with? I mean, if this isn't the breaker of that camel's back, I don't know what the hell is."

"I know. I feel so stupid and weak. When did I become that girl?" I felt for her. It had taken a lot of sticks and stones to get my sister-friend to this place. A shell was left where a strong woman used to be, I thought. She had drunk the kool-aid to become one of those women whose very existence depended on the presence of a man. In her case, a very rich man.

To be clear, though, she was no different than Peggy Sue in Idaho chasing behind Billy Bob or LaQuesha chasing behind Marcus in Compton. They were only separated by zip codes and the price of their boys' toys. The core, however, was the same...a woman led to think that she had no other options. No choice in the matter. When, in fact, she held all of the power.

"Enough is enough! I swear I will not sit through another lunch with you and hear the same story. You're better than this, and it's time you start acting like it. I don't care how much money he has, who he knows, or what your perception is of your own life... you deserve better."

Ruby took a deep breath and wiped her tears as the waitress dropped off our frenchies. We had decided to take it back to the martinis we shared a love for and that we'd cemented our friendship over. Silently, we sat there as more tears rolled down her face. We clicked martini glasses and began to sip on our drinks. I grabbed her hand that was resting on the table, rubbed it, and gave it a good squeeze. She looked around the restaurant and stared out of the window as if looking for her strength. Slowly, the tears began to dissipate with successive deep breaths. She knew the inevitable had to be done or she was going to be undone.

Reassured, she pulled her head up and straightened her back, "Let's eat. I'm starving."

"Cool. Rebecca invited me to work out with her at Equinox tomorrow. You should come, too. I know there are bound to be tons of guys there. The best way to get over one lover is to get under another."

Ruby laughed and smiled for the first time since I had sat down. She pulled out an elastic hair band and tied her beautiful hair up in a ponytail. "Sure, why they hell not? But, can we talk about the Literacy Gala some other time, I'm not feeling it right now."

"We can do whatever you want."

She smiled softly again and this time grabbed my hand, "Thank you."

"For what?" I returned the smile. "Now, for some light talk. Krissy met the most handsome guy the other night at the Rooster."

"Wow. Good for her."

"No, you don't understand. He runs a biotech hedge fund."

"First of all, how did you get Krissy to the Rooster?"

"Bribes. You know she went kicking and screaming. She was a total mean girl at first, and then we went down to Ginny's. It was a blast. I was dancing with Tina Jones when she met Justin."

"You remember his name?"

"He made that kind of impression on me. First off, I completely judged him by the way he was dressed. Not true. I judged him because of Krissy's track record."

"Yeah, she loves a project."

"A project insinuates that there is hope for development. Krissy likes dead ends."

"She's so busy. When does she have time for a relationship? Most guys are too needy for a woman like Krissy, especially the successful ones. They want you to be there whenever they want you. I don't see Krissy putting up with that."

"There has to be a median, which is why I am even bringing it up. Maybe you should think about not going for the Holy Grail on each adventure."

"Hard to teach an old dog new tricks."

"You're not old. There's enough time to give up your tricks."

"We'll see."

Chapter Five

A Good Workout

Global warming is no tooth fairy. How else can you explain ninety-two degree weather in April immediately following a snowstorm just weeks ago in March. My pale grey cotton shirt was plastered to my body from the pool of sweat on my chest that had accumulated while waiting on the train. Subway travel makes the heat in New York City much more of a burden than in other cities. But I couldn't justify the expense of a cab ride to work out. And just my luck, the train had decided to go express from 66th Street to 42nd Street, overshooting my 59th Street stop and forcing me to exit and walk the rest of the way. The New York Metropolitan Transit Authority – the MTA – a model of excellence and efficiency. A sarcastic complaint or two about the transit system is a requirement for any bona fide New Yorker. It is a part of your rite of passage and your right as a taxpayer.

Walking through the neighborhood that is home to the Lincoln Center for Performing Arts, I noticed how few people were on the street. Many of the soldiers had retreated to avoid baking in their business suits and other armor. I mean, even the trees stood still. But here I was on my way to – of all things – a workout.

Rebecca had asked me to join her at the Equinox located in her building at the Time Warner Center this afternoon to exercise, chat, and to lunch after. I was also secretly hoping to see one of the well-known celebrity members sweating it out on the treadmill. Misery loves company, so I'd convinced Vikki to join us, especially since she had been complaining about all of the food she'd eaten on her vacation with Dax. And, Ruby was equally excited to take the nudge I gave at our lunch to possibly meet someone new, and thus she had accepted my invitation as well. We'd decided to make a day of it and to lunch at Josie's after, a healthy choice.

Rebecca was waiting just inside as I arrived to the club. The purple and black Nike lycra workout ensemble was showing off the work she'd put in over the last few months.

"Damn, you look like you've already had a workout," Rebecca said as I walked up, drenched.

"Sorry, I don't have a driver taking me around the city, and the train is an oven today."

"I can imagine. Can you believe this in April? You still look good, sweaty or not." She started to walk toward the elevators.

"Hold on, we have to wait for Vikki. I won't even bother waiting on Ruby."

"They're already here and getting changed." The disbelief that Ruby was early was replaced by the realization that they were up there alone together. Although I'd alerted Vikki that Ruby was going through it with Steve, I wasn't convinced she'd discover sympathy for her not-so-favorite redhead.

"I'll head to the men's locker room and meet you all in a minute. I need to change into something dry."

"To get wet again?"

"True, but I refuse to be gross at the start of my workout. Who does that?" I'd seen plenty of people come in to work out after a run and always thought it was disgusting. My mind shifted as I walked through the luxurious gym with its cork walls, fresh flowers and plants, and some amazing art on the walls. It truly was an elevated gym experience that lived up to one of my friend's assessments as, "the most elegant workout in the city." I forgot about the oppressive plantation heat outside and got excited to get physical with my girls.

◆ ◆ ◆

"Y'all ready to get it?" Vikki asked exuberantly. All three of them were waiting just outside the men's locker room, seemingly as excited as I was for an afternoon of sweat and friendly gossip.

"I see you're all eager beaver," I replied through the hug and the wonderful smell that Vikki maintained.

"Do you not see this?" She grabbed a barely noticeable bit of pudge from her side. "I ate like food was going out of style on vacation."

Rebecca jumped in, "I can't wait to hear all about it at lunch, I absolutely love Cabo. And you stayed at my favorite spot, Las Ventañas. The last time I was there we partied with Eddie Murphy."

"I didn't see *The Nutty Professor*, but I did have the most amazing time. It's my new favorite place, too. We're definitely going back. "

"Steve cheated on me there with a bartender," said Ruby matter-of-factly. Rebecca put her hand on Ruby's back for comfort. Vikki looked at me with the warning that her tolerance of Ruby was short. Vikki was never in the mood for a pity party. I smiled a grateful smile. Just in time, we found of row of empty elliptical trainers and jumped on.

"More about this vacation," Rebecca demanded as she began working the elliptical.

"No, first things first. Ruby, how are you?" asked Vikki with a genuinely concerned air. My heart smiled. My best sister-friend was always able to raise her compassion to the occasion. For now, her patience remained, and our agreement was in place.

"I already broke up with him. I'm done. Seriously, and really done this time."

"Good for you! Better than being done with." And Vikki was right. It was much better to be the dumper than the dumpee.

"I agree, it's too many men out here to be taking some bullshit on a consistent basis." Rebecca uncharacteristically added her two cents. She was often very guarded about her relationship with Gerand and thus did not like to pry with others.

Just then, a very handsome tanned man jumped on the elliptical next to me and gave me a cruise. Vikki produced a big smile and nodded her head in the direction of the tanned flirt.

"What?" I asked checking on the guy and then quickly turning back to Vikki. "Don't start today. What about this vacation, hooker?"

"I don't want to gush, but it was great. Dax spared no detail..."

"Or expense. Las Ventañas ain't cheap," Ruby said

"No, he really outdid himself, and we got along well. Until the end."

"What happened?" I got scared as I asked this question. It was always something with Vikki's guys. I was hoping that Dax was the real deal fairytale. I prepared myself for the worst and got ready to do my job. First Ruby, and now Viks. No!

"He brought up the subject of marriage again."

I let out an audible sigh accompanied by "That's it!"

"Yeah, that's great. I couldn't get Steve to marry me if I were the last single woman on earth. Which it looks like I will be."

"Ruby, hush! We've switched gears. No more Debbie Downer," I said, turning my attention back to Vikki. "You said in Miami that you were going to say yes."

"That was before he bought a ring and popped the question."

"Love, that's not bringing up the subject...that's proposing," corrected Rebecca.

"When he did, my heart stopped, but not in a good way. Me and marriage aren't the best of friends you know. It's not for too many people I know."

"Well, you've got a point there." Was that really Rebecca saying that?

"You can never give up on love! Ever," I countered.

"Look who's talking," Rebecca countered back.

"I haven't given up. I'm just taking a break. I know that I will find the right man soon enough. Just not rushing the situation. I'm not pressed. In the meantime, Ms. Smarty Pants, you're sitting on a gold mine of a man. Literally and figuratively."

"But why can't we just have fun? Marriage complicates things," Vikki remained focused on her conundrum.

"At least you have the option," huffed Ruby as she sank lower on the elliptical and into her own sadness. "You all are successful in your own right. With careers. Lives. Me, I need a man."

"Girl, you don't need a man. What you need is to get you some business and stop waiting on a man to take care of you." I could tell by Vikki's blunt delivery that her cup of compassion was percolating to its brim. No sympathy from me this time because Ruby needed to hear it.

"If I waited around for Gerand to create my life...I'd still be waiting," added Rebecca.

"Ruby, you know you're talented. I tell you all of the time." I meant that statement, and the unspoken caveat was that talent wasn't the problem. If it weren't for the placement that chairing charitable functions gave her in society amongst Steve's friends, she probably wouldn't do that either. The duty at hand, however, was focused on encouragement, so I kept those thoughts tucked away.

"I'm almost forty. Fine time to start a career."

"Toni Morrison was thirty-nine when she published her first novel."

"Who?"

Ruby was smart but limited. So I went to her playground. "Oprah was thirty-two when she got the *Oprah Winfrey Show*."

"But I'm no Oprah."

Vikki let out an affirming breath that I'm sure she thought was an internal one.

"Look Ruby, you can either woe is me the rest of your life or you can get out there and get to it. I understand as much as anyone that it's difficult to take control of your life in the shadow of a man. But you can do it," Rebecca said with a convincing authority.

"Thanks, you all."

A perfect time for me to interrupt. "We've been on these damn ellipticals for too long. I'm ready to hit some weights."

"OK, Hercules. We can split up and meet in an hour," agreed our hostess. "Ladies, do you want to take a class with me?"

"I despise group exercise. I'm going to stay on the cardio machines. I need as much as I can get following my gluttonous trip," declared Vikki.

"I'll go with you Rebecca. It'll take my mind off of Steve."

"OK, in an hour."

◆ ◆ ◆

I finished my workout and went to explore while looking for the girls. Vikki's words about my four-year dating hiatus tolled in my ears the entire hour. I chuckled at myself as I walked up on Rebecca standing with a breathing work of art. "Oh, here's my friend I was telling you about," Rebecca said, slightly startled by my presence. "This is Dillon."

"Hi, Dillon. Nice to meet you." Dillon looked like he could be a trainer or decathlete or something that required him to constantly be in the gym. Or at least I had decided that he had to be constantly in the gym to achieve that kind of body. He clearly hadn't seen a carb since Prohibition. It was my way of letting myself off the hook and, admittedly, slightly hating. I had to give it to him, though. Whatever he did, it was worth it. He also had no problem showing it off in his spaghetti strapped dark-blue tank top and short, black acrylic workout shorts. Yet he still looked masculine in the very revealing outfit. His chiseled Paul Newman facial features with piercing ice-blue eyes, dark brown hair and distinguished cheekbones complemented the worked-out body. It was also clear that whatever he was talking about with Rebecca had put a smile on both their faces. His eyes were beaming looking at her.

"You ready to lunch? I'm done and starving," I asked.

"Um, yeah, sure. Ah, why don't you go find Vikki, and I'll grab Ruby and meet you guys downstairs." I felt every bit the intruder as Rebecca verbally waved me off.

"Why don't you guys join me for lunch at Landmarc here? The food is great. My treat," offered Ken-doll Dillon.

"That's nice of you, man. I don't mind eating here..."

"We have our mouths set for this organic place up the street. Thanks, though," interjected Rebecca, cutting me off. I followed her lead.

"Yeah, we've been talking about Josie's for a week. Thanks anyway, man. Nice to meet you. I'm going to grab Vikki. We'll see you downstairs, Becks." I walked away and peeked back at them through one of the mirrors. I was eager to find out what that was all about.

◆ ◆ ◆

We ordered our cocktails. The treats for a good workout. We'd chosen Josie's not just because it was healthy but also because it had a full bar. You only live once.

Vikki continued her story about the first stop on her vacation, a secluded place in the Fiji islands. "Yes, nothing to do but each other."

"Hallelujah, you broke the seal," said Rebecca, toasting Vikki with her martini.

"Yes, chile, over and over again. He may have gotten rich quick, but he's no quickie in bed."

"Damn," said Ruby. "Rich and a long stroke. I didn't think they existed."

"Me either. But not just a long stroke, his tongue game is…"

"OK, enough with the Taxi Cab Confessions. We get the point," I said not really wanting her to go on because Vikki could and would go on.

"Heyyyy, can't we live for a minute?" demanded Ruby.

"Have your *Girl 6* moment when I'm not around."

"How long did you stay in Fiji?" I knew Rebecca wasn't interested in any details beyond the mission confirmation; particularly in the middle of a crowded restaurant blocks away from her apartment.

"Four days. A perfect amount of time. We had an amazing time, but I'm good on the deserted island thing for a while. I was ready to get to Cabo."

"Isn't Las Ventañas gorgeous? I always get depressed when it's time to leave." Rebecca had often talked about the brilliance of one the best resorts in the world snuggled away in the Mexican resort land.

"Actually, we didn't leave that much even after being cast away in Fiji. But the option to go into the city was a welcome change. And, you're right. It's a breathtaking piece of property. Girl, the food is just to die for, which is why my ass was getting my Shaun T on in that gym. I had dessert and wine for breakfast. Then, dessert again," Vikki giggled. "Decadence, baby!"

"Does he have any brothers?" asked Ruby.

"Seems like another lifetime that Gerand and I went there on vacation. Damn, it seems like another lifetime that Gerand and I went anywhere together," Rebecca said, floating away into a reminiscent haze.

"Steve takes me places, but like some mute trophy. Asshole."

"I'm having an affair!" The words thrust from Rebecca's lips with the subtlety of a launched torpedo. This revelation came from whatever field is beyond the left one. Vikki almost choked on her water. Ruby was definitely awake now. None of us with a clue what to do or say. The entire room seemed to stand still like an extended freeze frame in an action film.

Rebecca's husband, Gerand, was an "International Businessman" with so many different businesses that it was almost impossible to categorize him as more or less than such. In his late forties, he was a decent-looking, stout, balding white man, but long hours and constant travel hadn't benefited him over the years. Plus, he lacked the cordiality that would've enhanced his looks. In typical fashion, what he lacked in aesthetics and personality, he made up for with zeros in his bank account. Unlike many of my sister-friends who were married to wealthy men, Rebecca had been with Gerand since the beginning when he was a young trader at Lehman Brothers.

Gerand, with Rebecca's help, had risen through the ranks and then left to pursue his entrepreneurial dreams. As the years grew on, the hours got longer, the trips became more frequent, and Rebecca often found herself alone in one of their seven homes across the globe. Atypically, Rebecca never felt the maternal yearnings that most women feel, which was fine with Gerand because he'd had a daughter while he was in college. Leaving no desire for any more children (or responsibilities). Business was his passion, and his companies were the only offspring that were going to get his love and attention. They didn't even have a dog.

Yet Gerand was no fool. He was well aware of the asset he had in his wife. The one whom everyone loved. When he couldn't arouse affection in his potential business partners, he'd call in Rebecca to seal the deal. They were a team, and for many years, that had worked for both of them. Until recently, when Rebecca had become suspicious that Gerand was having an affair. She had no concrete evidence, but women know. They just know. It had caused her to question the choices she'd made. The sacrifices to live the lifestyle she'd dreamed and wondered if it was worth it. The thought of his infidelity had smacked her in the face like a brick.

But she never asked him directly. Her fear of the answer prevented the confrontation. She knew he wouldn't leave her. His fear of the divorce settlement would keep him put. The first wives club typically lacked pre-nups. If Gerand were ever caught with his pants down, Rebecca would leave an equally wealthy woman. And the only thing that meant more to Gerand than his stable of businesses was the money he made from them.

"Um, OK," was the brilliant response I managed to string together in response to Rebecca's revelation.

"With the guy from the gym," she said intently.

"The one I just met?" I asked.

Then, with missile speed and near incoherency, Rebecca rambled, "Yes, Dillon. It's been going on for two months, and I don't feel bad about it at all. But I just had to tell someone. No one else knows." It was clear that she'd brought us here for that sole reason. But, I didn't buy the, "don't feel bad" bit as it was also clear that it had taken every ounce of courage for her to get it out.

"Um...OK." Brilliant again. We just sat there. None of us looking at each other. It was one of those uncomfortable moments that you hope will quickly pass, but it seems to linger in perpetuity, growing in discomfort. Someone had to say something, but what was there to say? I wasn't sure if this was a cry for help, advice, or did she merely need to get this off of her chest? I'm sure Vikki and Ruby were equally whiplashed by the sudden change in tone and theme. We were just talking about honeymoon-type splendor. Perfect breezes and settings. Now we were suddenly trans-ported to a reality that was neither anticipated, nor quite frankly, welcome. My senses were set for endorphins, organic foods, and tales of cocktails on the shores of clear blue waters.

"I know that came out of nowhere, but keeping a secret like that to yourself is a bitch. And I know you won't judge me. Well, not in the way that will make me feel bad."

Speaking for myself, I would try my hardest not to do so. Everybody's house has a fair share of glass, so throwing stones isn't safe. Vikki, on the other hand, might be a different story. Infidelity, as a subject, strikes a discordant chord with her because of all of the things she went through with Mark and, particularly, Paul. I said a quick prayer that she would let it ride. Ain't nobody got time for any more discomfort.

"Do you feel better, now that you've shared?" I asked with all of the tenderness I could muster.

"Sort of. Like I said, it's not that I feel bad. It's been a wonderful two months. I've discovered things and thoughts that I hadn't met in such a long time. I've been so comfortable in my life with Gerand, I'd forgotten so much."

"So are you saying you're in love with this guy?" asked Vikki with a little more bite in her voice than I'd hoped.

"Honestly don't know."

"Have you told him you love him?" I asked with a bit more compassion.

She paused and reluctantly whispered, "Yes."

Far more complicated than a drunken romp in the hay, it was clear she had developed feelings that extended beyond a mere tryst. It had gotten deep, and she was stuck. All evidence pointed to a call of distress. As much as I dreaded it, I couldn't leave my sister-friend in the middle of the quicksand. It was out of character for her, and I was sure she felt alone. Keeping a secret like that coupled with the dichotomy of enjoying an exciting love affair had to be driving her crazy.

"Do you want a divorce?" I asked. My phone rang loudly interrupting the cross-examination. I started not to answer it, but I'd seen four missed calls from Lauren while I was changing at the gym. Again, I discovered it was her calling as I pulled it out to look.

"The craziest thing is not at all. I haven't even contemplated it. Sure, I've fantasized what it would be like to experience every day like the days I spend with Dillon. But, I know that's..."

"Unrealistic," I added.

"Yes, I know. Completely. But, you know that things haven't been right between Gerand and me for quite some time. I signed up for something that I thought I was good with. Turns out, I'm not." Ruby probably had no idea that Rebecca and Gerand had been having issues, unlike Vikki and me. Couldn't worry about Ruby right now, though. This great day was turning into a walk through a cavern of crazy. I knew something had to be going on with Lauren, too. Prayed another silent prayer that God would direct my words.

"Was it the fact that you thought he was cheating on you?" I asked, seeking justification for her revelation.

"Only part of it. You know how one thing just triggers a domino effect. The time apart and lack of intimacy never bothered me until I thought he was sharing his time and intimacy with someone else." Vikki, who'd been sitting board-rigid since the story began, softened at this statement. Men cheat for sport. Women tend to cheat because they are deeply hurt by either their husband's infidelity or his lack of care.

"I just had the most random thought. Dillon and Dax. Wouldn't that be cute," said Ruby clearly in outer space.

"Shut up...please," said Vikki, whose social graces had long been thrown out the window.

I ignored them and asked, "Do you want advice or just an ear?"

"Both."

"It's a difficult situation all the way around. But what I do know is that if you want to save your marriage, there's no way you're going to be able to do that with someone else in the picture. Three's a crowd."

"If three's a crowd, four is a mob," Rebecca replied defensively.

"Ask him! Confront him about your suspicions. You'll know if he's lying. You've known him for over twenty years, most of which you've been married. You'll know. I think that's what you're afraid of...to ask, and then know."

"Do not ask him. You don't have to. Find out for yourself." Clearly, we were back on Ruby's playground as she continued, "I can help you break into any phone, email account, computer, bank account, you name it. I know how to find out."

"You never cease to amaze me, Ruby." Part of Vikki's comment was meant as a compliment, I think.

"And if he is?" asked Rebecca appropriately refocusing the conversation.

"You have to decide what you want and don't want. Is that a deal breaker? Not to seem like I'm not on your side in this, but do you really have any room at this point? If he has or hasn't, you're in the same boat. Same foul," I said.

"But, what about Dillon?" Rebecca asked.

"Fuck Dillon! Did he know you were married when you met him?" interjected Vikki.

"Yes."

"Well, fuck him! He has no rights in this. He entered into a situation that he was well aware of. You don't owe him shit."

"I have to agree with Vikki. Wouldn't have said it like that, but she's right. You don't owe him anything. He knew what he was getting into. Something also tells me that he's no rookie."

"Should I tell Gerand?"

"Hell no," I said emphatically. The male ego is as fragile as Waterford. A double standard I know, but if she wanted to save her marriage, being honest about having an affair wasn't going to do it. Dishonesty was rarely advisable, but this was one of those occasions. Men aren't generally equipped with the skills required to deal with the thought of some other guy screwing his wife. Especially not men like Gerand.

"How do you even start an affair?" asked Vikki with an unexpected naïvete. As I thought about it more, she might be genuinely naïve, having only been on the receiving end of adultery. Although I wasn't a cheerleader for cheating, I had experienced my own indiscretions in the past and was no saint. Ruby didn't have wings and a halo either, so Vikki might be the only one who had never experienced the all too common tiptoe down the road toward infidelity.

"I never intended to have an affair." Very few people set out with the intention. "We would see each other in the gym. He kept the same hours as I had with my trainer. It began with just small talk about this and that. And, soon the conversations got longer and longer. We had lunch and realized we had so much in common. He's a principal dancer with the Ballet Ciudad."

"I thought he looked familiar," I said as things in my mind began falling into place.

"You know how much I love the ballet. But you know how it is. A picture in a playbill is different recognition than in person. Once he said that, I was hooked into our conversations and encounters."

"It had nothing to do with the fact that he looks like young Paul Newman?" I quizzed, not believing that the foundation of this was all cerebrally rooted.

"Of course. He is gorgeous, but he is also spiritually connected, educated, traveled, and so very interesting."

"I can't," Vikki was on the verge.

"Calm down, Viks. This is Rebecca." Vikki might be the anti-adulterer, but we were sitting here with our friend. She needed to put up her past and hang-ups to be present for her. Or at least sit in silence.

"I know it sounds so cliché. I never wanted to be. Then the lunches turned into museum trips. Long afternoons. I had a man to talk to for the first time in as many years as I can remember. Not about an acquisition. Not about what gala we were attending and who I had to make sure I talked to. Not about the business of my life. About me and what I loved. The things I talk with you all about, but with a gorgeous and intelligent man who, by that point, clearly liked me. And then, one day he kissed me."

It would have been easy to get lost in the romance of the story. Meeting someone who naturally got your beats. The ones in rhythm with the rest of the world and the ones that were not. That person who you didn't have to explain yourself to from hello. Two souls that had been searching for one another in this busy and crazy world that was New York and finally had bumped into each other with the softness of meteors. It would have been easy, except there was Gerand. Her husband.

"It might be completely crass and out of line, but have you slept with him?" I cautiously asked.

"I hadn't had sex in two years four months and three days."

"Wow, really?" Ruby couldn't even imagine.

"Damn Rebecca. I know about taking care of your own business. But, damn." Vikki was starting to lighten and hear our friend. Not judge her.

"Let's be clear, sex was never a significant part of the deal with Gerand. Hell, it wasn't any part of it. I thought it didn't matter. He was a good man. He was going to be successful. He loved me. It was enough then."

"Getting older changes what is enough," added Vikki.

"That's the thing. I feel young again. I was feeling very old before. Reviewing it all and coming up with nothing but older. Don't get me wrong I am very grateful for all that I have. I know better than anyone that I lead a privileged life. Just realizing that it's not enough is a very difficult thing. When you think it's too late to make any changes. And just like that hope for something different walks right up to your face."

We all understood. An understanding that erased the traces of judgment any of us had. Conversations with the same thesis had swirled in each of our heads and through our lips to one or the other. Our methods and materials might be unique, but the hypothesis was the same. Had we reached the point of no return? Was this how it was going to be? Or, did we have the ability to change the course? More importantly, did we have the time? You can't criticize anyone's journey to the answers of those questions. It is why we sat there silently sipping on our drinks.

When our food arrived, I was no longer excited about eating something healthy. I wanted something fattening to counteract the weight of the conversation. Grilled salmon and some air-puffed fries were not going to cut it. I needed some grease and a shot of Patron. I ordered the shot and planned to stop off at Corner Social when I got home. A burger with bacon, cheddar cheese, grilled onions, and real fries. Comfort food has rightfully earned its name. I was looking forward to getting out of there and getting my comfort on. Then my phone rang again. It was Lauren.

Chapter Six

Husbands Gone Wild

The teardrops hit my shoulder like the beginning of a rainstorm. Evidence of what's to come. We sat on the floor in Lauren's pristine closet, the size of many New York apartments, underneath the names that noted her designer life — Urban Zen, Phillip Lam, and Alexander Wang. My rescue effort had been right on time. Calls like the one Lauren just gave me come with little warning and no decoder for the indecipherable whimpers of despair heard on the other end. But when you truly know someone, making sense is unnecessary. A cry for help is just that. So I had rushed over from my episode of *Cheaters* to find her crouched down like an unborn child wasting away in a pool of far too expensive tears.

The children were on break with her parents in France. No Josh. And there was no staff to speak of in sight either. During the call she'd managed to articulate that she was on the floor of the closet and that the front door was open. She was unable to explain much more or muster the energy to move from her position. I had no idea what was going on although a myriad of thoughts ran through my head. Different scenarios that all involved Josh. Had it been the kids Lauren would have certainly been in save-the-day mode and not crippled. She was fiercely protective of her three children, and I knew that her lioness instincts would have kicked in by now if it were related to their well-being. Whatever it was, though, was not fresh. For her to be in this space meant that it had been brewing for some time.

She cried in my arms for what felt like hours but was really just shy of one. I kept silent partly because it seemed like the right thing to do and also because I didn't have a clue what to say. Although my afternoon had been filled with unexpected announcements from Rebecca, I was ready to deal with whatever had brought Lauren to her knees. Even after the effects of the afternoon cocktails had long worn off, the weeping hour had afforded me the opportunity for multiple prayers and centering thoughts as I armored my own spirit in preparation.

The tears became less and less while her breaths became deeper. Lauren finally lifted her head from my shoulder and sat back against the wall. After wiping her beet red face and eyes she said, "It's all true."

I stared at her for a minute still not clear to what she was referring until my mind caught up with the moment. She meant the tabloids. I hadn't read any of the gossip rags or blogs myself, but the rumors were becoming so widespread that you couldn't avoid them. It wasn't the first time one of my friends had been the subject of a relentless storyline that was untrue so I hadn't paid much attention to it. Josh was a famous producer who was often covered by the so-called celebrity journalists because of his work with A-List talent and his early success. According to what had recently been reported, he was becoming more known for having a drug problem. I had chalked it up to exaggerated sensationalism because Lauren had never mentioned anything about it. Sure, we all knew Josh was an occasional partier, but never to the extent that would cause anyone to be worried. It was part of the Hollywood beat and certainly not unusual in the circles in which we all ran. The first time I had seen someone do cocaine had freaked me out beyond belief. I was definitely a square and stayed that way personally, but over time the occurrence became less and less extraordinary. It was what it was, and there was no judgment, especially if it wasn't regular. Looking at Lauren now, I got very worried.

"How long has it been going on?" I asked.

"For years. I knew Josh liked to have a good time when I met him. I know it sounds dumb, but I was attracted to the rock star side of him. It was so different than everything I had known, and it wasn't like it was every day. Hell, we had a good time together. We were young, and it was harmless, I thought. After we got married and the kids came, I just figured those days were behind us. And they were. For me."

Lauren came from a family of old money dating back to the printing press. A pedigree of pedigrees. She had the type of lineage that would've made the Mayflower descendants bow and curtsy. Josh's family was wrinkled wealth, too. Not as preserved or vast as Lauren's but definitely established New York elite. When they met I was so excited about her finding someone like Josh. Not only was he not after her money (as many past boyfriends had been), but also he had such an amazing energy that matched Lauren's. They were the fairytale couple. He was as handsome as she was beautiful. Both blessed with spirits, which overwhelmed their unquestionable good looks. Each the life of the party in their own unique, complementary way.

The first five years of her marriage undoubtedly lived up to the fairytale. Jessie came two years after the Cinderella wedding in Central Park and the Plaza. Jessie was perfection in the form of a baby. Lauren and Josh turned out to be as amazing parents as they were people. To see them together could make the coldest Scrooge warm up to love. Then, came J.J. (Josh, Jr.), followed by little Jordan (named after Josh's favorite basketball player, Michael). And, it would have been sickening if they hadn't remained the down-to-earth folks that made me love them in the first place.

Shortly after Jordan's arrival, the economy took a turn for the worse, and Josh, like many of his contemporaries, found himself in a financial quagmire. To be clear, over the course of two years, Josh lost over three-quarters of his portfolio and assets. During that time he discovered that his older brother had squandered the family business and much of the fortune with it. The saving grace was that Josh used his background, education and money to forge his career as a film producer. He'd boasted a string of indie hits and then got a crack at a big studio film that took him over the top by grossing nearly two hundred million dollars worldwide. That kind of success is hard to maintain, and after a series of expensive flops the studios stopped calling or returning his calls. Deciding he could do a better job than the experienced lens jockeys he'd previously hired, he tried his hand at directing and that went limp, too. So Josh committed the ultimate taboo — he started investing in his own films. It began to drain their pot of gold and him, too. In the grand scheme of things, they weren't as devastated as most due to Lauren's inheritance, which was substantial and secure. As I listened to Lauren recount the turning point of his drug use, I was baffled as to how she'd been able to keep all of this to herself.

"I haven't seen or heard from him in six days, and then this," she said, much more collected than when I had first found her. Lauren stood up and picked up her iPad from the dresser in her closet. She sat on the chaise lounge next to it and began to type. I joined her on the chaise. After finding the page she was looking for, she handed the iPad to me. It was a gossip site, and the image was a still shot from a video of Josh and an actor I recognized but whose name I couldn't remember. I scrolled up to read the headline: "Josh Billings & Flannery Redd's Wild Drug Night Rampage." "Press Play," she said as she stared at the screen. The video began to play a scene of Josh and the actor talking jibberish, both with what looked like traces of cocaine on their noses. "It gets worse," she said. And, she was right. As the video continued, it was clear that they were taking turns doing lines of blow or something off-screen only to return with more and more powdered noses. I wanted it to stop, but I knew she wanted me to see the whole thing. What was decipherable was a career sabotaging rant against the Hollywood machine. Names were included. Secrets were told. And, for the next thirteen minutes and twenty-four seconds Josh and his friend made it clear what they thought about everyone in Tinseltown from A to Z. No one was spared, and it was likely that Josh's career wouldn't be either. It finally ended with Josh proclaiming, "Fuck you! Time to party!"

"Yeah, that happened," she said and looked at me.

"What the hell was he thinking?"

"He's not thinking. He hasn't been for the past two years."

"This kind of shit has been going on for two years?"

"It started off with him coming home at three o'clock in the morning. Then overnight. Two days. Three days. He went to rehab after I threatened to leave him. We had a good patch for six months. Then it started all over again about two months ago."

"You've been dealing with this by yourself?"

"Who could I tell? What would I say? The man I love and married turned out to be a drug addict. Who do you say that to?"

"You could've told me."

"I thought I could fix it. And I know it sounds crazy, but he is still a great father."

"I don't understand how that's possible if this is going on."

"I don't understand any of it." She began to cry again. "I'm so embarrassed and ashamed." I grabbed her in a hug. As she cried, my hug tightened around her, telling her that I wasn't going to let her go. Now or ever. We'd known each other since we were in our twenties, and she'd instantly become one of my best friends. Her laugh was one that always evoked joy in my spirit. Lauren was the girl that you could always count on to be there for you. To do the right thing. To be a great friend. I actually learned how to be a friend from Lauren. She was always so supportive of her friends and happier for our successes than her own. She was a pure and gentle soul blessed with a toughness that made her quite special. All the reason why it was killing me to see her helpless in this predicament.

"For better or worse, right?" she said while trying to hold back more tears.

"How much worse do you have to put up with?"

"He's my husband."

I understood her commitment to her marriage. It's who she is, but I couldn't help wonder if the writers of those vows contemplated anything like this. Still, she was determined to stick it out, and I was committed to helping her figure it out. First, we had to get Josh home from Los Angeles and back into rehab. And then we needed to call a great publicist.

Chapter Seven

Gentlemen Who Lunch

I was ready to lunch, but Vikki was running late so I ordered a glass of Pinot grigio while I took in the sights at Michael's, one of New York City's most popular restaurants. Filled with priceless art from American modern masters like Jasper Johns, it was always an afternoon party of simplified elegance, power meetings, and the infinite flow of wine from around the world. Michael's was Vikki's favorite spot to have business meetings because she rarely entertained anyone for meetings at the *Designe* offices, except the editorial staff. We were meeting early to talk about the piece I had submitted to her before I met Dax for the first time. I was anxious about her feedback because it had been such a long time since I had written an editorial story, and I felt out of practice. Despite spending many hours agonizing over the task and making countless edits, I wasn't confident that it was good enough for publishing or for Vikki's nearly impossible standards. Even when we were in school, she was well-known for her take-no-prisoners perfectionism that intimidated me, who was equally committed to excellence. It was a good exercise, though, because it put oil on my mind's creative wheels that had recently ground to a screeching halt following the collapse of my last film.

As the waitress delivered the generous pour of the Italian wine I ordered, I immediately raised it to inhale the aroma and proceeded to take a long, soothing sip. It was good. To be honest, most wine was good to me. I hadn't acquired a discerning palate since vodka and tequila were my spirits of choice. No matter how much Rebecca or Lauren tried to teach me about the variances amongst the grape varietals, it always seemed as if school were out of session. We can't expect to master all things. I was particularly chastised because of my practice of putting ice cubes in wine that was not cold enough — white or red — and for putting red wine in the refrigerator. I can't count how many times someone I've been scolded about this "uncivilized" routine that "ruined" my wine. Nor could I count how many times I had replied, "The operative word is *mine*." Too many embarrassing moments for my friends relegated my consumption of red wine to home or a close friend's place. Actually, I had bonded with one of Gerand's billionaire business partners who reinforced that the correct way to consume wine or anything else was the way *I* liked it. I giggled at my irreverence for social graces and norms just as Vikki walked through the door. She stopped as the host greeted her with a familiar hug. As she waved to the many people she knew in the restaurant, she did not stop making her way toward the table at which she always sat and me. It was in the center of things, just like Vikki. She was radiant in an elegant, form-fitting powder blue power suit that was brightened by her wide smile.

"Damn, you look good, girl."

"Why, sweetie, thank you. I am meeting two very important men in my life. So, I had to dress the part." Vikki placed her oversized bag in one of the three open chairs as I stood up to give her a hug and a kiss. Like clockwork, the Maître' d' delivered a generous glass of rosé. She hugged him, too, in appreciation as she sat down next to me. "I don't know if that is a shame or just good service."

"I vote for good service. It's like your "Cheers" — where everybody knows your name."

"To a fabulous afternoon." We clicked glasses, and with that lunch began. "First things first, if you don't mind. I want to get our business out of the way before Dax arrives."

"Sure." The nerves crept back inside.

"The piece is fabulously written. I'd forgotten what a virtuoso you are." I began to smile and was beginning to ease up a bit as this was what I had hoped to hear. "But I need you to do a rewrite." Too soon, I guess. "I like your perspective, and it's a valid one. Gay men of color being represented one-dimensionally on television. And although my readership is very gay-friendly, they are still women. We need an angle that speaks to them directly. The representation of gay men is a side note. A secondary angle. The primary angle I'm looking for is how women, particularly women of color, have adopted so much of gay culture into their lives. Language. The way they dress. Etcetera. I want to explore whether or not that makes us more or less feminine."

"I get that," I replied.

"Ultimately, it's about does this turn on or turn off straight men? And what, if anything, do we lose by co-opting another culture's affectations. With all of these shows on cable, I think it's so fascinating."

"I agree. I can definitely adjust it so that is the focus. When do you need it by?"

"Yesterday."

"Oh wow, I have that much time."

"Sweetie, you know how it is in publishing. We're always in a rush. Plus, I love the writing so much that I want to push it in the print edition, online, and also in social media. It's so *Vanity Fair*, but for *Designe*. I might even send a personal copy to Graydon just to be a bitch." We both laughed. She wasn't serious, but Vikki was always in competitive mode. "So, we're good. Clear?"

"Loud and," I said.

"Perfection. Now, I am about to shit my pants for this meeting. Please be gentle with Dax.

I was determined to do better by my sister-friend, yet I had planned more interview than a grill over hot coals session. "I promise not to scare him away. Unless he needs to be."

"I think you will love him."

"I don't know if that's a good thing."

"By all means, if you get the sense that he is playing for any other team than team Vikki, please let a sister know."

"What other team is there?" boomed a voice that startled both of us and looked up to Dax. I stood up to greet him properly. He had to be at least 6'4," as he stood taller than me, with light caramel skin, curly hair and, I noticed as I reached in to shake his hand, a pair of grayish-green eyes that fit his face flawlessly. Dax was the kind of light-skinned, pretty boy fine that never goes out of style. Tyson Beckford's chocolate revolution or not.

"Nice to finally meet you." Dax's deep bass voice was a total surprise given his pretty boy looks.

"Same here, man! You've obviously got my gorgeous girl here excited."

"Actually, I'm the lucky and excited one. May I join you or are you still working?" he asked.

"Sit down, lover. We're wrapped," said Vikki. As he took his seat, she gave me a knowing look. She knew what I was thinking. Yes, impressed. And she was proud of herself. Not too fast, though. "You all don't have to stop the compliments on my account. I'm all set to sit here and let you both dote over me all afternoon. In fact, I've cleared my schedule just so you can."

"I'm sorry, my dear. You are fabulous, but this is about Dax."

"You mean this is about giving me the once-over," he laughed.

"Or thrice. I plan to be thorough."

"Ah, easy Hammer, don't hurt 'em," said Vikki.

"No worries, Viks, it's cool. And I expect it from any good friend. I'm a big boy. I can handle myself." Vikki gave him a validating look on his "I'm a big boy," comment. TMI.

"So Vikki tells me you met at an art showing. Are you a collector?"

"I'm learning man. The investment part is more fascinating to me than the artistic part. Vikki is trying to school me, though."

"I keep telling him that it's more than the money. It's art."

"What can I say, some of my caveman ways just won't go away. It's why I need you, baby." They smiled at each other tenderly. Puppy dogs.

"I'm actually with you. I don't know much about it myself beyond I know what looks pretty."

"The two of you. You don't say art is pretty."

"Well, what do you say then?" I asked.

"Something other than pretty."

"You stay out of this. Dax and I are talking. Know your place, woman."
I knew I could get away with that joke because Vikki knew it was a joke.
Dax held back his laughter because he wasn't so sure of his safety. He
just smiled slightly. I continued, "Vikki also tells me you have more money
than God."

He burst into laughter, partly releasing what had built up from the
previous statement. "I wouldn't say that, but I have done well for a boy
from Ohio."

"Oh, the Midwest. Me too."

"Where?"

"Chicago," I replied.

"A great city."

"It's a cleaner version of New York," I said.

"I don't know about that," said Vikki. My look at her prompted, "Oh
sorry, the woman is not supposed to speak."

"Not when you're talking about my hometown, Ms. Day-Tois. Detroit
can never talk about the Chi."

"Don't be mad that we're on the come up, Chi-raq."

"Low blow. Good. But low," Dax said jumping in on our light sparring
match. "Yeah, but I was very blessed man. I had a good idea. Had some
smart friends. But it's all the man upstairs. I was just a vessel."

I was speechless. Dax was speaking my language. It was a humil-
ity that was genuine and in synch with my own beliefs about life. "M.I.T.
means you're pretty smart, too."

"I work hard, man. I definitely wasn't anywhere near the smartest, but
I will work harder than anyone on the field."

"You played sports?"

"Football, soccer, and lacrosse."

"Fancy."

"More like strategic. I knew that it would be easier for me to get a
scholarship in soccer or lacrosse than football."

"I played soccer and hockey. My parents were, like, what about basketball and football? Sports they knew."

"What position in soccer?"

"Right wing," I said.

"Goalie."

"So you're used to being the man in charge."

"I think everyone at this table is used to being in charge." He had a point. It was a table of Type A personalities with Vikki probably being the A-plus. Just as much as Dax was handsome and confident, he was equally charming and genuine. I could sense an aura about him that most people probably mistook at first for arrogance. Instead, it was an easy persona that allowed him to navigate the world with those looks, that voice, the money, and still have the entire room like him. He was definitely a charmer, but not of the snake kind.

"So what about you? What's your story?" he asked, turning the tables.

"I'm pretty simple and ordinary. I'm no jet-setter like you and Vikki."

"Please. You put the fab in fabulous," Vikki corrected me.

"Yeah, I don't buy that man. Plus, Vikki has told me a lot about you. The TV shows. The movies. The writing."

"I pay her to say those things." I turned to Vikki. "The check's in the mail, boo."

"Heard that before."

"No, seriously, I have been very blessed, too. I get to do what I love. Sometimes at a high level. Sometimes, it's a struggle to be honest."

"The road less traveled often is, man."

Well put. Carving your own way in the world is a daunting undertaking, and there is no trail to follow. I was in one of those moments in life where figuring it out was more difficult than it had been. My initial goal was to conduct a thorough background check, and somehow sitting at the table with Vikki and Dax was beginning to inspire me. No matter how inspired I was or how charming he was, I was not going to forget the task at hand. For over two hours we bantered and I quizzed, trying my hardest to break through the exterior. We talked about everything from politics to gay rights to Buddhism. He'd used his early introduction to the good life not just to explore women, like so many young millionaires, but also the world and himself. He was very concerned about his spiritual growth and how he could develop into a philanthropic citizen of the world. With every discussion, he returned to a deep need to help other people and to make a difference. An exceptional breath of fresh air; vastly different from the other juvenile, financially well-endowed little boys running around New York and Europe.

No matter how hard I tried, and I was giving it my best, I couldn't find anything to dislike. No cracks in the armor. No inconsistencies. True, two hours is not long enough to discover the core of a man. But two hours is long enough to understand when someone is sincere. In most cases, even people who later disappoint you and don't live up to who they've professed to be have revealed themselves from the beginning. If only you had been aware. And for Vikki's sake, today I was keenly so.

Maya Angelou famously said, "When people tell you who they are, believe them the first time." And from what I was seeing, not from just what he was saying, Dax was the real deal. Quite frankly, I had never met anyone like him. Ever. By the end of the two hours, I was overcome. I wanted to know more. I looked forward to talking to him again. Most importantly, I knew he had the capability of making my friend ecstatically happy. He even had me smiling by the end. My spirit told me that it was no con act. And for that, I felt good. Relieved. Hopeful. Thankful, for Vikki's sake.

"Sweetie, Dax has to get to a meeting. I know you two boys are enjoying yourselves, and he'd never be rude to interrupt the party, so I must. We can reconvene over dinner," These were the first words I remember Vikki saying in a long time.

"See, this is why I love you. You keep me together. Unfortunately, it's true. I have a meeting in thirty minutes. But why don't you two continue to hang out? I'll meet back up when it's done. We can grab a bite and maybe hit the town," Dax said as he stood up, shook my hand, and then gave Vikki an "I love your dirty drawers" lip-lock. So much so I felt like an intruder.

Unlocked, Dax said, "Really, I hope to see you later. I've enjoyed the conversation. You're cool as shit. I was worried." We both laughed.

"Krissy is having a Cinco de Mayo party tonight at her house. Y'all should come," I said.

"Krissy and Cinco de Mayo?" questioned Vikki.

"I know, right. You can't ever predict Krissy. Plus, she has a new boo... Justin. Are you down, Dax?"

"Sure, sounds fun! What could be wrong when tequila's involved? But I gotta dash. See ya' tonight," he said quickly and glided to the exit with an understated swagger. Vikki and I sat there in a moment of silence as she waited for him to get out of door, never taking her eyes off him. Right before exiting, he turned around and waved 'bye to Vikki and dipped his head at me.

"So?"

"Well, damn...damn!" was all I could say! Vikki started to giggle, amused by my reaction as she motioned for the waiter.

"Two Goose gimlets, please. Time to get this party started now that's over."

"Quite honestly, Viks, I tried my best to do whatever I could to 'do you a favor' and reveal the fraud, but..."

"He's the real deal, Holyfield. I know."

"Yeah, it certainly seems that way."

"Look, I know I haven't been the best judge of character before when it comes to men. But this is different. Trust me, sweetie, my gaydar, cray-dar, whatever-dar was way up when we met. Even at the beginning I thought, 'Oh this'll be fun at least.' And then, I got to know him, and that's really who he is. I've met his friends. They say that's who he is. His mother was more concerned about me because she said Dax has always been this extremely connected and sensitive soul. Trust me, there is no ringer you could have put him through that I hadn't run several times already."

And as she said that, the skeptic that had been fought all afternoon reared his hideous head inside my spirit once again. No one is perfect. There had to be something wrong with Dax.

"I've decided not to marry him, though. At least not now."

Clearly, something was raising a signal in her spirit, too, so I continued my examination. "So, what's the problem?"

"I don't want it to end, that's all. I'm enjoying this too much!"

"Stop saying that!"

"I know what I have, and he's not going anywhere. Plus, who says marriage is the answer? There are plenty of sinner couples who have lasted longer than any married ones." True. The aisle walkers' win-to-loss ratio was way off. It was quite possible that Vikki was onto something.

"I give you that I have never met anyone like him, which makes my eyebrow raise."

"Wait! I have no doubts about him, the person. I have doubts about marriage, the institution."

"Oh! My bad. Crazy past or not, I am sure you will make the right decision. Either way, I am excited for you."

Chapter Eight

A "Bitches Brew" of Twirlers & Tequila

As much as I love Harlem, I also have a crush on the Upper West Side. Out of all of the other neighborhoods in the city, it seems the most diverse and although it has plenty of stores, restaurants, and activities, it retains a distinctive "neighborhood-y" feel. It also retains that common New York denominator — high rent. Thankfully, I had all of my sister-friends to visit to get my fix from time to time and then go back to Harlem's space and relative affordability.

It'd been almost a month since I'd seen Krissy, and I was excited for her dinner party. I skipped lunch to make room for the feast I was certain she was going to present. My contribution was a dozen cupcakes from her favorite cake place — Make My Cake. The generous-sized cupcakes and creamy frosting packed a wallop of moist deliciousness that both Krissy and I enjoyed. I knew she'd be excited to see both the cupcakes and me.

Krissy's building sat on Central Park West in a renovated insane asylum. It was a chic address for New York — 105th and Central Park West. The elegant but friendly doorman greeted me at the door with a smile.

"Ms. Jackson is expecting you," he said, motioning toward the elevators. It was always astonishing how the doormen in this city remembered all of the residents and their close friends. I would certainly fail at that job because my memory always leaves me stranded, especially when it comes to names and people. Probably has a lot to do with what Vikki and I smoked a lot of in college.

As I stepped off the elevator, the aroma in the hall lifted me up by my nose and carried me to Krissy's door. Behind it, I could hear Miles Davis's iconic album, *Bitches Brew* playing from the large floor speaker connected to Krissy's iPod. She might like her hip-hop in the club, but she almost always had jazz playing in her home. And, almost always Miles. Just as I stepped inside the door left ajar, there he was. Drop-dead Justin. Greeting me with that million-watt smile, pushing his locks from his face. He immediately pulled me in for a man-hug, as I stood there limp with my mouth opened a bit.

Shocked, I had not expected him to be at the door. I knew they'd been consistently dating, but door greeter status was a leap. Curiosity immediately replaced my shock, as I know my sister-friend very well. There was more to this dinner than having the crew over for some Cinco de Mayo fun, especially if Drop-dead/Hedge-fund is meeting guests at the door. I love a good adventure, so I was up for the ride.

"What's up man...Justin, right?"

"Yep. Nothing much, brother. Just happy, man. Good to see you. Krissy's in the kitchen, and some of your other friends are in the living room. I'll take the bag, and you go grab a drink. We got some margaritas and tequila flowing."

Wait. Hold up just one minute. Did he just give me the Benson treatment in *my* friend's house? Yes, I guess he did. I was feeling very Ricky Ricardo at that moment, "Krissy, you gots some 'splainin' to do." But the way he did it was so smooth I could do nothing except oblige. As I walked into the living room, I saw Vikki and Dax.

"You guys beat me here," I said as I hugged Vikki and shook Dax's hand. They'd both changed into clothes that if I didn't know any better were fitted to the Mexican occasion, but tastefully so. She had on a thigh-length black dress that was covered in colorful flowers and a long fuchsia scarf that draped over one shoulder and down her back. Dax had on a black bolero like blazer, crisp white shirt, jeans, and Western-styled boots. It would be too much of a coincidence if this were not intentional. But their designer costumes were a cute and corny touch. Clowning Vikki about this borderline cheesy effect would come later, but my first mind was focused on getting one of those margaritas and a shot of Patron.

"We just got here about five minutes before you did." In that short time she'd managed to get a drink and finish half of it. True form. True Vikki. Dax was empty- handed.

"Not drinking tonight?" I asked him.

"Nah, I am. Just trying to pace myself. You know how your girl rolls, and I can't keep up if I start too early."

"It's Cinco de Mayo, and the only thing I know about it is drinking. Man up," I demanded playfully.

"Ahh shit, am I being punked?"

"Baby, it would look as if you are. Man up." At her encouragement, I made my way to the mahogany and glass bar in the corner. It was a mod- est-sized bar, but it was definitely the centerpiece of Krissy's living room. She had a builder replicate it after seeing a similar one that Miles Davis had. Usually, there were a plethora of bottles for her guests' enjoyment, but in line with today's theme, there was just a crystal carafe of margaritas flanked by a variety of tequilas. After setting two matching crystal rock glasses on the black glass top, I filled them halfway with the surely strong, pre-made margarita and gave them a herculean workout by topping the rest with Patron. Several sharp-edged ice cubes took synchronized dives into each glass completing the task. Done to perfection, I delivered one to Dax and then raised the other in a celebratory toast to him and Vikki.

"Happy Cinco de Mayo!"

"Whatever that means," said Vikki.

"It actually has two meanings. In Mexico, it's a celebration of the day the Mexican army defeated the French. El diá de la Batalla de Puebla. Here, it's to celebrate freedom during the early years in the Civil War," Dax lectured.

"I just wanted to have some drinks," Krissy said as she popped up behind us grabbing my drink and taking a gulp that she'd soon regret. "Damn! You added more tequila to the margarita? I put in a whole bottle already."

"That's what you get for playing with grown folks' toys," I said.

Krissy grimaced at me and turned her attention back to Dax. "So, Mr. Textbook, how'd you know all that?"

"An ex. Isn't that always the case?"

"So, you had a little Chimichanga who schooled you, huh?"

"Krissy!" I was flabbergasted. Not only by the total political incorrectness of the statement, but it was my job to grill Dax. Bursting into laughter, he clinked my glass that Krissy still had a tight grip on and didn't look like she was letting go of any time soon. Leading me to return to the Miles Davis to make another. Equally as perfect.

The stately doorbell (more fitting of a massive Tudor mansion than a two- bedroom apartment) rang, and I knew it had to be Rebecca. I hadn't called her since our episode following our workout. The credit was only half-owned by me because I hadn't created the uncomfortable situation. Believe it or not, I had never been placed in such a predicament by any of my friends. I'm no prude, but when it comes to infidelity, homie don't play that. Not a judgment thing either because again, I was no angel, I just don't want to be put in an awkward place with any of them and their S.O.S. I had kept my indiscretions private and thought I was clear that I expected the favor to be returned. Guess I wasn't.

"Looks like the party already started. What did I miss?" As Rebecca turned the corner from the door the smile that I had planned to greet her with dropped with the sight of her paramour this time minus the spaghetti straps but in clothes that fully revealed his body. The beams that emanated from the expertly crafted face would've brightened the room had they not landed sourly on the realization that Rebecca had just brought her "mister" to a "family" gathering. It was clear that she had lost her moral compass and her mind along with it. A million thoughts shot like bullets through my head, all of them aimed at injury. I looked at Vikki, as the only other person in the room who knew what was going on, to gauge her reaction. On cue, her jaws were dragging the floor right next to mine, and her clutched pearls expression let me know she felt the same as I did. Krissy and the guys were clueless. I wondered how long that would last.

"Hi there, I don't think we've met. I'm Krissy. Welcome to my home." The overly polite tone in her voice signaled to me that her suspicions were aroused. Naturally so, as I couldn't remember the last time Rebecca went anywhere with any man (who wasn't gay) other than Gerand.

"I'm Dillon. Thank you for having me," as he and Rebecca stepped into the party, now realizing that all eyes were firmly planted on them. Surely, Rebecca should have warned him of the result of his unexpected presence. Then I began to contemplate Rebecca's motivation. If she had warned him and they'd decided to come anyway, it spoke library-full volumes. Not only about her, but him, too. And possibly them together. Certainly they were taking this farce of a relationship too far. Gerand's shortcomings or not, Rebecca was still a married woman. Rebecca and I would talk later.

"Dillon, good to see you again. We met at the gym." I extended my hand in a firm yet distant handshake. "'Becks, always great to see you, my love." I double- cheeked her in as cold a manner as possible without seeming like a jerk. I wanted her to know, but I didn't want her to feel uncomfortable. It was a catch-22 that I was quickly learning to manipulate. As wrong as she was to bring him, Dillon was here now so might as well not make it any more unpleasant than it was already. They continued their advance to the center of the room near the Miles where everyone else was standing.

Rebecca introduced Dillon to Vikki, who gave a polite hand and smile. "But I don't know who this is. You must be Dax." Dax greeted Rebecca warmly; oblivious to the fragrant smell of discomfort that was permeating the room. He and Dillon gave strong and welcoming handshakes as two confident men would. Dillon's confidence, which in this situation translated into arrogance, began to stir up the foul taste that had been accumulating. Their actions had gone beyond distasteful to downright disrespectful of not only Gerand but of us as her friends. It burst out of me.

"Rebecca, can I speak to you for a moment?!" If they'd not been in sockets, Vikki's eyes surely would've rolled to the ground. Krissy too was taken aback by the abruptness and directness of my request. Or rather, my demand. Not quite the delivery I intended; yet the one that was most natural (and appropriate). Rebecca followed me to Krissy's bedroom without question or pause. Silently, I prayed for compassion. I wanted my words to come from the deep place of love I had for my sister-friend and not from some other place. It had to be done, though, because we'd crossed a border that none of us knew had to be patrolled.

"Before you start..."

"Me? I'm not the one who brought their boy-toy to our friend's apartment." I immediately regretted my burst of indignation when I saw Rebecca recoil. "I'm sorry, I don't mean to chastise you. I'm just shocked." I paused. "Wait, I do mean to chastise you. What the hell were you thinking?"

"I really don't know what I was thinking, but we were already out and there was something badass about it that was...exciting."

"At the expense of your friends, though?"

"I know. I'm wrong for involving you." So she was being deliberate. That's when I realized it wasn't about us. This was for her, just like the big reveal at lunch was about her. Maybe she thought telling us would make her less culpable or that somehow we would accept it. For a woman as concerned about propriety as Rebecca, there was clearly something deeper at play here for even the consideration of such an arrangement in the first place. This latest stunt was her quest for the validation that she sought in her own mind from friends she knew who would not approve but would ultimately protect her and keep her safe. Ride or die.

"I could kill you."

"We'll leave." There was something in her resignation, the way her shoulders hunched that made me realize no punishment I could inflict was greater than the prison she'd built for herself. We needed to discuss this more. Now was not the time, and if she left it would just create more awkwardness. I could hear the party raging back on full blast, and we needed to join our friends. And Dillon. As we walked back out, the fire that had been brewing was sputtering, having been overwhelmed by a friendship much stronger than indiscretion. But no, I didn't like it.

Reentering the fold was almost as uncomfortable as "Lady Chatterley's" entrance to the party with Spaghetti Straps. I headed straight to the bar to pour a third cocktail, one I hoped to finally drink. The Infidel joined Vikki, Dax, Justin, and her Private Dancer, who had a drink waiting for her. How cute. Just as I was about to pour a waterfall over the two large rocks in my glass — straight Patron this time — Krissy stepped up, grabbed me by the arm, and whispered for me to come with her. For an intimate party, there were already too many intimate moments. It was Krissy's house, and I knew there was no way around it. Hell, even if it weren't Krissy's house, there'd be no slaking her thirst for information (or mine for Patron it seemed). That cat would rather be killed than not know something that was going on, especially with her friends. So, unwillingly I obliged, like a reluctant child being dragged behind his insistent mother in a mall. Except this time it was to the kitchen. My consolation was the preview of what was in the magic pots, which Krissy began stirring in rotation with one hand and the other on her hip.

"So?"

"So, what?"

"Please don't make me cuss yo' ass out. You know what. She's fucking him, ain't she?"

I avoided answering the question directly by raising one of the other lids to her coordinated stainless steel Calphalon pots. Krissy snatched the lid and put it back down then, placed her hand back on her hip, and formed a perch with her lips suitable for a crow. And that's exactly what she wanted me to do.

"What do you think?"

"I think Ms. Prim and Proper is getting her groove on." I gave her a look of confirmation, and she replied with a look of satisfaction. Krissy and Rebecca got along, but cordially so. At least on Krissy's end. She often thought of Rebecca as a sellout for not only marrying a white man but also adopting a purely white existence outside of our crew. Actually, outside of me. If not for the women I'd introduced Rebecca to, she'd have no African American female friends. It didn't bother me and my United Nations sensibilities. But it unnerved Krissy. Even

Lauren, as a white woman, found it a bit suspect. Vikki is so consumed with Vikki that I doubt it ever crossed her mind beyond when Krissy mentioned it.

"Let her tell you. You know I don't do gossip."

"Chile, please. Plus, between friends, it's not gossip."

"Just let her tell you."

"My lips are sealed. I just knew it from the moment she walked in with him. I ain't really mad at her, though. Gerand has been fucking around for years."

"You don't know that." As the words passed my lips I knew I didn't really believe it, and obviously Krissy wasn't into that charade either because she barely acknowledged the statement. As she began to turn down the fires burning on the pots, I was both relieved and excited that it was time for dinner. I definitely would be doubling up on the libations once we sat down. I prayed that nothing would get out of hand, but if it did, hopefully I would be too tipsy to care.

"What are you two up to in here? We miss you guys," joked Justin as he appeared in the kitchen.

"Hush, boy, you're just being nosey," said Krissy.

"I mean, who wouldn't want to know what is going with all of the sidebars?"

"The food is almost done. Everybody can sit," said Krissy, dismissing Justin's questions. He might not have known Krissy long, but he knew her well enough to do what he was told and disappeared back into the living room.

"You got him trained already."

"Chile, you know I don't play. And how do I tell him that one of my married friends just brought her sidepiece to my house. I don't want him thinking that's how we roll."

"True. This dinner should be interesting. I hope you have enough licka."

"Chile, I got bottles and bottles. Can you put these placemats on the table?"

Doing as I was told, I returned to the living/dining room just as everyone else was taking their seats. Dax pulled out Vikki's chair and took the seat next to her. Dillon did the same for Rebecca, prompting an exchange of raised eyebrow looks between Vikki and me. Justin returned to the kitchen to help Krissy bring out the dishes. After placing the placemats, I headed back to the Miles to finally get my drink. I needed a bigger glass to be sufficiently prepared for this sit-down.

"No side-by-side couples. Krissy's orders," said Justin reappearing from the kitchen with a bowl of arroz con pollo in one hand and huge bowl of guacamole in the other.

Krissy hurriedly came out of the kitchen to correct him, "it's OK, babe. People can sit where they want."

"But, you said..."

"I know, it's cool, though," Krissy said cutting Justin off. She smiled at Justin, begging him with her eyes to drop it. He obliged. They continued to bring out the food as I took my seat on the other side of Dax. He had been saved because I had planned on continuing the inquisition from earlier. Rebecca's guest selection had thwarted that mission. It would take all of my concentration to make it through the dinner issue-free. Just as I resolved to get to know Dax more some other time, Krissy and Justin brought in the remainder of the Mexican meal. She had outdone herself once again. In addition to the rice with chicken and guacamole, there was also carne asada, enchiladas suizas, and pork carnitas. Add in the freshly baked chips and tortillas she picked up from Rosa Mexicano and the tortillas; I was glad that I had gotten in a good workout.

"What a feast," said Dax. "It looks great."

"Wait to taste it first," said Krissy as she took her seat the head of the table. Justin sat at the other end next to Dillon, still adhering to Krissy's previous no side-by-side couples mandate.

"Sweetie, we all know it's going to be good," said Vikki, who then turned to Dax. "Krissy is the most amazing cook. As you know, I make great reservations." Vikki's joke lightened the tension in the room as we all laughed.

"Yes, I am quite aware that I am not marrying you for your domestic skills."

"So, you said yes?" asked Krissy.

"I hope that ring sitting on her finger means, yes." Dax was obviously oblivious to Vikki's apprehensions. It was probably a good thing. Even with everything going on, I was shocked to have missed Gibraltar on Vikki's left hand and at lunch she'd said she wasn't going to marry him. I was starting to get a headache.

"Have you two set a date?" asked Dillon.

"Not exactly. I keep asking Vikki when. I would do it tomorrow if she said she was down for it."

"No need to rush anymore than we already have," said Vikki.

"I'm excited to marry her, if you can't tell. But, I am willing to be patient. Just not too long," then Dax smiled at Vikki and leaned in for a kiss.

The dishes began to be passed around the table as each of us served healthy portions of the delicious-looking meal Krissy had prepared. Everyone except Dillon, who let all but the guacamole pass him by. This was not lost on Krissy, who had been watching with the eye of a lawyer and the sensitivity of a chef. As the dishes found their way back to the center of the table, Dillon's plate remained mostly empty.

"Not hungry, Dillon?" asked Krissy.

"He's on a strict diet," interjected Rebecca.

"Oh, really? Why?" snarled Krissy.

"He's going on tour in two weeks."

"Are you his spokesperson?" Krissy's claws were coming out.

"No, he's a dancer," I jumped into the fray trying to give Krissy a clue to back off.

"Can't he speak for himself?" She was not giving up easily.

"I can. Yes, I dance with Ballet Ciudad. I don't eat meat. But you're making me rethink that. It looks awesome." Krissy surveyed her carnivorous

meal and realized that the only thing a vegetarian could eat was the guacamole. There was probably some chicken grease in there, too.

"Oh, my bad. I guess that I didn't think about having a vegetarian over.
No one told me." The hostess in Krissy took over. "Seriously, I am sorry. I
can make you a salad or some vegetables."

"No, not necessary. I know I wasn't expected."

"You think?" said Vikki and from the look on her face I knew that
slipped out.

Dax jumped in, "Man, I tried to be a vegetarian once. For three weeks.
I started having dreams about bacon, and it was a wrap." To my knowledge, he was unaware of the situation, yet his timing was perfect.

"Bacon is your friend," was my contribution.

"I have to say I miss a bacon burger the most," said Dillon as the
general atmosphere got lighter than it had been all night. Those who were
aware had quietly resolved to be adults and get through it. Justin and Dax
might not have known the details, but they surely knew everything wasn't
easy and breezy.

"Back to you two," Rebecca seized the opportunity to move the nee-
dle from her seat and to Vikki. "Are you going to have a big wedding or
something small? I can understand since this will be number three for
Vikki."

Damn. Rebecca had just unconsciously raised the temperature in the
room back to hell. No one said a word because we all knew that we had
been turning off a path and Rebecca's comment had returned us to the
center of it. Vikki was visibly upset by her carelessness but chose to ignore it.

Vikki replied, "You will all get invitations soon enough." Skillful
shutdown.

"We'll be sure to send you our new address," said Justin who had
been motionless and without comment the entire meal. Krissy's eyes
pierced through him as she looked up. Had she not been so reactive I
don't think it would have been significant to any of us. There was so much

going on that Justin's statement would have been innocuous compared to the rest of the evening's story lines.

Then Krissy unexpectedly went for it. "Justin asked me to move in with him." Here I was thinking we'd had enough circus for the night, but Krissy's words assured me that I had entered an alternate *Truman Show*-esque universe. Less than a month ago, Krissy had met Drop Dead, and now they were talking about living together. This was Flo-Jo fast, especially for Krissy. As we had discussed the night she met Justin, her (bad) taste in men had thankfully kept her from falling too deep for any one of them. They were temporary situations that she could dispose of at any time, and she liked it that way. When she was done, there was no hassle. No long drawn-out emotional breakups. By the end, usually no emotions at all... at least for Krissy.

"I know it sounds ridiculous, but like your boy Eckhart Tolle says, 'It's about the power of the now. Right?" declared Krissy who had never quoted Tolle before but clearly was using his words out of context to justify herself. As if moving in with Justin was not some big deal considering that they'd only known each other for two seconds. I wondered if she knew his middle name. Or if he even had a middle name. His mother's name.

"Ridiculous, nah. Not at all." I gulped the rest of my drink and checked out.

"She keeps saying that you all would say that she was crazy, which is why we decided to have this dinner," said Justin. Krissy looked directly at me, waiting. The entire table seemed to turn their energy toward me.

She *is* crazy was the sole thought I had. I was beginning to believe they all were. The last couple of months had been a whitewater raft ride with no breaks or breaths. All hell had broken loose — no end in sight. There was no more normal. I cringed at the thought that I might have to accept that this *was* the new normal.

"Love has no rules. Why the hell not?" I said. And I believed that in theory. But moving in with someone you barely knew? There were definitely rules about that.

My statement mostly relieved everyone, though there was a tinge of shock on their faces that it had rolled off that simply. I did take a big brother position with Krissy, but I was unable to play that role tonight. I wanted all of the curveballs to be straight again, so I rolled with it.

"We're going to take our time. It's where we're headed, though," rationalized the real Krissy, who had finally decided to show back up in this conversation.

"When you know it's right, you know it's right," said Dax, who was on board and who annoyed me for the first time the entire day. Stay out of it.

My thoughts must have translated to my face because Vikki switched the subject with no consideration of finesse. "How's the planning for the Literacy Gala going?"

"Great. It should be the best we've done yet," I lied. I actually had no idea what was going on with the gala. Ruby and I hadn't spoken in weeks. She attributed it to letting me focus on work. It was understandable and appreciated because I was busy working on the article and trying to stir the pot for a new production. However, I could have contributed and known more.

"You must be excited," said Rebecca.

The mention of the gala and the thought of being out of sync with the planning made me remember something I read about one of the planets being in retrograde or something to that affect. Saturn must definitely be crashing into Mercury. "I can't wait," was all I had left.

Chapter Nine

Reading Between the Lines

It was such a beautiful evening; I decided to walk to the Schomburg Center where the Children's Literacy Gala was scheduled to take place. It was another unseasonably warm night that I welcomed because when the weather is good, New York has no rival. Feeling like Fred Astaire in my charcoal grey Joseph Abboud tux, I strolled happily along Lenox Avenue in Harlem, ignoring the stares. There was a time when a dapperly dressed man was the norm, not the exception. How did we devolve to the point where a man in a suit was a sight to see but a thirty-year-old man's underwear overflowing from his sagging jeans an everyday thing?

Faults and all, I loved Harlem for all of its richness of character, not only in the people but also in the smells, the buildings, the sounds. There was no place on earth like Harlem, where people of such varied socioeconomic backgrounds all lived together in a tiny stretch of green and brown. I would miss the neighborhood as I knew there was nothing that would come close in L.A.

My stroll included a couple of Astaire-like skips as "Singin' in the Rain" played in my head. Nobody could be blamed for staring then, but I didn't care. I was happy. Happy to be doing some good for the community. Happy to be dressed up in my "good clothes." And happy I'd get a chance to catch up with Ruby. This would be our fourth year of co-chairing the gala together. Although Ruby and I had been out of touch recently, we always had a ball at these events — drinking too much, dancing and doing the New York gala thing.

As a teenager, I dreamed of walking red carpets. Wasn't quite sure why, but I knew I wanted to do it. By now, I'd walked plenty and I'd gotten to the point where I only liked to walk a carpet if I had a purpose. And if they knew who I was. What could be more embarrassing than a walk down a red, pink or purple carpet and having no one want to take your picture? It had happened once, and that was one too many times. Tonight, they definitely knew who I was, so I was going to walk it proudly.

The Schomburg Center for Research in Black Culture is really a part of the New York Public Library but was renamed to celebrate Arthur Schomburg, the famed historian who devoted his life to highlighting the contributions made by Afro-Latin Americans and Afro-Americans to society. It was befittingly placed in the heart of Harlem on Lenox Avenue where so much of our culture was birthed and cultivated. Approaching the steps, I marveled at the thought of the many folks that had preceded me in this space. I wondered if Langston, Zora, and Baldwin would be proud of us today. There was still much work to be done, but we were a long way from where we began and in such a comparatively short span of time. The thought made me feel good walking up to the black carpet just outside the entrance.

A young guy in his twenties wearing a headset with clipboard in hand ran up to me. Must be my escort. "I take it you're assigned to me," I said with a smile.

"Yes, sir."

"We'll only have a problem if you continue to call me sir. Do I look like a sir to you?"

"No, sir. I mean, no...you look great."

"Why thank you...um, what's your name?"

"Adam."

"Adam, cool. Let's do this. Do you know if my co-host, Ruby has made it here yet? We usually do this together."

"Yes, she came in about twenty minutes ago with Mr. Somers, I think." Really? I'd timed my arrival perfectly to meet Ruby on the carpet to do our traditional entrance. I looked at my watch. I was on time. Plus, Ruby and

Steve together? Still? And Steve walking anything in Harlem was even stranger than the weather. This was going to be an evening of surprises, I thought, as the bulbs on the carpet began to snap, crackle, and pop. It was show time and so I plastered a wide smile on my face and began to make my way down the carpet. My first stop was my friend, Janet, from the local newspaper in Harlem, the *Amsterdam News*.

"This marks the fourth year you're chairing the gala. Why do you keep doing it?" she asked.

"If you can't read, the odds that you will remain in poverty are exponentially increased. Unfortunately, illiteracy rates in our communities remain at unacceptable levels, and it becomes a never-ending cycle in families. For me, education was the great equalizer, so I feel it's my duty to give back and provide young people who may not have had the same opportunities I had a chance." The question focused my mind back on the task at hand. I was there on a mission, and so my friend drama had to be put aside so I could put my best foot forward to highlight the work of the foundation. No matter what, we had raised a lot of money to help children, and my ego needed to take a back seat. The black carpet took about forty-minutes and had been exceptionally long compared to other years, which was a good sign that more people were interested in the cause. It was also because Ruby and I had done our best to invite celebrities and notable New Yorkers who attracted the kind of attention and dollars that the foundation needed to do its work. I wrapped the carpet feeling just as good as I had felt walking up Lenox Avenue to the event.

Inside, I was greeted by all of the friends and colleagues I'd invited to attend, but when someone asked about Ruby my focus turned to finding her whom I had yet to see after almost an hour of being there. I couldn't be rude or phony, so I stopped to chat with all the guests I knew, which took another twenty minutes as I made my way through the crowd. Then, I saw them — Ruby and Steve.

A smile came across my face, and I waved. Ruby, however, looked away as Steve gave a nod of recognition. Someone must have thought it was warmer than it was outside and turned up the air conditioner considering the chill I felt. I stopped to process the response and then walked over, resolved to get to the bottom of this. Despite my frustration with all that had transpired and the bubbling tension, I had to acknowledge that Ruby looked amazing in a red strapless gown with a black strip of velvet fabric going down the side that trumpeted into a short train behind her. The dress itself would have been elegant but plain had it not been for the incredible diamond necklace with a dazzling ruby at its center around her neck. I wasn't quite sure if it was real or not as many of the women at these events sport crystals or CZs because no one will dare challenge them. I had also come to know that very few people actually knew the difference upon casual inspection. Yet there was something about the sparkle of these diamonds accented by that ruby that said it was real.

"You did the carpet without me."

"I had so much to get in and do. It's been a crazy night."

"What can I do? You've done so much. Let me take it from here."

"It's OK. I've got it under control. Let me go make sure they're prepared for the program. You look good." Ruby uncomfortably flitted away, grabbing Steve's hand. He looked back at me. "Good to see you," came from his pale lips, as dry and cold as he and Ruby's reception.

"Steve," I nodded standing there dumbfounded. Surely, that wasn't my sister-friend Ruby. And surely, she didn't just do that to me.

"Don't you look smashing, my dear." I turned around and was greeted by two brown, perfectly round melons propped up and pointing directly at me. Tina. The chill I felt earlier quickly vanished, thanks to the warmth of Tina's sex appeal. There were so many things that she could get away with. Always having her 'girls' on full display was one of the things she owned with an appropriateness most other women could not sell. It was never vulgar, but consistently stunning. Tonight, she and her girls had slid into a muted silver wrap dress that hugged her curves like a toddler hugs his teddy bear.

"Damn, girl, you make a brother rethink some things." I leaned in to give Tina a hug and the essential air kiss. As usual, her smell brought back those good memories of the women I knew growing up. Your favorite aunt, the loving teacher, your mother. The big-bosomed smell of love and familiarity. I think that is what I liked most about Tina. It wasn't the fabulousness (although she was extra fabulous). It was the familiarity. I knew Tina. And, I'd loved many Tinas in my life. Tina takes care of you. That's probably why it was so easy for her to get so many knights in shining.

I squeezed her tightly. Partly because she looked good, mostly because she'd instantly provided comfort. I listened to my spirit and believed Tina's appearance was God's reminder that all was good in the world and my sense of vulnerability in the moment with Ruby and Steve was nonsense. I was here to have a good time and not get intertwined in Steve and Ruby's incessant drama, which was undoubtedly the root of the issue. Again, I had let myself get caught up and distracted from the cause at hand.

"Let me stop before some tall and handsome comes and gets upset with me."

"No worries, gorgeous. Ms. Tina is flying Lindbergh tonight. I knew all of my pets would be here, so I wanted to play and be petted. So get a good grip, but after we get a cocktail. I am beyond thirsty. And, at the price of these tickets, I expect to be right and toasty when we saunter out of here." We strolled into the back section reserved for VIPs or people who had paid enough to be considered so for the evening. It was nice to have Tina there because she knew far more people than I did, and she could do most of the talking. Once we got our drinks, I reveled in her ability to hold court with the best of them, thinking to myself that we should hang out far more.

All of Harlem's elite passed by us at one time or another and even more drinks passed our lips. I was having so much fun that I lost track of time and consideration of Ruby's crazy behavior (for the most part). Then one of the staffers ran into the room in a panic, an abrupt contrast to the festive atmosphere we had all been enjoying. Tina and I watched as the young woman with studious glasses, crisp white button-down shirt, and long chocolate satin skirt frantically looked searchingly around the room. Then, her mousy-brown eyes zeroed in on me, and she scurried our way.

"The program has started. We were looking everywhere for you. I'm supposed to be assigned to you. This is my first event. They're going to kill me. We need you now," Mousy spewed at the speed of light in exasperation. I was exhausted for her.

"No problem, sweetheart. It's OK; I'll make sure no one kills you. Tina, will you join me? Showtime."

"But, of course."

I grabbed Tina's arm, placed a calming hand on Mousy's back and motioned for her to lead the way to the stage. Behind her, Tina and I gave each other a look and smiled. We'd both been there. Young, eager and ready to please. Thinking every little thing could break your chances of becoming what you've dreamed. Not understanding that most of it is inconsequential, and it always works out. Always. A reminder that you couldn't pay me to be an early twenty-something ever again.

We made our way through the crowd, sending silent hellos and waves while the executive director of the Literacy Fund, Charlene, was welcoming all of the satin, sequins, and silk to the Gala. You certainly couldn't tell the country had come out of a recession not too many years ago by the looks of this room. And, although Wall Street was booming main street was still looking for a living wage. The wardrobe budget alone could feed all of the hungry in Harlem and then some. Social commentary aside, it was good to see black, white, brown, and all of the colors of the rainbow dressed to the nines in their finest and it was for a good cause. You can't be sad or serious all of the time.

I was extremely grateful to be there and for everything that had gotten me there. It humbled (and sobered) me as we made our way to the front of the crowd. Ruby had just taken the stage, so I decided to wait until she introduced me for my remarks. As she spoke, I beamed with pride. We'd done it again. Another successful night. Another successful collaboration, even if this time around it was a bit lopsided. Maybe she had been thinking of me. It didn't really matter at this point because when Ruby and I worked together for this charity, it was always a good thing.

I lost myself in the sentimentality of the moment until she said, "And so, thank you so much for your support. I hope you enjoy the remainder of the night. DJ!"

Instantly, I felt all of the twos and fours on me in the room. Surely, she'd made a mistake, or I must not have heard my name.

"She didn't even mention you. What's up with that?" whispered Tina in my ear. For the second time in one night, Ruby had blatantly dissed me, this time in front of the entire room of guests. I stood with my feet frozen to the glossy hardwood floor, unable to move. Brain on pause from the shock of the moment. Once unfrozen, my brain went through the chain of events of the past months with computer-like speed. She wasn't being considerate. This was intentional. I had been squeezed out. And Ruby had done it all on purpose. But why? I hadn't done anything to her to deserve this treatment. A façade of a smile came across my face, and I began to applaud along with the rest of the star-ing crowd.

I grabbed Tina's arm and walked back through the crowd as if everything had gone as planned. I despise gratuitous public displays of affection but not as much as I loathe public displays of dissension. Inside, however, my spirit was burning, and my heart was a barrow of bricks. With each step, the weight of it all slowed me down. I prayed that my legs would remain sturdy and not buckle under the load. Thankfully, Tina held me steady by the arm.

"I missed it, didn't I?" panted Krissy as she ran up on us almost out of nowhere. A good thing that she had missed Ruby's dismissive antics; otherwise things might have turned up to a level that was better suited for her old Harlem days. She was the sister that you called when the school bully had gone too far.

"What's wrong? I'm really sorry I missed it. Long story. But we'll save that for another day." I didn't respond through my painted smile. Krissy took one look at me and immediately stopped the questions. She realized my mood had nothing to do with her being tardy. She probably could also tell from my pace that I wanted to get to a private spot as soon as possible. She and Tina, with her ebullient waves and smiles, pushed me through various partiers attempting to stop and engage. We found the bar first, then a small section in the private lounge where we finally stopped and formed a small, tight circle.

"I know this has something to do with Ruby. What did that bitch do?"

"She was completely out of line. I was flabbergasted. She acted as if he wasn't here," explained Tina.

"I'ma fuck her up!"

"Not necessary. Definitely not the time," I said trying to calm down.

"Seriously, she's always been sometimey to me. Whatever she did, I know it was foul. And I know you didn't deserve it," said a fired up Krissy who had no intention of calming down.

But, she had a point. It was completely undeserved and it reeked. Ruby was a hard sell to many people. I'd seen her bad behavior and mistreatment of other people for personal gain. Never expected I would be on the receiving end. I always took pride in the obviously unfounded belief that our bond was special and different. Deep down I hoped this was all a misunderstanding. But I also knew it wasn't. I was anxious about the conversation we would definitely have and more so about what I would discover.

"We're gonna talk, believe me. Right now, I want to enjoy the rest of this party and act like I'm the host of it." Krissy reluctantly yielded, and Tina went to grab some more drinks. As the night progressed, I didn't see Ruby or Steve again. I presumed they'd left shortly after the stage. Probably for the best considering I had a wildcat with me who was ready to pounce. It also allowed me to come out of the seclusion of the private lounge and mingle with the main party without having to deal with my issues with my lovely co-host and her fake necklace.

Before I got too petty, I decided to focus on my impending trip with Lauren and Vikki to St. Barth's for Memorial Day. One of my favorite chefs,

Jean-Georges, had opened a new restaurant at the Eden Rock Hotel there since the last time I'd been, and in low season it was less of a scene (and less expensive). Lauren needed a break since she'd asked Josh to take a few weeks in L.A. while she decided what to do next, and it would be fun to play with the kids. It could not come fast enough.

Chapter Ten

Getting Clear

The air was dry from the sun and lack of consistent breeze as we walked out of the comfort of the air-conditioned airport in St. Maarten to the shuttle that would take us to the plane. To be clear, the use of the word *plane* was a stretch since the impending aircraft was far inferior in size to the bus we had been riding in to meet it. St. Barth's was definitely an elite, grown-up playground reserved for the very rich and the very famous, particularly during high season in December and January. A scene that I didn't mind because any jaunt there translated into an opportunity for business nestled under the guise of pleasure. To see the jet set at ease in an accessible environment made the extravagant price tags on everything from lobster to water worth it. This time, however, we were going during the relatively calm time of Memorial Day Weekend. Sights were to be had and plenty, but not in the abundance of the Jingle Bells and Auld Lang Syne time. Vikki was appropriately chic. Her floppy hat conjured up old Hollywood glamour, and she went for silent film melodrama by highlighting the look with Marlene Dietrich-style sunglasses.

The bus driver greeted us with a wide smile and a hello, and we were met with stares by two couples already seated. Either they were shocked to see persons of our dark hue, or they were trying to figure out if we too were a couple. Either way, it didn't matter; my plan was to decompress and get away from all that had transpired back in New York. The sun always had a way of rejuvenating me from the outside in, and although I was not a big fan of beaches, some time by the ocean was definitely on my mind. I knew Lauren was still reeling from her issues with Josh, but we had pledged not to dwell on the tragic while in paradise's lap. Vikki was the perfect addition because she was comparatively low maintenance and high fun. A more perfect vacation could not have been imagined or planned — I was beyond enthusiastic about it all.

The catch is there are only two ways to get to St. Barth's. Either by short plane jump or an extended, bumpy boat ride. Simple sounding but not. The runway on the island has an infamous history of not only being shorter than my block in Harlem and thus only capable of accommodating the smallest of small planes but also being notoriously over and undershot by these crop duster pilots. In preparation, I downed a Valium with some water while my sister-friend looked on with a bit of pity and slight disdain. Her judgment didn't bother me, though, because nothing was going to separate me from the rest and relaxation I'd been dreaming about for weeks. Nothing. Not even a small-ass plane. We deboarded the shuttle bus and walked up to the pilot and the ground person who helped us all step into the door right off the wing. We jumped in first so we could sit in the third and last row because I wanted to be as far from the pilot as possible. Still, if I reached my arm far enough I could graze his shoulder. I began to recall the pristine beaches, the pillow-soft sand and the never-ending cocktails from my last visit five years ago. These thoughts would soothe me until the medicinal relaxer kicked in — in one, two...three. I was ready to fly.

Once in the air, it was easy to forget the peril I was putting myself in for pleasure. I was lost in the wonder of nature as we soared over the rolling waves and waters jumping with life. It wasn't long before the engines began slowing down and we climbed over the mountains to prepare for the U-turn required to land on the tic-tac-sized runway. Despite the help in pill form, I tensed slightly. This was the main event. It was midday and clear so there should be no chance for pause or issue, but you never know. After my prayer, I went somewhere else and it was over. Now, idled down to a purr, the engines stopped their hum as the door opened and the effort was complete. I could see Lauren's silhouette just inside the small airport waiting for us, and I was relieved to let the relaxation games begin.

Lauren stood solemn. As we got closer, a smile broke across her face — not forced, but not full. Well, we were going to correct that with this trip. The plan was leisure time together doing nothing except enjoying each other's company, good food, and a cocktail here and there. With the kids along for the journey and the general laid- back nature of the island, we'd definitely be in bed early each night. Vikki would undoubtedly liven it up a bit. She would push us to have some fun beyond the daily activities and, given her popularity, the house party invitations would soon be aplenty. The relief that we'd made it safely, coupled with the thoughts of the great vacation that lay ahead of us, cracked a humongous happy grin on my face that widened Lauren's smile when we embraced.

"It's so good to see you," said Lauren with a breathiness that gave away her slight exasperation. She grabbed one of Vikki's bags and turned toward the car waiting on the side of the road just outside the airport. If you didn't know it, you would think the island was some undiscovered territory, with its dirt roads and other rural qualities. You would never guess it was the place where the wealthy came to play. But it was the island's rustic nature that attracted the elite here. They could walk around in sundresses and casual attire — all the work of the world's most fabulous designers who attempted to make even the expensive beachwear look effortless. Lauren had on a beautiful ankle-length dress covered in small but intricate pastel flowers loosely held on her shoulders by thin straps. If she had been fuller-bosomed it might have been too much, but with her slight body it was sexy. Her hair was pulled up in her signature loose, I'm-gorgeous-without-trying updo. She may have been going through it, but you couldn't tell by her appearance.

"Sweetie, you should have seen him on the plane. He winced and whined the entire way. It was downright embarrassing for such a hunk of man to act like a little girl."

"Are you starting with me already? You know damn well those tiny planes scare the hell out of me. Always have. And I'm not ashamed."

"You should be, you big creampuff."

"Kiss it. All you need to do is look at the incident rate of those small planes to understand why. Give me first class on a 747 any day. You can keep your private jets."

"Look, Lucy and Ethel, are you hungry?" Lauren asked while laughing at our back-and-forth.

"I could eat," I said because it was usually the truth.

"Yes, I could use something, too."

"OK, well we should stop at the market because it's between lunch and dinner now and I have to get a few more things for the house. You can grab a sandwich or salad from the deli next door. Does that work?"

"Perfect for me. I just want to take a moment at the house to recover from that treacherous plane ride."

"Enough with the dramatics already. Works for me, too," said Mean Girl Vikki.

When we arrived at the café I was reminded of two things: how non-fancy my palate is and how expensive this island is. I just wanted a turkey or tuna salad sandwich, not the exotic fare that was presented, mostly in French, on the café chalkboard. But I would figure something out.

"Je vais avoir le couscous aux légumes, veuillez," said Vikki to the man behind the counter.

"What did you order?" I asked.

"Couscous with vegetables."

"No, thank you. What are you getting, Lauren?"

"A cheese sandwich."

"Can someone order me something simple? Meat. Bread. Lettuce."

"You really need to learn another language. As much as you travel," scolded Vikki. Again, she was right, but at my age I couldn't even begin to wrap my mind around learning another language. Anything remotely close to school made me recoil. I had done well in school only because that was what was expected. I certainly did not like it in the least, and once I was done I vowed never to return.

Lauren then ordered for both of us, "Je vais avoir du fromage sandwich. Il aimerait avoir un sandwich au poulet sur pain de blé avec de la laitue et brie." I looked at her impressed and confused. "Chicken breast on wheat bread with brie," she translated to me.

"Awesome. Now we're talking. Should we get something for the kids?"

"No, Maira has them covered."

"I wish there were nannies for adults." I envied the kids because Maira was from Honduras and knew her way around the kitchen as evidenced by her very healthy figure. I know they ate something great, hearty, and pronounceable. Sure, I liked sushi, caviar, and foie gras from time to time. I preferred, however, a good old steak and potatoes if it was an option. My tastebuds never quite caught up with my lifestyle or my friends. I had no intent of changing that fact. After I paid for our lunch, we drove around the back to the market. Lauren encouraged us to get whatever culinary creature comforts we would need for our stay. We split up and met back at the register.

A parade of various grocery items passed along the conveyor belt. Vikki and I added only a couple of things because what Lauren had placed in the cart covered the entire store. I could tell by the assortment of meats and naughty snacks that she was picking up things with our diets (or lack thereof) in mind as well. Always a gracious hostess in spite of whatever she was dealing with personally. Lauren had a way of moving forward no matter what her circumstances were. It was a quality I admired about her, especially given her extremely privileged upbringing. A spoiled little rich girl she definitely was not. She was a fighter in the most refined way, and her resiliency came from a deep place that is innately who she is. It was a tribute to her parents and family who never gave her or her siblings a sense of entitlement because they were rich. She was raised to believe that life was a tough ordeal and that we'd all have to overcome setbacks and obstacles. It gave her the resolve to continue to search for her light in the darkest of moments. That type of attitude is what attracted me to her when we first met and what continued to inspire our friendship. A bit of her sparkle was coming back as she was much more buoyant than when we first arrived. Being around friends will bring out the shine in you and lift you higher.

The groceries totaled nearly five hundred euro, and Lauren handed the counter woman her Amex. The woman ran the card through the machine and then waited with a strange look on her face. She ran it through the machine again before handing the card back to Lauren.

"Avez-vous une autre carte? Cette carte a été diminué," said the woman. I didn't have to speak French to understand that Lauren's platinum Amex had been declined. I had never seen that happen to her before. Her cards always go through. She's Lauren.

"I'm sorry. I only brought this one. The others are at home."

"Sweetie, no worries. It has happened to the best of us. You probably just need to let them know you're abroad. In the meantime, I've got it." Vikki reached in her purse and gave the woman one of her cards. Lauren's spark fizzled, and a look of embarrassment overcame her face. Having your card denied here or there may happen to the rest of us, but it was not something that Lauren was used to have happen, ever. Just like that, things were tense again as I loaded the groceries in the trunk while Vikki and Lauren slid into the front two seats of the car.

"Thank you, Vikki. I will withdraw some cash on the way to the house."

"Sweetie, it's the least I can do. You're providing free room and board. I should have offered in the first place. Plus, I'm sure there was some mistake. You'll clear it up when we get back to the house. No matter what, we are here to have a great time and there will be nothing that stands in the way of it. Problems left in the States," Vikki said. The effect on Lauren wasn't instant, but it was a start.

◆ ◆ ◆

Vikki stormed onto the deck of the pool where Lauren and I had been sitting watching the kids take one last dip. "Can you both be ready in an hour?" she asked startling me out of the light sleep I was enjoying, intermittently nodding off between the requests for "Uncle" to watch this trick or that race. The kids were so caught up in the splish-splash of their water play that I'm not even sure they realized Auntie Vikki had made a grand entrance onto the deck in a brightly patterned chiffon caftan and in-style turban covering her hair that was still drying from the earlier all-in swim time. Neither Lauren nor I responded quickly, but by the way Vikki stood there I knew she wasn't taking no for an answer. Since our arrival, we'd spent the great majority of our time over the last two days in the house except for our lunch adventures to the Eden Rock and to Taiwana to see who else was on the island and to break up the monotony. Although I don't think either Lauren or I minded the downtime in the privacy of the beautiful home. Everything we needed was in the house, so there really wasn't much incentive to leave. We had food. We had kids. We had libations. We had each other. In my book, nothing else was required.

"What have you been in there cooking up?" I asked. "I knew you were up to something when you disappeared and jumped on your phone. You haven't been on the phone since we arrived. Except to make reservations"

"Sweetie, we're heading over to Randy's. He's having a little soirée at his house."

"The music guy?" I asked in slight protest.

"Yes, he throws the best parties and always has interesting artistic, handsome people. You might meet someone."

"Please take a thousand seats. If I'm not interested in meeting anyone in New York, what makes you think I came here lookin'?"

"For Pete's sake, we're on vacation. We can't just sit in the damn house playing Rummi every night," said a frustrated Vikki.

"I love Rummi," said Lauren who I also knew was not up to some industry party crowd night.

"Look Rummi is fine, but we are not the fucking Golden Girls. Both of you get your asses in gear, put on something cute, and be ready in an hour. End of story." Immediately following her declaration, Vikki returned back inside the house with clearly no further word on the subject to be tolerated. Lauren and I looked at each other with the understanding that there was no choice, and I felt more like the kids we were watching than the nearly forty-year-old man I was. But Vikki had spoken, and she meant what she said, so my brain started rummaging through my suitcase. If I was going to be around the music business, I was certainly planning on representing the movie business well.

As it turned out, we all represented well by stepping up our style game more than we had since we arrived. I mentally regarded how good we looked as we walked up to the enormous door of Randy's house. It sat atop one of the mountains, though you could barely see it until you traveled farther up the winding road. Lauren's house was very nice. But Randy's house was classic music business "I have arrived" impressive. One thing you had to give it to the music folks for was their belief in the motto, "go hard or go home." They were mostly nouveau riche people, many of whom were essentially street hustlers. But I admired that about them. They were unashamed of excess, and the more success they enjoyed, the more access they had. So it didn't matter if the bluebloods or the black bourgeois (who tried hard to forget their beginnings) criticized them for being garish and gauche; they were determined to get money, spend money, and get more of it. And in this society, money opens doors. Which ones that opened primarily depended upon how much money you had. Jay-Z has dinner with President Obama and Bill Gates and now Oprah, too. Jay-Z used to sell drugs for a living. The American dream at work, and I wasn't mad at it.

Randy was a bit of an anomaly in the music business, though. He'd come up through the ranks as a sound engineer. For almost all of the 80s, he was the go-to guy if you wanted the best mastering and mixing. But Randy started as a sought-after studio session pianist in the 70s. Then he was forced to switch over to engineering when he lost two fingertips in a car accident and could no longer play. The injury also inspired him to develop an automated soundboard that would adjust all of the levels on the board via a computer. Nothing like a big, game-changing idea to change your life. After that, he began producing for everyone, leading him to run his own label imprint under a major. Actually, he and Steve were industry rivals, which made him not too fond of Ruby either. Go figure.

I had met Randy before, but I wasn't sure he really remembered me any of the times we'd run into each other. He was the kind of gentleman that made you feel as if he knew your life story even if he didn't remember your name. That had clearly served him well in the business because, unlike Steve who had many enemies, he was extremely well regarded in and outside the music business. With that said, I was still uncertain as to what I should expect from the evening. It was music industry folks, and so you never know what could happen.

It seemed as if Vikki had barely pressed the doorbell when the door opened up, and there was Randy's gorgeous wife, Kari. It was his fourth try, although they had been married for over ten years (his longest) if my math and memory served me correctly. Like Lauren, she was a blonde white girl. A former model type who was far more intelligent than your typical trophy wife. Unlike Lauren, she had definitely been around people of color her entire life because if you closed your eyes you would swear that she was from Brooklyn and not Berkeley based on the way she spoke. If you can imagine surfer girl meets hood chick then you would get Kari. Though had I not experienced her firsthand, I would find it difficult to imagine. She definitely was not one of those white girls that like to play-talk "black" with inappropriately employed colloquialisms and idioms.

"Heyyyyy! So glad you made it. Come on in," said Kari as she pulled the door open wide and with a big motion. She was barefoot with a tight tank top that made her voluptuous breasts even more pronounced. They were greeting us, too. With a big time hello! Once we stepped in past the foyer, the true beauty of the property was revealed. The living room, dining room, and kitchen were all open-air leading out to the grounds, which ultimately led down to a pool that seemed to surround the house on all sides. It was beyond anything I had seen in St. Barth's, and this was the place were the property was known for making a grand statement. The seemingly hundreds of candles placed around the room complemented the darkness of the night with the lights from town flickering as reminders of the evening business that was happening hundreds of feet below.

Although the openness of the space made you aware of it, we were certainly away from it all. To top off the Zen moment, eucalyptus was burning throughout the house with just enough force that made you notice it, but not in an overbearing way. It reminded me of an elegant spa in St. Tropez and made me think of how nice a massage would be at that moment.

"Vikki, so glad you made it," said Randy as he came down the stairs behind us. I hadn't previously noticed the stairs were flanked on one side by a rail and open air that seemed to lead to the sky. But that was not what struck me the most. The last time I'd seen Randy he was definitely a music fat cat both figuratively and literally. The Randy that descended the stairway to heaven was more feline, having shed the equivalent of two medium-sized Guatemalans.

"Randy, my God. You look amazing," said Vikki, equally surprised by the drastic transformation, as he gave her a big hug as Kari looked on, all smiles.

"A lot has changed since I saw you last. Had to do it if I wanted to keep living." Then Randy turned to Lauren and me, looking at us both with recognition. It didn't matter this time because I was still in complete shock at his altered appearance. He actually looked great as a thin man. It's hit or miss when large people lose a significant amount of weight, as some don't look healthy afterward. I was definitely one of the ones who preferred chubby Luther over skinny Luther (God rest his soul). But I had never even contemplated Randy being handsome because underneath all of the weight his features were indistinguishable. Slimmer, he was truly a handsome guy. Not GQ magazine cover handsome but better than average, and he certainly was in amazing shape now.

"Sweetie, you remember my friend, don't you?" asked Vikki.

"Yeah, we hung out at the Image Awards a few years back, right?"

"That's right. Backstage with Jilly from Philly." Maybe the weight loss equaled memory gain.

"Yeah man, cool. Great to see you."

"And this is my friend, Lauren, who we're here visiting."

"Lauren, a pleasure to meet you, beautiful. I have seen you before, though."

"Yes, around the island in season. Thank you for having us. We brought this as a gift." Then Lauren followed protocol and handed Kari a magnum of rosé Veuve.

"Thank you, Lauren, I will get Tomás to put this on some ice, and we can have it after dinner," said Kari, who literally went a few steps to the kitchen and handed it to a gentleman in a chef's coat, presumably Tomás, who was busily prepping something along with a younger woman, both working in silence.

"Speaking of, I think dinner will be ready in just a bit. Would any of you like a pre-dinner cocktail?" asked Randy, who was layering on the charm in a way I had not remembered. New body. New outlook.

"Why yes, sweetie, a little aperitif sounds delish," said Vikki, who had slid into charm mode as well. "What are you having?"

"Water. But, don't let me stop y'all."

"Well, no, if you won't then, we won't. And who are you by the way? What happened to Hollow Leg Randy?" asked Vikki.

"He was going to kill me. I'll tell you all about it after I pour you all something to drink. I insist. Plus, I had a little herbal essence before I came down, so it's only fair."

We all laughed at this revelation. I loved when people referred to marijuana as the "herbals" or "the medicine" or "the get-lifted." I had one girlfriend who called it "the ritual." I preferred the creative monikers to "weed" or "pot," which were pedestrian to me. And since "Mary Jane" was now legal in multiple states (and counting) it seemed only fitting that it acquired a less common nickname. Although I was not a habitual partaker in "the ritual," I did enjoy it from time to time with friends at home. Vikki and I were bona fide "pot heads" in college, but that subsided by the time we hit our late twenties. Not for philosophical reasons. I just think we'd smoked so much at Northwestern that we got tired of it. Quite frankly, I was a major champion of legalizing it across the country. It was a better and safer stimulant than alcohol, which all too often led to problems in far too many people who could not control themselves. The herbals evoked only a few things in people: laughter, the munchies, and sleep.

"I'll have both," declared Lauren."

"Of?" asked Randy.

"I'll take a cocktail and a bit of your essence, if you don't mind."

"Whatever Lauren wants," he sang. "I'll have to run upstairs for the herbals. In the meantime, what can I get you to wet your whistle?"

"A glass of Pinot grigio," said Lauren.

"I'll take a glass of that as well," requested Vikki. "I'm the designated tonight."

"OK, so you're both going to make me sound like the drunk because wine would put me to sleep right now. Do you have vodka or tequila?" I asked.

"Either."

"I'll take a Goose on the rocks with two limes and a splash of water."

"Well, alright. That's what I'm talking about," said Randy.

"On second thought, that does sound good. I'll start with that as well." Lauren was joining the party. I knew it would be seconds before Vikki jumped in, too.

"Ah hell, why not? I'll take that, too. It should wear off by the time we leave. If not, we can call a cab."

"Or you'll just have to stay here. I haven't reformed all of my ways," said Randy as he winked at Vikki and then walked toward the fully stocked bar in the opposite corner of the living room. "Have a seat. Actually, do whatever the hell you want. The house is yours." Just as we were taking our seats, looking out onto the town of St. Barth's, Kari reappeared with a glass of wine in her hand. She sat down next to me with her legs crossed Indian style on the charcoal brushed suede sofa. We all silently took in the wonder of the view as the fire crackled behind us and the ice cubes danced in the glasses of the drinks Randy was making. The sofa was so sleek that it didn't look comfortable, but the look was deceiving.

It was indeed very comfortable, which was the best word to describe the moment. The energy throughout the house was calm and relaxing, so we all settled in for a good, intimate night. Definitely not what I'd anticipated.

Randy returned with a tray of drinks and placed it on the lacquered black log coffee table with a mirrored top that was in the center of the living room. The glasses were humongous, and I knew if he had adhered to my request for a splash of water that we were certainly going to be feeling it after one.

"Cheers! Thanks for coming over. I so much prefer this to going out in town. At least for dinner," said Kari as she raised her glass.

"Salud, thank you for having us. It's already a lovely evening. Although I expected a turned-up party, but I prefer this, too," said Vikki as we all toasted our glasses and took sips of our respective beverages. "Well, damn, Randy. Your hand sure didn't lose weight," exclaimed Vikki while grimacing at the power punch the drink packed. And Vikki was no lightweight. Neither was I, but she was right. I think Randy thought the ice cubes constituted the splash of water because mine was all vodka.

"Too strong?" he asked.

"Mine is just fine," said Little Miss Lauren. I wasn't sure what she was feeling, but she was feeling something. I certainly wasn't going to disturb her groove because that is exactly what we were here for — to get our grooves back and on.

"Excuse me. Let me run upstairs and grab a couple of happy sticks. Hold tight." Randy dashed up the stairs as we returned to the silent admiration of the post card-like view.

"Kari, I heard you're starting a new line of active wear," asked Vikki, breaking the silence (although I was enjoying the moment).

"Yes, I just approved the first round of designs. I'm so amped. I wanted a line that could go from yoga to the grocery store or to lunch with just an addition or subtraction of a piece here or there."

"That's so the L.A. lifestyle," said Vikki.

"Exactly. Everything is so spread out, and who has time to go all the way home and change just to run a couple of errands or meet a girlfriend to lunch." As she said, "to lunch," I liked her even more. I thought we were the only ones who used it as a verb.

"We should talk, I would love to cover the line in the magazine."

"That would be fantastic. Thanks!"

"How's the transition been from New York?" asked Vikki.

"I love it. Randy loves it, too. He was nervous at first since he's lived in New York for so long. I'm a Cali girl originally, so I knew I would be alright. He really didn't have a choice when the label was sold and moved the offices there. But it's been real good for him and for us."

"I'm taking the plunge and moving to L.A. too," I said.

"Really? When?"

"Probably at the end of the year or in January. Right when it gets cold and I won't feel so bad for leaving."

"Trust me, you're going to love it. L.A. has changed so much. Plus, there are tons of New Yorkers and artists there now, so it's not as plastic."

"We don't want him to leave," said Lauren, who had gotten through a little over half of her drink. "We're going to fall apart."

"I don't know about all of that, but it is definitely not an easy decision. It's for the career."

"Dude, I feel your pain. I protested so much when the big brass told me I had to go west. I contemplated leaving the business altogether to stay in New York. But after the first month of being out there I can't imagine going back to live in New York permanently." Randy jumped right back into the conversation after returning from upstairs. He sat on the other side of Kari and immediately sparked one of the three happy sticks he'd retrieved.

"You're not helping our cause here Randy," said Vikki.

"I'm being serious. You're in production, right?" asked Randy, who continued to amaze me with his newfound memory.

"Yep, and a writer."

"Let me tell you that there is no better place for you to be. The business is so plentiful there that I'm even making movie deals. Everyone you meet has some angle in the biz."

"Which is actually why I have been so reluctant to move there all of these years. I liked being special in New York."

"You'll like being rich more. I guarantee you that with your New York hustle you'll make shit happen quick. They really don't like to work out there, and that's what gives New Yorkers the edge."

"Baby, that's not true. They just work differently," said Kari.

"Translation: As little as possible for as much as possible. I'm not knocking it, babe. I'm just saying if this man comes out there on his New York grind, he'll be golden." The joint had made its second time around to me, and I pulled in what Randy was saying as I was pulling on the herbal, which was already having a positive effect.

"All of my friends out there say the same thing."

"Speaking of new, you gotta spill it about this," said Vikki as she motioned toward Randy's body.

"We were skiing in Vail, and I came down on my leg the wrong way. I was over three-fifty at the time and really had no business being on skis. Plus, I was drunk. Definitely not a good look. I shattered my leg so badly that I had to be airlifted to the hospital. I was scared as shit lying there in the snow while they tried to figure out how to get my big ass out of there. A lot went through my mind. What I'd done right. Wrong."

"They said his body was in shock, so he was semiconscious," added Kari.

"Yeah, that's what they say, but my memory is clear as today. I met God that day."

Randy's words hung in the air though not heavily so, but I did feel an instant emotional reaction. It could have been the smoke. However, there was an understanding in his words that probably was not lost on Vikki and Lauren either. Aside from movie scripts and Shirley MacLaine, it wasn't often you heard someone say they'd met the Creator. Even for me who was a regular churchgoer and considered myself spiritually connected, it was the first time I had heard anyone speak those words in real life. I had certainly felt the spirit of God before and definitely bore witness to miracles. But to say that I actually *met* God was something I could not honestly do. Randy's declaration confronted the questions of my faith head on. With all of the belief I had my entire life, it was not without doubt from time to time, which I wrote off as being human. However, hearing someone say they actually met God, I was surprised that the first thought that popped into my mind was, "Really?"

"I know that sounds ridiculous. Had someone said that to me before it happened, I would have laughed at them. Especially for a proud sinner like me. But it's true. I had a real and bona fide encounter with God." Was Randy reading my mind? I was sure he'd met skepticism in prior retellings of this story so he was probably reading our collective minds.

"It actually doesn't sound ridiculous," said Lauren. "We are far more connected to the spirit world than we allow ourselves to be aware of." I wasn't surprised by Lauren's statement. Back in the day, she was always preaching about our connectivity to the universe. The birds. The trees. The wind. I used to call her a 'Rippie' (rich girl hippie). You believed that Lauren believed everything she said. It had just been quite some time since she had said anything like it.

"Well, what did God say?" The journalist in Vikki was kicking up sand.

"Nothing was said. I was just standing there surrounded by light and in front of an even brighter light. A felt a sensation come over my body like I was being touched by hundreds of hands at once. I didn't see anyone — no man or woman. But, it felt like God. I can't describe it any other way."

"So that's when the transformation began?" Vikki continued her questions.

"Naw, I'm hard-headed. After they operated on my leg, I went home and resumed life as usual. I didn't tell anyone about it although I thought about it every day."

"He didn't even tell me," said Kari.

"I mean how do you really say, dude, I just met God? I kept having these dreams, though, of me being on the edge of a mountain about to fall. Then, I would wake up right before I fell. You know I was raised by an all-day-praying Pentecostal grandmother who believed that dreams mean something. And with what had happened in Vail, I was starting to freak out."

"That's when he told me about it. Of course, I was in shock because it didn't sound like Randy. Mr. Practical. Mr. I-Pray-at-Thanksgiving-and-Christmas. So I told him he should see somebody to help him figure it out," said Kari.

"I still kept putting it off. First, I was going to see a dream interpreter. Then, a preacher we know up in Harlem. Then, a psychic. But I never went to see any of them. Then I passed out one day in the office."

"Did you meet God again?" I asked in more of a joking manner than I intended. The herbals.

"Ha! No, not that time." Thankfully, Randy had a sense of humor and hadn't taken my question disrespectfully. "That's when I found out that I was prediabetic. Even though I didn't encounter God like before, I took that as a final sign that I'd better shape up or I was going to ship out. I hired a nutritionist and a trainer. Stopped drinking. Changed my work habits. And just got focused on living better. My new saying is "when you get clear, the trivial disappears.""

"I love that," said Lauren who was in a not-so-clear state but hanging on Randy's every word.

"Dude, I tell people all the time that if I could change my ways, there's hope for anyone. Y'all know the music business is wild, and I came up in the 80s and 90s when there was nothing but excess. Before the Internet and technology kicked our asses."

"Randy's actually started speaking about healthy living and lifestyle changes," said Kari as we watched Randy take the last pull of the joint. The irony was not lost on him.

"A man without some vice scares me," he said, laughing as he exhaled.

"No judgment from me, man. The herbals are from nature," I said.

"True. True. Right now, I got the natural munchies. Y'all hungry?" He asked.

"I definitely could eat," said Vikki.

Randy said, "Let's get to it then."

• ◆ ◆

By far, Governor Beach was my favorite on the island. A trek from Lauren's house but worth it because it was the calmest on the island. The people, the waves, and the nature were all the ideal of beach relaxation. I played with the soft sand between my toes as my feet hung off the oversized beach towel still not long enough to accommodate my entire body. I had put in three days of solid tan work and was rather pleased with the caramel color of my body. Vikki began to hum some song that I couldn't decipher and didn't mind because of the pleasantness of her voice. She was reading, and obviously something had triggered the melodic memory. The kids were in and out of the water that was a just right temperature when I jumped in for a brief swim. Lauren watched them intently from underneath an umbrella as she'd reached her fair skin's half-day limit of sun. The island and the company seemingly had worked medicinal magic on her spirit, which softened into more of its natural form as the days progressed. She was still a bit distant, but the joy of seeing her children happy and unaffected by and mostly unaware of the true circumstances of their life clearly grounded her and gave her peace. I could tell she was feeling better because there had been more smiles, particularly after the night at Randy and Kari's house. More jokes. More laughs. More of all of the things that I loved to see come from my girl.

Vikki put down her book and closed her eyes under the sun. She had also benefited from this down time and was glowing. In the hustle and bustle of big city living you can become unaware of the necessity for rest. Something usually triggers it — your body shuts down or some crisis occurs. As Randy's story reminded us, the movers and shakers never realize that they need less moving and shaking until it's too late. One of the many difficulties about living in New York is the lack of understanding and appreciation for balance. It's always go. Never stop. I often encourage newcomers to get out of the city as much as possible for this very reason. It is the key to survival in the first year and beyond. I was so grateful for this opportunity to remove myself from the busyness of the city and the craziness of everything that had been going on before we left. I had allowed my cell phone to die, and so had Vikki. I checked in via a nightly and purposefully brief visit to the computer. I'd been successful at temporarily curing my Instagram and Facebook addictions. Even Lauren was able to leave her cell phone behind because the kids were with us, and I think she pointedly needed a break from Josh. Understandable. Glad she did.

"That conversation the other night at Randy's has been on my mind. It was encouraging," said Lauren. I knew it had affected her since that evening because of the way she took it in and the shift in mood that followed the next morning. However, I hadn't questioned her about it because I was happy that she was moving away from the fragile edge we sensed when we first arrived.

"How so?"

"To be honest, I came here ready to give up on Josh. I didn't think I had any more chances to give. But Randy's story reminded me that there's always space for change. No matter where you've been or what you've been through."

"That's definitely true," I said.

"It also got me to thinking about how I've changed. I can't remember the last time I meditated or went to yoga," she analyzed.

"I know. It's been a minute since I've been to church. Going to fix that when I get back," I said.

"Me, too. I'm so grateful for this trip. I needed it on so many levels. Thanks for coming."

"Thanks for having us. I needed it too."

"I miss Dax," Vikki said abruptly without opening her eyes as a smile extended across her face. She hadn't spoken much about Dax, and I didn't press it fearing that something was awry. I didn't want to say I told you so, but no one is *that* perfect. And to be clear, I wasn't hating on him in the least. I'd just never met anyone so pulled together who didn't come unraveled at some point. There were no visible cracks in the armor, and that level of faultlessness was seldom faultless. I didn't share my feelings because for the moment she was happy, and that was all that mattered.

I knew these moments all too well and all too often. They'd come and go and come and...go. I assumed this was going to be in the same step and stance as all of the others. Yet I didn't want to profess my cynicism for fear of discouraging the goodness of the moment. Plus, Vikki was no fool.

"Have you spoken with him?" Lauren asked.

"We Skype at least twice a day. He's in Brussels on business, so me being away is not a big deal. I'm going to meet him after I get back to the city and take care of a few things." So I had been far off in my assessment of their relationship status. Not only had it not ended; it was still in full gear as indicated by the plastered right parentheses on her face that had not left since her first mention of his name. "That man, I tell you. He draws my baths. I have a new bouquet of flowers in my office almost every other day. And talk about smart. He knows so much about so much. There's never a moment when we don't have something to talk about. I won't even begin to talk about how he lays it down. Oooohhh!" Her body shook a bit as she let that one out. I wasn't sure if Vikki was talking to us or had gotten lost in a daytime dream that she was speaking out loud. Her eyes were still closed and the smile was still wide.

"Don't you think he's a bit too perfect?"

"What do you mean?" Vikki slowly opened her eyes and aimed them at me, sitting up slightly to signal that some regret was in my future.

It was too late to recant, so I continued, "I've just never met anyone like him before. He seems too good to be true...at least to me."

She sat up fully in the portable beach lounger, now directing all her energy and attention at me. I could feel she was about to go in for the kill. I'd seen this preparation to pounce too many times before not to brace myself.

"I resent that! For the first time in years, maybe ever, I find someone who fully gets my crazy, can keep up, and loves me. And you poo-poo it because he's 'too perfect'? I call bullshit."

I had braced myself, but the statement I'd made didn't warrant this level of force. We'd always been honest about who we dated and our thoughts about them. Something struck a chord, and I couldn't decide whether it was her truly being upset with what I said or whether I had stirred some of her own doubts. Either way, I was not about to ruin this lovely afternoon to prove a point. I would retreat from this battle with my opinion between my legs.

"Vikki, I'm sorry if I offended you. That was not my intent."

"What was it then?"

"Just talking. Probably out the side of my neck."

"You're jealous!"

"C'mon. Let's not go there." She was making it difficult to keep up the white flag of surrender.

"You took us there. You're jealous that I found someone. Vikki is no longer single with you, and you can't take it." She was fuming (and talking about herself in the third person), and I knew there was no way I could get out of this one except just to accept that I'd upset her.

"I'm sorry."

"I'm going to marry him, so whatever you're feeling, just stop it now." The train crashed into the side of the building, causing Lauren to look at Vikki in disbelief. Talk about coming out of nowhere. She hadn't even mentioned his name in three days and now she was going through with marrying him. It was perplexing to say the least, and questionable, but I'd already stepped deep enough in it for today, and I knew if I kept going I'd be knee-deep for a much longer time than I had the patience or stamina for.

"Good for you," was all I could honestly say and mean. It was a good thing that she felt strongly enough to marry him. Despite her suggestions of jealousy, I was not. Protective, yes. The suggestion to anything otherwise was offensive, and we would deal with it later. Now, I would just leave it at "good for her."

"I wasn't expecting that either, but you know we just want you to do what works for you," said the blonde diplomat. The gladiator fell back in her lounger, still steaming a bit from the exchange that really wasn't about us. I knew it. She did too. The best thing about being best friends for so long is that you're allowed to fly off the handle, within reason, with no major consequence. She also knew that it was time to calm it down before it progressed further.

I had to close it out with, "Seriously Viks, you know we will always have your back and be happy for you!"

"Thanks." With that, it was over for now. The saddest part being that if she was really serious about getting married, we couldn't even celebrate the way we should have. I would think of a way to make it up to all of us when we got back to the house. It was best to continue the beach afternoon without any additional incident.

Just as we were all settling back into the sun and the breeze, an almost in-shape, lanky brunette with a whining toddler in tow approached where we were sitting. Governor Beach is pretty bare, with no restaurants or the like… just people. The reason why most on the island come here is to get away from the scene that can be St. Barth's. So it was odd that someone was coming over to us considering we had stationed ourselves as far away from the rest of the beachgoers as possible. I didn't recognize the woman as one of Lauren or Vikki's friends, all of whom we'd seen over the course of our holiday. And her walk was determined as if she were on a mission. Immediately, I looked for the kids to see where they were. Maybe they'd hit her brat or something while playing, which was not like them, although not out of the question. Kids will be kids. Whatever it was, I had the feeling I was not going to like it or her.

"Lauren dear, how are you doing?" asked Lanky. She said it with a tinge of patronizing sympathy. My instincts were right. I didn't like her.

"I'm fine. How are you?" Lauren responded with no familiarity.

"You must remember me, we met at David Parkinson's house last Christmas. I'm Julie Babcock. Kevin's wife." Lauren smiled politely and nodded, even though it was clear from the confused look on her face that she had no recollection of the encounter. "In any event, I just wanted to come over and offer my concern. You must be so worried, and to still be able to vacation is applaudable." Now it was Lauren's turn, and she sat up in her seat with raised eyebrows. What the hell was Lanky talking about? "Oh, wait, you have to know…maybe, um."

"Know what?" Lauren reluctantly asked.

"About Josh being arrested." Nope, it wasn't that I didn't like Lanky. I hated this bitch. She knew good and well that if Lauren had known Josh had been arrested, we would not be on this damn beach.

"Excuse me, Judy? What the hell are you talking about?" Vikki obviously didn't like her either, intentionally messing up Lanky's name.

"Oh geesh, I didn't meant to..."

"You did. Now what are you talking about?" The gladiator redirected her venomous focus.

"Well, I was just reading online that he'd been arrested for drug possession and DUI in L.A. I'm terribly sorry, I thought you knew."

"You can leave now." With Vikki's dismissal, Lanky crawled away, armed with her false sense of horror about what she'd done. I knew when she turned her back she probably smiled. Rich women can be the worst sometimes. Always trying to knock each other down a peg, especially those on the higher rungs. Lanky was the least of our concerns as I looked over to Lauren, who had lost all of the peace she'd reclaimed. The cavern had returned, and she was stuck to the position she'd been in when she first sat up.

Then she said plainly, "I have to go." And so we did.

Chapter Eleven

The Titanic Hits the Iceberg (& A Vintage Sofa)

I should have been exhausted from taking the red-eye flight back from Los Angeles, but I was too anxious waiting in Starbucks for Ruby to arrive. Quite the contrast from the laid-back afternoon and early evening meetings that had consumed the entire ten days I was away. The meetings I was able to secure encouraged me that I was indeed not a washup, but still relevant. It had reinvigorated my hustle so much so that I couldn't recall a single daytime minute that I wasn't meeting with a studio executive, production company, or someone who could be a catalyst for my transition. The grind reminded me of one of my old sayings, "Just because your bank account hasn't caught up with your hustle doesn't make your hustle any less righteous." Somewhere, that had been lost, but it had crept back into my spirit while plotting my move to Hollywood. I was also able to see my friends, who were more excited about my relocation than I was, especially the ones I'd known in New York. There were plenty of transplants there – mostly other creatives and entrepreneurs that had been outpriced and outpaced by New York City. L.A. was no longer the plastic parade of Barbie's and Ken's it used to be and every one of my friends that had moved there seemed to love it, which surprised both them and me.

Partner the good fortune of the business meetings and my friends with Hollywood's best asset — the weather — and the decision to go left was becoming increasingly the best idea I'd had in years. I worried though that leaving all of my sister-friends now when they were in various states of turmoil and transition was not a good idea, but I would always come back to the fact that I had to live my own life. Plus, they were all grown and, despite acting like it way too much, I wasn't their daddy or their man.

I also went out west more refreshed than I had been in a while. Even with the dramatic climax, St. Barth's did my mind and body good. Josh was released from jail on bond and immediately returned to rehab, which also shuttered the film he was working on. Lauren was existing. Nothing more, nothing less. Vikki was moving ahead with her wedding and had decided to make the destination Jamaica. It had been awhile since I'd spoken to Rebecca or seen Krissy. I was going to change that this afternoon when Krissy and I lunched. I'd plan to catch up with Rebecca soon, too.

The present moment, however, was about clearing up whatever was going on between Ruby and me. Well, what was going on with Ruby because despite being played, I still didn't feel any true ill will toward her. Sure, I didn't like the way I had been treated, but friendships sometimes hit a bump for a myriad of reasons. In my book, there weren't many things that would justify throwing out so much history and love merely because of a disagreement or patch of bad behavior. Still, it had been over a month since the Literacy Gala, and she and I had not spoken directly in the same amount of time. My voicemails were returned via text messages; my text messages, if returned, yielded a terse email. The events of the past few months completely baffled me. The bad friend behavior on her part had soared in from outer space without provocation or warning. A UFO sighting, but this time all of New York had seen it.

During those weeks of waiting for this meeting, I'd received countless calls from our friends, acquaintances and people who I hadn't spoken to in years. Offering their condolences as if a relative had died. Most also said, "I knew she was like that, but I didn't think it would happen to you." Turns out, everyone but me saw the big O (for Opportunist) emblazoned across Ruby's forehead. The consensus was that I was no longer needed, and our relationship stood in the way of her true goal, Steve.

In walked Ruby, washed face wearing gold plated, dark sunglasses and carrying a shiny new (six months' rent) handbag. I might not have noticed the handbag if everything else about her had not been blank and expressionless. She'd had her old bag — a high, five-figure, Fifth Avenue impulse purchase squeezed from the balance of her settlement from Alex — for the past five years. When it was new, it reminded people of the immense wealth she'd enjoyed. As the years progressed, the bag became increasingly tattered from overstuffing and over usage, a reminder of how far she'd fallen down the crystal staircase.

Starbucks was busy with people creating and doing what people do in the stiffly priced coffeehouse-turned-office for students, creative folks, and startups. For a moment, we stared at each other in silence. A standoff that was both dramatic and preposterous. Even with all of her one-sided forest full of shade, we had not had a real fight per se in recent memory. Not a disagreement. Nothing, which should have brought us to this O.K. Corral surrounded by ten-dollar chai lattes.

Breaking the ice, I began, "Thank you for meeting me. It's good to see you." All of a sudden the action that was once loud in my ear became still in the silence that followed my opener.

"No need for this to be overly dramatic."

"Huh? For what to be dramatic? I'm still trying to figure out what the hell is going on." I said, starting to get pissed already.

"I just think it's time we both move on."

"Is that so? When and why did you come to this conclusion?"

"It's been a minute."

"Oh, OK. The reason being?"

"Look, like I said. I don't need this to be some dramatic scene from one of your movies. Let's just agree to keep it moving."

"What the fuck are you talking about, Ruby? You're the one bringing the drama, and for no damn reason," I shot back. Her nervous twitch of twirling her hair commenced as she became visibly more uncomfortable with the confrontation. Then I saw it. The cold reception I was getting, had been getting, was coming directly from that sparkling, round iceberg sitting between the middle and pinky fingers on her left hand. It sat there ornery, daring me to challenge it. Already the victor.

"There's something toxic about this relationship. I mean, it's not like any of your friends like me. Or that we really do anything except lunch and drink. And I just think we've spent way too much time together over the past few years, and it has stunted growth for both of us. At least, it has mine." Every expletive imaginable quickly flew through my mind. I was stunned by her words that were indeed recited like lines from a script written for her by someone with whom she, in fact, did have a toxic relationship.

"If that's what you think of our friendship, then I guess we should move on." There it was. Nothing left to be said. If I had been confused walking into the Schomburg or here, I certainly no longer was.

"Good luck to you, Ruby. I hope you get everything you're looking for," I said as I got up from the table, walked out, and started up the street. Once a good distance away, I shut my eyes, hoping my eyelids would serve as a dam for the flood of tears threatening to flow like a river. It would've been far more tolerable, understandable, if I'd actually done something to her. But to be cut off from a friend's life like that was foreign to me. I couldn't remember anything remotely similar ever happening. I had lost friends over the years, but not so coldly and abruptly. Broadsided or not, I knew deep down that the truth was I had too much information, and it was she who could no longer look at herself through my eyes.

Ruby was no saint and definitely had enough buried bones to fill up Arlington Cemetery. Now that it seemed she had gotten what she wanted from Steve, I threatened the safety of that with what I knew. I had to be handled, which made me realize that this probably was all Ms. Ruby, and there was a good chance it had not been orchestrated by Steve at all. Ultimately, it didn't matter either way, and at least now my own blind spot had been removed and I could see clearly. Twenty-twenty vision or not, I had no intentions of bringing up Ruby or what had just happened when I met Krissy to lunch later.

◆ ◆ ◆

The lobby was sterile and cold—typical of a law firm. Law firms and funeral homes gave me the same discomfort. The legal profession, in general, is a peculiar one. Praised by many for the prestige and hard work it takes to become an esquire, despised by most for the dubious acts of the few that taint the entire profession. It was a loveless relationship for those who practiced within its halls. Most lawyers ultimately left the profession within the first few years and were considered by those with fewer options to be the lucky ones who found a way to "get out." The unlucky ones would remain, caught in golden handcuffs and confined by the glass ceiling. Krissy was an anomaly even among the exceptions. She was a lawyer's lawyer who loved her job and the practice of the law, and she excelled.

Sitting next to all the suits who were also waiting, I felt underdressed and somewhat inappropriate in my jeans and polo shirt. As various firm employees passed by, it was clear I was the one out of place. But to watch the consistent countenance on the various cogs of this firm's wheel pass in and out, it felt good to be the odd man out. No one was smiling. Even when they made eye contact, a polite smile would be forced and then quickly disappear back into seeming despair. Or maybe that was just my way of making myself feel better. I couldn't imagine what it must be like to go to work every day and hate it. Particularly in an environment as charged and difficult as a law firm. Many of my friends compared the first years of working at a firm to a nonstop fraternity initiation ritual; being hazed daily by older associates and partners. I remember when Krissy first started there had been a female partner who would throw her phone at any associate who brought her bad news. Evilene with a law degree. A good thing she never threw it at Krissy because even as much as she loved her job and exhibited extreme professionalism, I couldn't imagine her being able to hold Harlem down if she had.

I had been there about twenty minutes and was beginning to get restless waiting. For one, I was hungry. I attributed the fact that we hadn't seen each other to our conflicting schedules, with me traveling to St. Barth and Los Angeles and her new love with Justin. I know new lovers tend to get caught up in one another early on as they discover each other. It was allowed to an extent, which is why I had insisted we lunch today. I also knew she was caught up in a major trial that had recently made the papers. Two things were true if Krissy's firm was representing the defendant — he was rich and in some serious trouble. Nothing and no one in this firm came cheap. You got your money's worth though — whether you were a good or bad person.

I had to hear about the case from Vikki as I don't watch or read the news. I've been accused of sounding unintelligent after making that statement on more than one occasion. But it keeps me sane and happy. The news always leads with murder, mayhem, and rape, instantly transforming a good day into a color-coded fear of Armageddon. No, thank you. I choose what information I put into my brain carefully. I'm up on things that have a direct bearing on my life, like elections and the weather. However, I long ago relinquished any desire to know about the issues that repeatedly plague the world that are well beyond my control. I prefer things that feed my spirit and make me smile.

A thin woman in an inexpensive grey pinstripe suit approached me. "Ms. Jackson will see you now." Her formality took me aback because although I understood the need to be professional, I was going to see my girl. I was not a client. Then I thought, "Exactly why are you mad?" She didn't know who I was and was just doing her job. She meekly walked down the hallway, and I followed peeking in the various occupied or empty offices of the firm. One thing was consistent; everyone looked very busy. My guess was that some actually were busy and others were feigning busyness to maintain the firm's "work harder, bill more" culture. As we arrived at Krissy's comparatively massive corner office, I could sense from the fact that she was on the phone, pacing back and forth behind her desk that something major was going down. Which explained the long wait in the lobby of the dead.

Krissy pulled the phone away from her mouth and covered the receiver. "Chile, I'm so sorry. I know you saw the news."

"You know I don't watch…," I replied but stopped, realizing she probably didn't hear me, having immediately turned back around to her call.

"Katie, please close the door," snapped Krissy, still facing the floor-to-ceiling window that looked down onto Wall Street. I stood there not quite knowing what to do, and I guess she could sense that because she turned around and whispered, "Just one more minute" while motioning me to take a seat.

"Take your time. I've got my phone," I whispered back as I lowered myself into one of the surprisingly comfortable armchairs facing her desk. When I noticed the lavender, ultra suede sofa with a bounty of cushy lilac, silk pillows along the wall, I contemplated moving and stretching out but then rejected the inappropriate impulse. Instead, I took in how she'd decorated her office. It was signature Krissy. Everything in its slightly flashy, perfect place. A massive brushed steel desk with a glass top with coordinated designer adornments thoughtfully placed on top of it. No stacks of papers like I'd grown accustomed to seeing in lawyer's offices. No dust on the degrees and awards covering the yellow accent wall. A major feat considering how many degrees and awards she had squeezed onto the wall. If you didn't know she was successful, the wall reminded you. It was probably a reminder for her as well on the rough days. I don't care who you are, top of your game or not, you're going to have some sandpaper days, and you need to be armed with the tools that remind you to keep going.

"Chile, they are working a sista's damn nerves today," she said as she put down her phone next to a headset on her desk. She had options. She could take calls in the old-fashioned way or she could give you the other Ms. Jackson circa the *Control* album with the headset. Another reminder of how powerful and successful my sister-friend was becoming. I got an instant kick out of that. By her well-informed account, Krissy was practically a shoe-in for partner this year. She'd been bringing in big business for the firm since her second year, which is unheard of for a new associate. According to her, she was for all intents and purposes a partner already with the level of autonomy she enjoyed compared to her peers. Her office supported her claim. She just needed to benefit more directly from her hard work in the form of firm equity enjoyed only by the partners.

"No probs, sweets. Are you still able to lunch?"

"Actually, I had Katie order us some lunch while I finish up. I want you to go furniture shopping with me, and I don't have time to do both." Shopping was the last thing I wanted to do. I wouldn't complain, though, as the point was to spend time with her. So I stopped myself from pouting as Katie brought in our lunch on perfect cue. I was definitely being bribed because lunch was from Luke's Lobster — a Wall Street staple. Krissy knew how to butter me up, figuratively and literally, with the fresh melt-in-your mouth lobster rolls we were about to devour.

We both ate while she worked, and I watched her in prideful amazement. Krissy was such a testament to the fact that hard work pays off. Refusing to accept the circumstances of her childhood, neighborhood, or family history, she used education and perseverance to change the trajectory of her life. The focus and belief in herself landed her in this beautiful office in one of the most prestigious law firms in the country. Seeing her in overdrive encouraged me to be more confident in my decision to move. Sitting there reminded me of something my mother had told me when I was very young, "Surround yourself with people you want to be like because that's what you will be." And that was the truth. Krissy was exceptional and by virtue of her (and the rest of my friends) being in my life for so long and for so strong, I was starting to again believe that I was also. Austin Powers was starting to get his mojo back. "Oh, behave!"

◆ ◆ ◆

A chauffeured SUV was our chariot to ABC Carpet & Home — the premier place for furniture in the city. The SUV was definitely a nice treat considering it was sweltering outside. And who doesn't like a little first-class service from time to time, especially when it's not on your dime? OK! It was, however, a special convenience for Krissy today so that she could get in and back to the office for the rest of the day. One of the perks of working in a big firm like Krissy's was they went out of their way to make it convenient for you to do more and more work. Free lunches, dinners, chauffeured cars to run your errands, but not without a high price.

Although it was not what I had in mind for the afternoon catching up, a trip to ABC was not your normal shopping experience. It was filled with gorgeous furniture and home accessories from around the world that you couldn't find anywhere else. It was more like an art museum than your typical retail experience. A veritable designer's paradise of sparkling specialty items at spectacular prices. The only drawback was that my friends tended to get lost inside. Not Krissy, though. She liked the activity of shopping only slightly more than me. She was an oxymoron for the ages: a fashionista who didn't really like to shop.

Inside the palatial store, mission-driven decorators and their high-powered clients traced through the endless rows of unique and over-priced home wares while dodging the tourists soaking in the wonder of this grand store. I was like a teenager dropped into a toy store. I didn't want to like being there, but I did. I could've gotten lost looking at all of the wonderful wares, but I had to keep pace with Krissy, who zoomed through like a skilled operative. As we made our way through the gorgeous lights and fixtures on the first floor, I realized that I had no idea why she was furniture shopping anyway considering her apartment had been recently redesigned with brand-new furniture. We squeezed onto the elevator, and Krissy hit number two. "Second floor – Modern & Vintage" is what the directory read. I understood the "Modern," but "Vintage" and Krissy were definitely not friends.

"What are we here for exactly?" I asked as we stepped off the elevator onto another beautifully appointed floor. Krissy looked at me with apprehension and then cracked a crooked smile. But no answer. She kept doing the Krissy pump forward with a clear intention that indicated she knew where she was going.

"Did you ever talk to the Wicked Witch about that shit she pulled at the Gala?" She asked, changing the subject.

"Who, Ruby?" Damn lawyers and their intuition. I wondered if they all secretly had ESP based on their collective and uncanny ability to ask the right question at the right time. I guess there was no avoiding talking about what had happened this morning after all.

"Yes, the broom rider. What did that heffa have to say for herself?"

"Hmm, you wouldn't even believe it."

"I bet I would."

"I actually saw her earlier today. She said our relationship was toxic, and basically friend dumped me."

"That's jacked up. But I'm not surprised. That bitch is crazy. You know this has nothing to do with you, right?"

"She's definitely confused. Half of me feels sorry for her."

"That bitch ain't confused. She is about her paper, and instead of getting a job like normal people; she has to get some man. Steve knows it, and that's why he plays her simple ass the way he does."

"I know, but I just don't think she knows any better."

"Please. Don't be naïve. She is grown enough and smart enough to know she has a choice in the matter. That bitch has a degree from a fierce school. She ain't no dummy. She's a lazy opportunistic user. That's what she is."

"A little harsh, Krissy."

"Look, what you won't do is sit here and defend someone who just shitted on you. The point is you were dispensable. I wouldn't be surprised if Steve told her exactly that."

Her points were hitting home a little too hard. I was still recovering from the earlier blow, and although I heard her, I didn't want to hear her. At least not right now. I would deal with what had transpired between Ruby and me in my own time, and that time was not now.

"Enough about Ruby. My trip to L.A. was excellent."

"Yeah, fuck her. Actually, we can drop it if you just say those two words."

"What two words?"

Krissy stopped and got close to my face and hissed, "Fuckkkk herrrr."

"C'mon." She got even closer and put one hand on her hip, signaling that she was not going to budge until I relented. "OK, fuck her."

"A little more feeling."

"What the hell is this, Actor's Studio for cussin'?"

"Do it! Fuck her!" She was getting loud, and although Krissy didn't care I did, so I gave in again.

"Fuck her!" Just my luck a group of Asian tourists passed from behind me and began to giggle. Angry black man on display was an added tourist attraction for the day. I just hoped they didn't start taking pictures with one of their many cameras. Each of us successfully living up to our prevailing stereotypes. It was actually kind of funny, and it did work to relieve some of the tension.

"Good job," said Krissy as she returned to her pump forward. "Nowwww you can tell me about L.A."

"I met with some studios who are hiring. Went well. I also ran into an old friend from Northwestern who has done pretty well for himself. Worked at Goldman for many years and just founded a hedge fund that invests in films. We're going to meet when he's back in New York."

"He lives here?"

"Yep, ironic. But, seriously, why the hell are we here? This has nothing to do with Ruby or L.A."

Krissy slid down onto a gorgeous cream (vintage looking) sofa. As she stretched across it in a pose that reminded me of an around-the-way Marilyn Monroe I could not help laughing. Her biggest talent was the ability to make any situation fun. Rubbing her perfectly manicured hands across it from side to side, she flipped her hair back and forth over her shoulder now, reminding me of those cheesy models on *The Price Is Right*. She sat up a bit and patted the space next to her, inviting me to take a seat. I happily obliged.

"What do you think?" she asked.

"Of?"

"The damn sofa."

"I mean, it's nice. You have a sofa, though."

"I know, but Justin and I want this sofa…for our new apartment."

"What? You're moving in with him? Wait! You said…"

"It was too fast. And it is. But fuck it. You only live once, right?" A humongous smile covered her face as she dipped her head into her shoulder to wink at me. Her happiness was my happiness even if the decision to move in with Justin after such a short time was every bit impetuous. But I agreed that life only comes around once, and you must live it without too much restraint.

"I swear y'all are like lesbians moving in this fast. But go for it. What's the worst that can happen?" I asked.

"First, you are dead wrong for that comment."

"Allowed."

"Whatever. Yeah, it's fast, but I think it's right. I'm going to keep my crib, chile, just in case. But I'm not worried. He knows I will cut him."

"Baby, that's all that counts. Step into it and get your life."

"Sit down. Try it out." I sat down next to her on the sofa and she put her head on my shoulder. "What about you?"

"What about me?"

"I just worry. That you're lonely."

"What makes you think that I'm lonely?"

"When was the last time you went on a date?"

"I go on dates. They're just not worth talking about. I refuse to introduce every Tom, Dick, and Larry that I go on a date or two with to my friends."

"The clocks are a ticking, you know."

"Um, your clock may be ticking, but I don't have a clock. So speak for yourself."

"I guess it's different for men, especially if you don't want any kids."

"Who said I don't want kids? I could see myself with some kids. With the right person."

"Then the clock is a-ticking. You don't want to be seventy-five at your kids' high school graduation. Having to take Geritol just to get to baseball practice."

"I'm not even forty. There's time."

"Let's say you meet the right guy tomorrow. You won't have kids right away. It'll be at least a couple of years and bam! You're forty-two. Plus eighteen equals sixty at graduation. Not cute."

"Kids are not a definite for me. So still no rush. I'm willing to wait."

"For how long? Forty-five?"

"Yep."

"Fifty-five?"

"If it takes that long. I would rather have ten years of happy than twenty of 'this motherfucker right here.'"

"You know you're not going to find Lawrence's twin."

"I'm not looking for his twin. That didn't work out, remember."

"I just know that you've dated some pretty nice guys since you broke up with him. And you found something wrong with all of them."

"Look who's talking."

"I'm changing my ways. Not trying to be in a wheelchair at the altar."

"I hear you." I did hear her loud and clear. I couldn't argue with her point either because she was speaking truth. Although I did not have a biological clock ticking per se, the universal clock of time was definitely moving forward. And, although another relationship was not my priority at the moment, it would be nice at some point. "You're still nuts for moving this damn fast. Changed ways or not."

"I know I'm crazy as hell!"

"This is nice." I said, mimicking her earlier game show display movement. "Can I have your other sofa?"

"No!" She said as we both laughed and stood up. Then she went and bought the ten thousand dollar sofa that was vintage.

Chapter Twelve

A Greek Tragedy in the Hamptons

July is the middle of high season in the Hamptons. New York's elite travels by car, train, or jitney eastward to the storied seaside addresses of the rich and famous. The first time I went to the Hamptons, its beauty, the over-the-top extravagance, floored me. Houses here rent for sums equal to yearly salaries just for the months of June, July, and especially August. Depending on whom you're with, it can be every bit of the bitchy elitist New York scene, transported just three hours away. Vacation, but not really.

Pomp, circumstance, and phoniness aside, I enjoyed a couple of trips out each summer because of the company I was blessed to keep. One of my favorite events was Lauren's annual "Love-Art" fundraiser for inner city arts organizations across the country. Not only was it a fabulous afternoon party stocked with the who's who in entertainment, business, and beyond, it was also for a cause that was near and dear to my heart — access to arts education for children who might not otherwise have it. Lauren and Josh usually went all out with Lauren taking the helm of the planning herself sans an event planner. This year would definitely be different with them separated and Josh in rehab. It surprised me that she hadn't canceled it altogether, but then again Lauren wouldn't. I decided to arrive a day early to make sure everything was going as it should and she felt supported.

I pulled up in the cute little hybrid I'd rented for the weekend. A line of party vans and trucks were parked on the long driveway. Several workers carted chairs, curtains, pillars, and other decorations to the back of the house. As I walked through the front door, I felt the energy of preparation for the big event. It definitely was not the somber mood I'd anticipated. I was glad. Had the house not been full of strangers, I would have just yelled for Lauren and the kids. I was pretty sure the kids weren't there, though. She usually sent them to prearranged play dates on event days so they would be out of the way. Lauren took her parties seriously, and she was not the type of mother that would be dismissive under any circumstance so, instead, she removed potential conflict. I kept walking to the kitchen, which was also full of hired hands busy doing prep work, but no Lauren. Rather than spend the next fifteen minutes or more trying to track her down in the massive house and grounds, I put modern technology to use and called her cell. A smart decision because she picked up right away. She was upstairs but on her way down.

She bounced in the kitchen with a buoyancy that told a different story than reality. Not only was Lauren looking well, she seemed excited and greeted me with a warm hug. It felt genuine. Unexpected, but definitely genuine. No surprise that she was dressed super causally in some khaki pedal pushers and a crisp yellow cotton Ralph Lauren shirt that was open just enough for it to be sexy, with sleeves rolled up just enough to be comfortable. Her hair was wrapped in a blue and purple scarf, and she sported a little bang. Lauren was definitely out Martha Stewart-ing Martha Stewart in this ensemble, and she looked great. My once-over alleviated a great deal of my concern. It also made me realize that this might be just what she needed — a distraction from the crazy that had become her life. She was a master party planner, and from appearances this year would be no exception.

"I'm sorry that I don't really have time to talk. I have so much to do."

"It's cool. I dropped off my things at Vikki's house and I stopped by to see if you needed anything. Looks like you have it under control."

"I'm glad it looks that way. Feels like I'm running around like a chicken with its head cut off. How's the house?"

"You know Viks. It's fabulous. In Wainscott with a massive pool, Jacuzzi, tennis court, etcetera, etcetera."

"One can never accuse Vikki of being understated or outdone even in a rental. And thank you for checking on me. I'm good." Lauren stopped moving about the kitchen to look at me directly with a sincerity that let me know she was aware of my intentions. She was fine and doing something that clearly brought her joy. I was satisfied and could let her get back to work. I had to meet Rebecca for a quick breakfast anyway. It was a relief that Lauren was doing so well because I knew it might be tense with Rebecca given the two months of intentional distance.

"Let me go. I'm meeting Rebecca for breakfast."

"Oh, really. You must have a glass of Champagne before you leave then. You'll need it. Rosé?"

"Since you're forcing me. One can never refuse a good glass of the bubbles."

"Now that would be uncivilized."

♦ ♦ ♦

Main Street in Bridgehampton was definitely alive with the Fourth of July holiday movement. Parking had been difficult, and it made me late. Despite my tardiness, the rapid thump in my chest forced me to maintain a slow, unrushed pace. My feet felt like cement. A few faces here and there recalled prior meetings, but there was no one familiar enough to warrant anything beyond a polite nod in acknowledgement or a slight smile. It too might have been apparent that the next stop on my agenda was not one I looked forward to even though the location, Pierre's, was a choice Hamptons staple for me and I was meeting a woman I loved dearly. I thought that Rebecca might be concerned about my lateness. Then again, she might not be in a hurry either. My mission was to make sure what happened on the fifth of May didn't repeat itself on the fourth of July. Whatever trick she intended, Rebecca's new friend would not be welcomed at Lauren's party. Period.

A group of passerbys by kept moving, which cleared the view to the restaurant as I jaywalked in the middle of the block. As they did, I saw

Rebecca sitting at an outside table for two. The all-black sunglasses that sat tightly against her face were the first thing I noticed. Far better suited for Norma Desmond than Rebecca. She stood up as I arrived at the light brown wooden table right on the edge of the entrance to the restaurant. The smile I conjured didn't warm the chill that was in the air. Her expressionless, makeup free face was a clue that the glasses were covering up something. She wore a wrinkled grey linen shirtdress and a dainty silver Cartier locket hung around her neck as her sole accessory. True, it was a casual lunch between friends, but this was just not the typical casual of this particular sister-friend.

"They're holding a table for us inside. I know it's a beautiful day. But do you mind?" She stood up and limply caressed my shoulder and hung there as we walked inside. The white cotton linens on the tables were brightened by the glow of the sun shining through the windows. A smooth, pulsating energy danced around the restaurant. More familiar faces but no friends, so we didn't stop for conversation. The hostess led us to the back corner, which was desolate and energy less. Rebecca was silent, but whatever was on her mind pounded loudly, pushing the thump in my chest up to my throat. A change in game plan was required. Don't talk, just listen.

It all became clear when Rebecca pushed those blacked-out spectacles onto a headband, exposing the puffy red eyes they'd been employed to hide. I was inadequately prepared and speechless. When her eyes began to release the water that remained in the wells that probably should have been dry by now, the glasses came back down. And so did the droplets, each one gliding down her cheek and finally stealing the crispness of the tablecloth in various places. She let them fall. Those glasses and our table position being the only camouflage she could manage.

"He asked for a divorce." Upon the utterance of this statement, the tears flowed anew, accompanied by audible sobs that fairly choked her. In our many years of friendship, I had never seen Rebecca cry, let alone this type of release.

When the tears subsided and breath was restored, she began to re-count the previous night's events. Unexpectedly, Gerand had returned home early from a business trip and requested that they have dinner at their house in Amagansett. She arrived to candles, dim light, and course after course of her favorite foods and wines. The opening, their chef's specialty, Maine Lobster bisque that, by experience, I know is so full-bodied that it could be a meal in its own right. This had put Rebecca in a romantic mood. Two bottles of the 1999 Chateau Le Pin Pomerol rescued from their wine cellar only for the most special occasions continued to fuel her happiness. Rebecca was surprised by the attention Gerand had paid to detail. They were traveling down a veritable memory lane of their long marriage. By the time the coq au vin arrived, she knew she was in store for some unique, unexpected news. His excitement and tenderness made her assume that another company had fallen under his conquest. It must be a major one, she'd thought to herself. She'd felt something for him, their relationship and future she had not felt in a long time. She even disregarded the diet of which she had been so recently conscious and indulged in a slice of key lime pie. When they retired to the back veranda, she had intended to curl up with him and continue talking about whatever news he had until bed.

"Where's Dillon tonight?" Gerand asked with a matter-of-factness. The shock shipwrecked her off Fantasy Island. She couldn't lie or pre-tend she didn't know what he was speaking of so she said nothing, which was a monologue in itself. Gerand laid a manila envelope on the table and instructed her to open it. When she refused, he did it for her. First, there was a picture of Rebecca and Dillon at lunch, her hand on his, which easily could have been interpreted as innocent affec-tion between acquaintances, she thought, hoping for a way out. But the pictures progressed. Kissing as she left him at the stage door. A three-in-the-morning date stamped picture of her leaving his house. And the pièce de resistance, Dillon taking Rebecca from behind in the kitchen of the West Village apartment she and Gerand kept for out-of-town guests. There'd been investigators. Cameras installed. Gerand showing her pictures from her blatant escapades with Dillon and her total disregard for discretion was his way of beginning to make her pay for her indiscretions. The remainder of the evening was the polar opposite of how it started — high drama full of accusations. I felt so bad for her, and there was a part of me that thought that the manner in which Gerand exposed her was out of line. But there are no Emily Post rules on this, so there was nothing neither she nor I could really protest. His intent was to hurt her deeply; it was cold-blooded, calculated and successful — completely in sync with Gerand's style.

"What did he say about his affair?"

"He never had an affair. He had an answer for every assumption I had made. I didn't want to believe him and told him I didn't. But I did."

"What are you going to do?"

"I have no idea. If I know Gerand, and I do, his mind is made up. There's no turning back. I guess I'm getting a divorce."

◆ ◆ ◆

It was a parade of pastel sundresses, designer polo shirts, seersucker shorts and sandals. The Hamptons has an unwritten, but well-known dress code. Proper attire is yet another indicator of your place on the social ladder — whether you've climbed or are climbing. To be clear, everyone must climb the ladder at some point, no matter what anyone says, as it is not wholly dependent upon wealth (which can be either made, married, or inherited). No, social status is definitely earned in New York, but based on some of the most arbitrary and superficial criteria. And it's as fickle as fashion; "one minute you're in, and the next minute you're out."

Usually, Lauren began planning her party in late January, brainstorming a theme. Past themes were "An Afternoon in Tunisia," "Alice in Wonderland," and my favorite, "Heaven on Earth," where she transformed the entire expanse of her backyard into an imagining of heaven — pearly gates and all. As party planning went, Lauren had a special gift. This year, we walked into a "Grecian Garden" with living statues, columns, and a botanical garden. The waiters were all in ancient Grecian attire, but not the cheesy togas you see at a college frat party. No, their outfits had been designed by the up-and-coming designers Jayden Eliot and J.Ford. Every year, she somehow managed to outdo her biggest rival, who was always and only Lauren. Some people just have a flair for things, and she had a flair for creating a festive atmosphere that was sophisticated, relaxed, and fun. A trifecta not easy to achieve in the rarified Hamptons.

After the tear-filled breakfast, I was late again meeting Vikki and Krissy at Vikki's rental. Good thing Krissy's jitney was delayed getting there, or I surely would have heard it. No one likes missing a minute of one of Lauren's parties. One of the few occasions where people arrived on time and left only when it was over. Every year there would be one or two early arrivals, which Lauren had become accustomed to and was thus always ready ahead of schedule.

"This bitch does not play with a party," said Krissy as we strolled along the back lawn to the bar. An afternoon soiree in the Hamptons was hit or miss depending on how humid it was. I've seen many a coiffed "sistah" leave looking like a wet puppy. This afternoon was perfection, though; we luxuriated in a consistent breeze and tons of shade created by the imported botanical garden. I sought out a margarita, and not a skinny-girl version. I wanted the full-on taste and calories. With all the extra time I was putting in at the gym, I'd earned that privilege. With Patron, of course.

"Honestly, I don't know how she does it all by herself," replied Vikki as we arrived at the bar made out of pewter Grecian columns and draped with lilac chiffon fabric. The alcohol had been transferred from bottles to urns with pouring spigots. Instead of glasses, there were ancient Greek miniature goblets like you see in the movies. As we ordered our drinks, I got excited because I knew a good time was in store.

"Cheers, ladies, thank you for being my dates," I said as I raised my goblet to toast my gorgeous sister-friends.

"Oh, is that Abigail coming in? Oooh," whispered Vikki. Krissy and I turned to see the "red-headed motor mouth from the south." Vicki and

I had nicknamed her that many years ago because, as sweet as she is, she will talk your head off at a racehorse pace with a strong southern accent. Her husband, Vlad, was the exact opposite, a very quiet, famous writer who seemed to have at least two best sellers every year. All his books were pretty much the same, but the masses loved them, and he consistently churned them out. Abigail was his first editor and had quit her publishing job after marrying him following his third best seller. She'd gone "in-house" and edited all of his books since then — thirty years ago.

"It looks like she's alone. Where's Vlad?" I asked.

"You didn't hear? Vlad left her for a twenty-something secretary at his agent's office," said Vikki.

"Typical," I said.

Then, Krissy asked, "Weren't they married like thirty years?"

"Yes, and the sad thing is that the entire time she was editing his books, he never paid her for it. So now they're in a bitter battle. She hired David Zeiter to represent her. It's going to get ugly," said Vikki as we all shook our heads out of sympathy for Abigail — motor mouth or not.

"That's fucked up! She gave him her best years and now he's dating some ho? I wish a motherfucker would. Harlem would kick so fast back up in my ass... and his."

"Shhh Krissy, she's coming this way," I whispered as Abigail rapidly approached.

"Abigail, you look amazing. I see you've gotten some sun already this season," complimented Vikki.

"Thank you, Vikki. I've been spending more time out east this summer and less in the city. I needed a break from it all," replied Abigail. The more bourgeois of the New York elite referred to the Hamptons as "out east." Somehow they think it makes it sound less pretentious when in fact, the opposite is true. It sounded even a bit more ridiculous on Abigail with her strong, unshakeable southern accent. Never understood why people who live extraordinary lives try so hard to make it seem as if their lives are ordinary. As if private planes, yachts, and second homes in the Hamptons were merely jingling bells. None of them had a clue what the life of a common person was like. Some people meant well, others were voluntarily ignorant as to the level and extent of their privilege.

"Abigail, it really is great to see you. It's been a while," I added to the conversation, giving her two air kisses on either side of her freckled ginger face.

"Always a pleasure, my dear. What y'all drinking? I need something quick."

"Margaritas," I said.

"Hope none of that skinny gal madness. Ruining a perfectly good drink."

"Trust, it's not a game," said Krissy holding up her glass.

Realizing that Abigail and Krissy probably had never met, I introduced them. "Abigail, this is one of my dearest friends, Krissy." They politely shook hands.

Then the racehorse stormed the stable, "I'm sure you've heard what that bastard Vlad is trying to do to me. I made that son of a bitch and now, because he's fucking some romper room floozy, he wants to kick me and thirty-one years aside. Well, I got another thing coming for his ass. Don't you worry about me. Hmmpf!" As the words left her lips, I knew she was talking more to herself than to us. She was worried and secretly hoped that by repeating herself over and over again it would somehow become something she could believe.

"Divorce is a bitch. You know I know," added Vikki empathetically.

"But did either of your ex-husbands try to destroy everything that you ever worked for? That punk son-of-a-bitch is trying to erase me from the face of the damn earth. And the fucked up thing is that he's taking so many of our so-called friends with him. People I've known longer than him are not returning my calls. Assholes!"

"Sadly, had one of those, too. Men can be pieces of shit."

"Hey," I said. "But it's true that the best way to find out who your friends are is to need something."

"I don't need jackshit from them. Just a returned call would do kindly. I tell you; people are so full of it here. Once this is all over, I'm packing up what belongs to me and going back south. These phony-ass people can kiss my ass."

Krissy began to giggle and, like an avalanche, it turned into a full-bellied laugh. At first, I looked at her mortified because it was clear Abigail was in a very fragile state, and I didn't want her to get into a showdown with Krissy. But just as I was about to pinch Krissy, Abigail burst into laughter as well. Then Vikki... and finally, I bowed to the pressure of the moment and began to guffaw, too. We laughed so hard that we caused a bit of a scene, catching Lauren's attention from across the lawn.

"I guess I did come in with the grace of a double-barreled shotgun."

"It's cool. I know what you mean, girl. These phony-ass people can kiss my ass, too," said Krissy, still laughing while high-fiving Abigail. "OK!"

"Really Abigail, if you ever need anything, please don't hesitate to call me. You've always been so gracious to me, and I do understand what a difficult time this must be for you," said Vikki with sincerity. If she said it, she meant it. Just as we were calming down, Lauren walked over in a curve-kissing crème column dress draped in scarves that billowed in the wind. She was an angelic vision as she strolled toward us. I got a little nervous because she was surely coming to chastise us for being so loud.

"Well, you guys seem to be having all the fun! Abigail, you changed your mind and came. That makes me happy," gushed Lauren.

"You're one of the few friends I have left. Wouldn't have missed it."

"That's not true. Everyone loves you," said Lauren.

"No, everyone loved the wife of the famous writer Vlad fucking Willem. They didn't love me, I'm discovering."

"I can't imagine what you're going through. Still, I'm glad you made it. It will be a fun day. And then, I hope you all stick around for a little post-party rundown. Cocktails included, of course. The kids are at overnights and I have cars on standby for the evening, so no need to worry about driving." It was miraculous how composed Lauren was with no signs of the trauma that we all knew was going on with her. We'd made an unspoken agreement not to bring up Josh's issues or absence. Silently, I knew she appreciated it.

"Y'all stay right here, I'm going to get a stiff one," said Abigail as she bolted her way to the bar. We all watched her walk away, relieved that a potentially explosive situation had turned out to be a bit of fun. All of us were filled with either sympathy or empathy for what Abigail was going through.

Lauren said, "You just never know. Do you?"

"Unfortunately girl, you never do," agreed Vikki.

◆ ◆ ◆

Abigail had a great time at the party. Inarguably, she had the best time at the party. With the aid of three too many "stiff ones," she left half-erect, carried out by her driver. It would have been far more embarrassing had she not been the life of the party, easing everyone's internal tension caused by the knowledge of her situation with Vlad and Lauren's with Josh. She made it comfortable to laugh with her and at her, which was quite an achievement in that room and under those circumstances. And like the true southern lady she is, she knew exactly when she had sung her swan song. Oftentimes, too many stiff ones also weaken your ability to decipher between amusing and annoying. Abigail crept right to the very edge and then, expertly, knew it was time for the not-so-fat lady to sing.

As the staff finished the last bit of cleanup, Lauren, Vikki, Krissy, plus two of Lauren's other friends and I sat around a final round of cocktails in the kitchen. At any house party in any neighborhood, you will find people gathered in the kitchen. Theoretically, the living room should be where people congregate, but without equivocation, the kitchen seems to win hands down. The kitchen is the soul of the house, and a warm kitchen typically means a warm house. Lauren's spirit emanated throughout every home she and Josh owned. They were all impressive addresses and properties, but you definitely could put your feet up and enjoy yourself. Lauren's exceptional hospitality made you always feel welcome and always sad to leave.

One of the drawbacks of leaving a party too early, though, is that you are usually the first topic of discussion. Not necessarily from a place of nasty gossip, it's just naturally the thing everyone in the room can share, particularly when a large party has been reduced to an intimate circle of friends. Harmless gossip with no intent except a review of the night, especially no ill intent.

Krissy jumped in first. "Abigail sure was lit." I chuckled to hear the kettle being called black by the pot. Krissy surely had her fair share of stiff ones, too. Being twenty or so years younger and in better practice gave her a slight edge in being able to still walk a straight line. But only ever so slight. A permanent smile was plastered on her face, and several hairs from her formerly straight wig had lost their place. The lipstick had been reapplied, but not as expertly as before. And her bra was playing peek-a-boo with us every now and again. Not a complete mess, but she'd clearly had a great time, too.

"She really enjoyed herself. I was glad she did," said Lauren as she pulled up a seat to the granite-topped island in the middle of the kitchen. I saw the stiff one she poured, and it was definitely the stiffest one in the room. Well-earned and much deserved considering the party raised over a million dollars for charity. A million dollars not only goes a long way in supporting the organization but it was quite a haul for the relatively small guest list. Another testament to her party-throwing talents — always picking the guest list with exacting precision. Too many boring deep pockets can make your event a yawnfest. Too many exciting but financially challenged guests (usually the models, actors, and entertainers) would leave the charity with pennies and promises. So the perfect blend was key to success; something Lauren understood better than anyone I knew.

"I just can't believe Vlad is treating her like this after so many years and all she's done for him. Besides editing all of his work, she raised four kids," proclaimed Lauren.

"My second divorce was definitely the most difficult thing I've ever had to go through," said a tipsy Vikki.

"We're broke," interjected Lauren out of nowhere, causing all of us to stop in the tracks of our thoughts. She couldn't be serious. Broke? Impossible. Sure, Josh had made some bad choices, but broke was inconceivable. Her version of *broke* was probably another man's "set for life." The seriousness on Lauren's face made me nervous, though.

"Not quite broke, but if we don't do something fast we will be. I don't get another disbursement from my trust for five years. And we've been hemorrhaging money on all of these films and other failed projects. The children's tuitions. Rehab. The multiple houses. I could go on." No amount of stiff ones could have numbed me to the sting of this news. We all sat silently while I rapidly searched for some comfort to share beyond the questions that were prevailing in my mind. By the looks on their faces, everyone's minds. Stories of MC Hammer and other reckless celebrities losing their fortunes were not uncommon and no surprise. For Lauren, on the other hand, this was the last thing any of us expected to ever hear from her. She and Josh lived a big life, but they could afford it. Then she acknowledged the elephant in the room, "Not to mention the drugs." Josh's drug habit was well documented by the tabloids and obviously far more expensive than any of us could have imagined. Drugs are ain't cheap, and when you have a vast amount of wealth at your disposal it can get ridiculous. There's no one to stop you. And no receipts to show. Taking a big swig of her drink, Lauren had put up a good front all day or had gotten so lost in the party planning that she'd been able to push it aside. In the relative quiet of the current moment and the comfort of some of her closest friends, she could no longer put on any semblance of airs. She had probably been waiting for this all day. Had made it a part of the plan, hence the strong invitation and preparation with the fleet of cars waiting outside for all of us. For the first time, I considered whether or not she could afford the expense of something. It just wasn't anything you ever worried about with Lauren. Times had changed. "I feel responsible for not paying attention. Who lets their drug addict husband handle their finances?"

Lauren had a point, and we all knew it. It seemed so completely out of character to be that disconnected from their affairs, especially since the bulk of their money was hers. Smart women do dumb things for the sake of love. I get it but will never understand it. Her rationale was that she was so busy with the children, charities, and running several households that she hadn't the time to pay attention. The truth was probably a lot more grey. She wanted Josh to preserve some of his manhood and allowed him to assume a traditional role even though their circumstances were far from conventional. It was also unbelievable to all of us that her family's advisors had so easily relinquished control of such a large fortune. Although I chastised her in my mind, as I am sure everyone in the room did, verbalizing it would not be helpful. The good news was that she'd had enough foresight to place a huge chunk of it in trusts for the kids that neither she nor Josh could touch. Even if they were broke for the time being, the children certainly were not. In the meantime, we needed to come up with a plan.

"Can you ask your family for an early disbursement?" I asked.

"No. Even if I did, they'd say no given Josh's history. They'd require me to leave him or something like that. I definitely don't want to be under their control."

"Sweetie, I can loan you some money," offered Vikki.

"Thank you, but that's only short term. I will figure it out."

"Why don't you get a job?" asked Krissy emphatically. At first, I thought her question and its delivery were insensitive until I until I glanced at Krissy. She was dead-ass serious. It made me think she might be on to something. Normal people can't go to their families or friends to borrow millions. Normal people work, and maybe it was time for Lauren to do the same. She'd long let Josh have at a failing career while she maintained their homes. Speaking of which, I'm sure they could downgrade in many areas. Krissy was right. Instead of this pity party, Lauren needed to take some action. Her passivity had allowed this situation to get to where it was, and now she needed to put her big-girl panties on to save her family.

"I haven't worked in over ten years," she offered.

"Girl, you worked today. You've been an event planner for years," I said.

"But that's just for charity. For fun."

"On a resume it's not for charity or fun. You've handled countless major events with big budgets all by yourself. Just because you 'donated your fee' doesn't mean it wasn't work. Make lemonade, Gorgina! You are a fabulous event planner, and you love it. No better job. And you can start tomorrow. My friend Anthony is getting married. He's rich and gay! He was going to use Colin, but I will make him go with you. He owes me a favor or three. And I know his ass is going to spend a load of money and he'll tell all his friends you're fabulous because you are. And once you have the wealthy gays on your side, you're set. We run the world. Plus, with your contacts? It's a no-brainer."

"Thank you. But what about the children?"

"You have a live-in weekday nanny and one for the weekend. Use them. And it doesn't stop with event planning. Look at Martha Stewart. You don't have to do the cooking part and all of that, but you definitely got her on event planning. Books. TV shows. The whole nine yards. You can do this, and we're going to help you."

"He has a point," added Vikki I know you must feel devastated by all that's happened. But you gotta pull yourself up and keep going. It's the only way. Trust me, sweetie, I know from experience." We all began to extol Lauren's virtues as an event planner and the myriad opportunities we could connect her with using our collective resources. From the budding twinkle in Lauren's eyes, I saw the pep talk was beginning to sink in. She wasn't as defeated as when she first opened up. Still, I could tell she knew there was a lot of work ahead — on her spirit, a potential career, and finding her own way. She would also have to deal with Josh; all while starting down a new path. But she had the dream team behind her, didn't she?

"Why the hell not?" she said. "I'm gonna kick Martha's ass!" With that, we all raised our stiff-ones and toasted.

Chapter Thirteen

The Help

Summer Saturdays in New York City are brilliant. She, the sleepless city, awakens even more, particularly with thousands of curious people trying to discover her. Visitors and inhabitants alike. The constant sense of urgent work to be done calms a bit, and a day is simply allowed to be enjoyed. With the increased amount of playtime in the sun, friendships are strengthened and relationships get a little heat too. She is romantically charged with a kinder, gentler energy that makes you want to be out — not just outdoors but outside of typical. It's what summertime is about, and New York understands summer better than most. With many of her busiest worker bees flying out for the weekend, she's no longer spilling with a tidal wave rush of caffeine-pumped type As. That makes her pleasant. Never boring, she's just a softer version of herself still filled with endless possibilities. That makes her fun.

Sure, there is some work that finds its way to the weekend, but an afternoon meeting can turn into lunch and then into hours of cocktails. It is exactly what I'd been doing for the greater part of the afternoon with Krissy and one of my producing partners, André Christopher. Out of the blue André called with great news: The new network "Alive" had reconsidered a talk show we had pitched almost ten months ago. *Confronting America* would feature a rotating cast of energetic and unique talking heads delivering facts and commentary with a flair not currently seen on TV (or at least that's how we pitched it). We were meeting to discuss shooting the pilot, and Krissy was going to be one of the regular legal experts. Television wasn't something she had considered, but as with everything, Krissy was a natural and got it fairly quickly when we used her while shooting our sizzle reel. She was so spot-on that the network specifically asked that we include her in the pilot. We wanted her to be a mix of Judge Judy and Judge Maybelline—irreverent, in-your-face commentary with a big dose of her unique style. Krissy was fully onboard for her role, and André had all of the production details mapped out, so we wrapped up the business and jumped into catching up on everything that wasn't work. Life. Cocktails. The other good stuff.

We'd chosen Cafeteria, a summertime must in the city. Perfect for an al fresco meeting and some serious people watching. The beautiful people seem to burrow throughout the five boroughs all winter, emerging in early summer when no layers were needed. The transformation begins in innumerable gyms in the late winter and is on full display by summer's chime. New York is an aesthetically gifted city, and the beautiful creatures know it. It raises the stakes, but everything about her does. Luck is no lady here.

Andre firmly stated, "I need another drink" with a force that made us all laugh.

"You meant that!" joked Krissy.

"Is grits grocery?"

We were in great spirits, and I knew our bill was going to prove it. But it didn't matter; it was summertime in New York. We'd deal with all of that in the fall. It was an opportunity to celebrate being alive in the greatest city in the world. So we ordered another round. And we meant it.

"How's Justin?"

"Good, I guess. The closer we get to the move, things are alright. I mean, it's all good for the most part. Just a couple of things. The other day we went out for dinner and his cards didn't work. None of them. So I had to pay."

"Trust me, I have seen it happen to the best of us. Not really a big deal. Did he explain?" I asked, remembering Lauren's unfortunate incident in St. Barth's and several of my own.

"Yeah, he said he'd put some office stuff on his cards, and it was blocked for fraud alert."

"OK, that's happened to me many times," said André. "Your boy here never wants to put anything production-related on his card. So who's stuck with getting reimbursed and the bills? Me."

"I do creative. You do credit. That's why they call it partners."

"Whatever!"

"But if it were just that I wouldn't be even mentioning. Other things also bother me. For instance, I came home one day and he'd rearranged my living room. Said it functioned better his way."

"And you, of all people, didn't go off?" I asked.

"I know! But no, not really."

"What? Let me do that. You would have blown a gasket."

"Right," Krissy chuckled. "I would have cussed *your* ass out."

"True and true!" Andre exclaimed.

"But I'm not planning to move in with either of you. I mean, I have to get accustomed to everything not being just my way, right?"

Andre and I kept silent.

"I don't know. There are just some inconsistencies in his behavior. Nothing major, just little things here and there."

"How long have you known him?" asked Andre.

Reluctantly, Krissy answered, "Four months." Judgment flushed Andre's face, and Krissy sat up defiantly in her seat. It did sound ridiculous that she was moving in with someone she'd known for such a short time, but Krissy had made up her mind and there was no one going to challenge her. Except Krissy.

I felt compelled to defend her, particularly since I had encouraged her and felt responsible for the meeting, "Justin is a great guy. He runs a new biotech hedge fund. The brother definitely has his shit together. And did I mention, he is fine? I'm proud of Krissy for being open."

"Open is one thing. Crazy is another. You don't know him," protested Andre.

"Well, this is the longest relationship she's been in years." Krissy shot me a half-mean look, but she knew I was right. She was a perpetual "monthagamous" — just usually with thugs and deadbeats. Two months here. Six weeks there. Never too long to really develop into anything. She liked having a companion until they got too close. Krissy and her career were in holy matrimony, and three was definitely a crowd. Justin was not only a breath of fresh air resume-wise; he'd interrupted her noncommittal patterns. Krissy was maturing when it came to relationships. It was very fast, but at the end of the day, I knew Krissy would take care of Krissy.

"Let's just drop it. No biggie boos. Was just talking my mind. I'm straight." My phone vibrated with a new text message. I usually put the phone away at restaurants with friends, but something told me to look at the text.

"Excuse me, guys," I said as I read the text message. "Oh, Daniel is having people over for drinks and wants me to stop by. Interested?"

"Is grits grocery?" André asked again.

"Live for Daniel. Always fun," added Krissy.

"OK, let me tell him I'm with you," I said while replying to the text. Daniel was like a mentor to me. He'd made several well-regarded films, including one that had been nominated for an Academy Award. He was also wondrously crazy. A joy to be around, plus he always knew very interesting people. A summer afternoon fête at his apartment was as close to guaranteed fun as you could get. "He said, 'cool.'"

I got excited as we finished our mostly liquid lunch. Impromptu parties were also a frequent treat on a weekend during the summertime. Everyone loves an unexpected dose of fun. And we had finished working so we could continue to play without guilt. "Work less hard, play a little harder" was the summer mantra. The season was handcrafted for practicing it on repeat.

◆ ◆ ◆

As we pulled up, there was a receiving line of drivers and cars waiting to greet us. A Bentley, a Rolls-Royce, two Maybachs, and a blacked-out extended Cadillac Escalade. Daniel lived in one of those kinds of buildings, so it didn't strike me as abnormal. It wasn't until the smiling uniformed man opened the door to his apartment that I realized this wasn't your average afternoon cocktail situation. There were muscular and attractive men walking around in black pants, black form-fitting button downs, and miniature white bow ties with trays of plated appetizers and flutes of Champagne. There was definitely no "self-serve moment before plopping back on the sofa with your feet up" happening tonight. Immediately, I felt underdressed and unprepared. Earlier, for my meeting, I'd thrown on some distressed jeans, a red polo shirt, and sandals. Not befitting a catered and staffed event. Andre and Krissy were extremely casual too, which made me feel a little better. But only just a little.

As we walked in, I realized my apprehension was well founded as I surveyed the room full of people in seersucker suits, sky-high red-bottomed shoes and elegant summer dresses. Krissy leaned in to me, "Isn't that...?" Before she could finish, I nodded and smiled back at her, noticing too that the room was full of celebrities and tastemakers. Very important people. And not your fly-by-night Instagram sensations. These were people who ran New York City and, therefore, the world. I wanted to kill Daniel. He could've given us a heads-up that the party was an "event." Just as I started looking for him, he suddenly appeared, with shoes off, wearing a flowing jacquard silk pajama pants and an oversized, muted-grey caftan shirt and looking much more relaxed than we were. So I knew we were cool.

"You pretty motherfuckers, I'm glad you made it," he yelled at the three of us, wrapping his arms around Krissy's neck. Daniel had a way of making you feel completely at ease even in the most extraordinary circumstances. The thing I admired most was his ability to be fabulous without being a freak. He was down home folk and made you know it. If you put on a pretense around him, you were quickly embarrassed, either directly or indirectly. No matter who you were. The sincerity with which he conducted himself allowed him to get away with it even with the most persnickety princes and princesses.

"You know, I'm mad at you. You could've told me this was a high society event," I said.

"Boy, fuck these people. This here my juke joint. We're here to have some damn fun. The waiters and shit is just 'cause I'm lazy."

"Thanks for having us," interjected André.

"No probs. Now go get a cocktail and some food. I have to change the music. It's a fucking funeral."

Just as he walked away, I noticed André Leon Talley, the legendary former editor-at-large of *Vogue* magazine. I'm not the biggest fashion person, but Mr. Talley transcended the industry. Everyone knew who he was and could easily spot his very specific but all-his-own style. It didn't hurt that he towered over most crowds at 6'6", but with the gentility of spirit that made him an even bigger giant. I had met him briefly during an interview for one of my television shows profiling an up-and-coming designer. He was exceptionally pleasant and possessed mind-baffling knowledge about fashion. I was excited to see him again because I was sure he was going to be gracious, and I wanted the other "whose-its" to see me speaking to him. Monkey see, monkey do in these types of settings. As insincere as it sounds, it was an undeniable game, and I'd long ago learned how to play it. They'd see me speaking to André and instantly wonder who I was, looking to find out quickly. He was speaking to a woman, but her back was to me and all I could see were her brown tresses, of which there were a lot, and a skin-tight brown dress that displayed some serious curves.

"Mr. Talley. I interviewed you two weeks ago for my show on the designer Tracy Reese," I said as I stuck out my hand to him.

He smiled a glorious smile and grabbed my hand. "Yes, of course, that was a wonderful interview. I just adore Tracy."

"Yes, thank you so much. You added a great deal to the show."

"When does it air, again?"

"In September during Fashion Week. We'll send your office a copy for sure."

"That would be just fabulous."

"André, you're being so rude," said Ms. Hair and Body, turning around to reveal the full frontal cornucopia. "Hi, I'm Mariah." I wanted to say, 'Yes, I know who you are, Ms. Butterfly Honey Vision of Love."

I almost fell down but, thankfully, my legs held and I was able to respond. "A pleasure to meet you." You got to keep it cute even if you are unexpectedly bombarded with one of the biggest stars in the world, particularly in such an intimate setting.

The anxiety was starting to kick back in until she said, "No, it's true. Had this whole singing thing not worked out, I would have been a hairdresser."

"Darling, I can't believe that. That would've been just a dreadful waste all that talent. Furthermore, you would have been a hairstylist, not a hairdresser. Charging five thousand dollars a day. Fabulous is in your blood," said Mr. Talley.

"Either way. It's true."

"Excuse me," I said, realizing that I was struck by the enormity of this star and could not deal at the moment. I'd been caught completely off guard and needed a chance to regroup.

"Of course, dear, you make your way back over." The anxiety would've been overwhelming had Ms. Honey not been so sweet and down to earth. You never know how celebrities of that stratosphere are going to be, but she was surprisingly normal.

I decided to walk over to my friend Keith, who was talking to the opera diva Letitia Moore whom I'd met through Lauren, and although she was definitely a diva in the true sense of the word, I at least knew them both. As I got closer, I realized that they were not having the most amicable conversation.

"There's plenty of Champagne. I'll get you another glass," said Keith, who laughed as he looked around for a waiter.

"Young man, wasting Champagne, true Champagne, is no laughing matter." I quickly made a detour from that stop.

"So spill the tea, bitch," said Daniel grabbing my arm and pulling me over to a back corner. I was happy he'd saved me because Krissy was talking to someone I didn't much like and André had vanished — probably to smoke a cigarette or a joint. The smell of both was wafting in the room from the balcony. For a moment I thought about partaking but then remembered my rule of not getting high at big parties. On the other hand, this was probably a safe environment considering most of Daniel's guests had more to lose than I did. Weed needed to hurry up and get legal because right now it would have relaxed my nerves tremendously.

"What tea?" I asked.

"Bitch, I hear you're taking the plunge and moving to L.A."

"Yep, I think it's time for me to shake some trees out there."

"You gotta job yet?"

"Not yet, but I should be cool once I get there."

"Let me know if you need my help. Those assholes have been on my nuts since my last film. I just can't take all that phony bullshit. You don't strike me as down for it either."

"I'm not. But I'm also not down for standing still."

"I get that shit for real. Oscar or not, this business is hard for black folks trying to tell black stories."

"Which is crazy to me because every time they let a great story through, black or not, it works out."

"Do you know this one studio asked me if I wanted to do a cartoon for them? A motherfucking cartoon! I didn't even respond in the meeting. I just got up and left. Dumb cunts."

"Yeah, you and a kids' movie don't really seem like a good fit."

"Fuck kids. I hate kids. Except my own damn kids. I love those l'il fuckers. Everybody else's kids can suck it. I'll be right back." Daniel went over to one of the waiters to bark some orders and probably make an inappropriate pass from the look of trepidation on the waiter's face which quickly turned into an uncomfortable blush as Daniel stared hard at his retreating ass. My host was certainly a character, and the party was now in full swing with old-school Tribe Called Quest playing on the system. It was apparent that people had started to feel the free-flowing cocktails. I hoped no one else wasted any more of Ms. Moore's Champagne. I then realized I'd yet to have a drink as, upon arrival, I was still feeling good from the three delicious but potent wild berry mojitos I'd consumed at lunch. But the effects were starting to wear off, so it was time to refuel.

Daniel's apartment was a modern oasis, mostly open space appointed with deliberate choices of glass and steel here and there. More California minimalist than midtown New York, the style suited me better than the overstated opulence of many fancy apartments I'd been in recently. Still, the space was full of opulent people, so the room rang with a regality that was intimidating yet also encouraging. In prior years, I would have felt uncomfortable being in the presence of these people. As the years progressed and I found my own lane, it was reassuring that I'd earned the right to be amongst the glamorati. Now, as I was getting older, I realized that we all have the right to be wherever we want to be, no matter who else is in the room. The cycle is quite funny and made me laugh at myself. In the beginning, I was so thirsty to be accepted. Then, I was so proud that I was. Older, I cared less and less what people thought, and it made me feel good that I'd found my place here amidst all the noise. I still wished Daniel had been more specific about the caliber and nature of the party. I thought about it for a minute, and I guess it didn't matter because I would have come anyway. Before, I would have gone shopping to spend money I didn't have to impress people who were far too busy trying to impress each other to care.

While I was waiting for my drink I surveyed the room so intently that I almost failed to notice the strikingly handsome bartender. I couldn't tell if he was Black, white, or some exotic mixture. He looked like a very well-tanned Greek guy with the most amazing set of pearly whites had seen in a while. Those gums weren't natural, but they didn't look as fake as most dental work does these days. I felt guilty for questioning how he could afford such impressive and obviously expensive work. He must be an actor, I thought, dismissing him. My next thought was how often I did that to guys. Maybe my girls were right. And what if he was an actor with a mouth full of veneers? He was fine as hell. And what if it was time for me to step out of my comfort zone and step back into the dating ring. I certainly was well overdue.

"What you having?" asked "Zeus."

"Do you have lime juice...to make a gimlet?"

"I've got whatever you need," he said with a smile.

I returned the smile. "Cool, I'll take a Grey Goose gimlet."

"My kind of man. One strong Goose gimlet coming up."

"Who said anything about strong?"

"I'm good at what I do. You like them strong." I just laughed and turned my head away at the awkward moment because he was surely good at whatever it was he was doing. My question was whether he was doing it on purpose because he was hired to do so or if because it was my drink he was making. Either way, I was content to soak up the attention and give a little back.

"So, do you have to pass a screen test to work for this company? All of you are gorgeous."

"Well, it would be kinda messed up to have a company called Model Waiters with bad-looking waiters."

"Ah, I see." Daniel had stacked the deck and hired all gorgeous male waiters on purpose, which I noticed for the first time. I'd been aware of the abundance of fine men walking around in black. But I had not noticed they were all men. I loved Daniel. As I was coming to my realization, Zeus sat my drink in front of me and turned his attention to the next "customer."

"What can I get for you, pretty lady?" I guess that answered my question. He was paid to be good at what he does. And that was that.

As I sipped on my fresh and strong cocktail I realized I had lost track of Krissy and André a long time ago, which was a great sign. They were comfortable and having fun. It could be difficult bringing some people into a room like this with all its potential for discomfort or insecurity. As things go, they were the perfect two compadres to be with me that day as they jumped right in, never missing a beat and ultimately leaving me to my discomfort and insecurity.

Krissy floated over with one of those grins that was either induced by good spirits or meeting a good spirit. I assumed she'd met a celebrity or some really cool person. A great conversation with a previously unmet friend can serve as a platter for happiness just as well as a lover. Meeting good people is always fun, no matter the outcome or intent. It's also why encountering lesser spirits can be taxing. And now one of those taxing spirits was also approaching from across the room: Karen Parks, the wife of the famous television producer Richard Parks. I was hoping she would choose a different path that did not include me. Yet as a precaution, I braced myself for the energy that never seemed positive. Had to be nice, though, because of work. A necessary evil, but I always kept it quick and cute.

"Something has you glowing," I said as Krissy got closer, beating Karen.

"Maybe," replied the giddy Krissy. Without second thought, I knew she'd met a guy, but what about Justin? She wouldn't be this happy if it were just a nice person or potential new friend.

I began to spell, "J-U-S-T-"

"Hush! It's not like that. He is fine, though."

"Lord, Krissy, which one is it?" I began to look around the room, but my eyes ran into Karen, who had quietly pounced upon me. I stepped back, startled. "Karen, I didn't realize you were standing there."

"The room's only so big. You had to see me coming over."

"I was hoping I was important enough for you to say hello. In this room, especially."

"You know I'm never rude." Actually, I didn't know. She was always rude and just didn't realize it. I don't know which is worse: people who are intentionally nasty or people who don't intend it but can't help being themselves — I think the latter. At least the former is not out of delusion. You can move out of the way of a moving train, but a train whose conductor doesn't realize it's in motion is far more dangerous.

"Of course not. You know my friend..."

"Krissy," sliced in Karen. "Many times. How are you?"

"I'm good. And you?" said Krissy whose mood had understandably frozen.

"Well. Now, what's this about a boy you've met?" How the hell had she heard all that? I wondered. Maybe she was indeed an alien (as many speculated).

Krissy thawed a bit at the thought of whatever gentleman in the room had caught her eye. "Like I said, it's not like that."

"Spill it," demanded Karen. "Which one is it?" Her thirst for knowledge was more of an inquisitive gossip than a curious girlfriend. I doubted Krissy would continue the conversation, but she shocked me.

"It's not who you think it would be."

"There are only a handful of straight, single guys in the room. The pickings are slim." Karen was right, there weren't that many options present unless it was a married guy, and I knew Krissy didn't roll like that so it forced me to get curious.

"Who is it then?" I asked.

"That guy right there. Mike." Krissy nodded her head in the direction of the open kitchen.

"Oh, honey, not the help," exclaimed Karen with the most condescending tone as we locked eyes on one of the waiters. I too was shocked that in this room, which was billowing with billions, she'd settled on one of the waiters. I then recalled my moment with Zeus, so I was in no position to say anything, but it was different for me. Not quite sure how it was, but it was. It was probably because I thought Krissy was back to her old ways. She'd hit a couple of bumps with Justin, and she was back in her worn old saddle. To her credit, though, billions or not, he was the best-looking option in the room.

"It's actually his company that supplies the staff. He only hires models. But, again, it's not like that! We were just talking. He's very interesting."

"You don't come to a party like this and go home with the staff," Karen retorted.

"That's not the issue," I shot Krissy a knowing look. She and Justin weren't married, but they had made a commitment. I didn't want another Rebecca situation at hand.

"Y'all are tripping. I'm just talking to the man. And it was far better than this conversation." Krissy pivoted and went back to her waiter.

"Oh shit, here comes Flo." Karen exited stage left far away in a flash as the celebrated gossip columnist Flo Anthony approached. Flo had originated the celebrity journalist role for black people with her long-running syndicated radio segment, "On the Go with Flo." She'd seen it all from Michael to Whitney to Beyoncé. Flo's career had spanned the ages, and if you wanted to know something going on in "Black Hollywood," you called her. She'd been my friend for years, and we always had a good time over laughs, gossip, and Chardonnay. As gossip columnists went, Flo maintained a heart of gold, which kept her firmly in the game and on everyone's guest list.

"Did that heffa Karen just run away from me?"

"So it would seem. Are you after her?"

"Her sleazy husband is about to get sued again by another female production assistant. There are witnesses that saw him grope her on the set of his new series. At least it's a woman this time."

"Why do they even stay together? She hates him. He doesn't even realize she exists."

"Who else is evil and greedy enough to put up with that l'il Napoleon besides her? She's so happy to be Mrs. Parks that he could screw a donkey in the middle of Times Square and she'd stay."

I burst into laughter. Flo had an excellent way of throwing shade hilariously that lacked the venom of many others. Plus, she was consistently supportive of my projects, and we'd developed a great friendship over the years. "When did you get here?"

"I just got here. Obviously, you haven't heard yet. Gerand had a massive heart attack. He's at Mount Sinai. It's all over the news. I just covered it for CNBC."

"Oh, my God! Rebecca!"

Chapter Fourteen

When the Heart Stops

I hate hospitals. I know everyone does, but my disdain for hospitals is so profound that my skin literally itches each time I have to be in one. My extreme aversion for the sterile palaces for the sick began when I was a young child and visited my Great Aunt Ilene who, prior to her stay in the hospital, was a plump butterball of life. When I saw her in the hospital, she had withered away to an emaciated shadow of herself. The next day she died. She was my grandmother's sister and my favorite. It wasn't just the abundance of candy and cake she had at her house, I felt as though "Auntie Peaches" understood me like no other person in my family. Unfortunately, a pattern formed for years after that, and when I would see family members in the hospital, within days of my visit they would die, so I stopped visiting people in the hospital altogether for about twenty years. After a dear friend was sick for a prolonged time, he begged me to come and see him. Krissy gave me so much flack about being an adult and that it wasn't about me, but about being supportive, that I gave in by paying him a visit. He didn't die.

The Mt. Sinai hallway in which I was waiting for Rebecca was still eerie, but my skin itched less than usual. Although Gerand's critical condition could likely bring back the hospital curse of my youth, I had made some progress regarding my fear of death. Before, death scared me with such a force and fear that it contradicted my faith in God and challenged my belief in heaven. For some reason, I'd always had this morbid idea that I would not make it to many of my milestone birthdays, leaving this world not having done all that I was intended to do. With the passing of more milestones I'd previously thought I wouldn't make, my irrational thinking began to wane, and at the same time my faith strengthened.

I was getting lost in my own crazy thoughts, so I reminded myself that my purpose for being there was to support Rebecca. She had maintained a vigil at Gerand's side and only left briefly here or there to take a walk or get something he needed. She'd jumped back into the role of dutiful wife without pause or question. Just days prior, the two were spiraling down an abyss of bitterness, revenge, and incessant blame. Gerand's most recent priority was making Rebecca's life a living hell. After the confrontation in the Hamptons, Gerand's hurt-inspired wrath came down on Rebecca with the force of the Greek god Nemesis. Bank accounts were frozen, keys no longer worked, and once overly friendly doormen were palm-pressured to join the offensive line. By allowing her to use the one-bedroom apartment they kept in the West Village for guests, he did not completely displace her, but that was for poetic justice. The scene of most of her indiscretions was now her prison. He was ruthless to an extent I didn't believe even he was capable. It was the kind of displacement you read about in the tabloids or hear as one of high society's urban legends. And with every blow he inflicted, it became clearer that Gerand had been so devastated and embarrassed that he would not relent until Rebecca felt the same pain via the only power he thought he had over her — their money and their possessions. To her credit, she owned the guilt and responsibility of it all, which paralyzed the force of her defenses against the brutal attack. And so, she accepted the rush with minimal opposition. Then, his heart stopped.

"Do you mind if we get out of here? Let's lunch." Rebecca startled me out of my comatose review of the past month's events. A good thing, because the anger I had against Gerand was hardly appropriate given the fact that he was clinging to life. I couldn't be mad at him and support my girlfriend at the same time. The despondent look on her face was further reminder that I was here to fulfill a role, and it didn't involve rehashing what had been. That would be helpful to no one, especially my main concern, my sister-friend who by the paleness of her now honey-less skin revealed for the first time her forty-one years and her need for support.

"Sure, where you wanna go?"

"Anywhere. He's sleeping, I just need to get away from this smell."

I knew exactly what she meant. The staff of hospitals strived to make it as sterile an environment as possible creating that distinctive smell. You can be blind and know when you walk into a hospital. Life is not supposed to be sterile. It's supposed to be dirty and filled with complexity. But calling a hospital sterile was also something of a misnomer since hospitals tended to be Petri dishes for disease and infection. It's why I sanitized my hands every chance I got as we walked down the hallway to the elevator. I suggested we eat at The Boat House in Central Park. The dense, lush green and colors of the park's foliage in August would be a stark contrast to this place and would hopefully infuse some energy back into my visibly worn-down friend.

We rode the elevator in silence and walked out into the afternoon sun, the heat of which had aroused the New York summer sewer stench that accosted virgin visitors and intoxicated inhabitants. Semi-foul air or not, it was a welcomed change from the stink of that supposed sanitary chamber of dread and gloom. Again, I stopped myself from thinking such uncharacteristically morbid and gruesome thoughts. That's what hospitals did to me. I couldn't really help it.

We continued along the short block without words, and then I grabbed Rebecca's hand and gave it a tight squeeze that pushed out the first smile I'd seen from her since before the breakfast in the Hamptons. The side street was pretty desolate compared to the midday traffic and taxi parade barreling down Fifth Avenue. I could feel some of the tension release from Rebecca's hand as we arrived at the corner. The environment change was already having a positive affect, and I knew a great lunch in a beautiful setting would further effectuate the job. It also freed my mind from the conundrum of overly dramatic bad thoughts I was having in the hospital. I was now firmly focused on the task at hand. There's a trickiness to the timing of tragedy. The way of the universe to balance itself. Not even two months ago, I dreaded seeing Rebecca and the chastising I felt obligated to bestow. To see her now, lifeless with worry, made me ready to give anything to go back or move forward. I hailed a cab, we jumped in, and she immediately slid over to the far door and looked out the window. I wasn't sure if this was a good time to begin a conversation or if the quiet was what she needed.

"Life's a funny bitch," Rebecca broke the ice for me. "You know I'm not one for praying and church and all that," she said still looking out the window. "I mean, I believe in God, but we haven't been that close. But all I've been doing is praying."

"Good thing to be doing."

"I just don't want to be one of those hypocrites. Calling on God only when I need him. Or when it's convenient."

"I don't think God cares. Like my pastor says, don't put human characteristics on him or on faith. The fact is you're calling to Him. You believe. The Word is pretty simple when it comes to the requirements. We're the ones that get it all jacked up."

"Do you believe in heaven?"

"Funny you should ask that. I was just thinking about that very thing last night. Honestly, I don't know. I do believe your energy transitions to another form. But the way people describe heaven doesn't seem quite right."

Rebecca turned to face me. "Really? Explain."

"I certainly don't believe in hell or some maniacal devil that's out to get me. I think it's contradictory to believe in God's omnipotence and then believe that He can't defeat some measly fallen angel."

"Wow, I would never have expected you to say that. You're so religious."

"That's the thing, I'd say I'm spiritual. To me, being religious is someone who only follows a set of rules and rituals. I put God first in all things, yes. But, religion without true spirituality has caused so many problems. Religion enslaved us and said we were three-fourths human."

"You have a point."

"The things people have done and the persecution people have suffered in the name of religion, especially Christianity, is cray. I think if more Christians actually followed the teachings of Christ, we'd be much better off."

"Amen to that." She then turned back to looking out of the window. "They look so happy. In the park." I looked past her to see the activity and life of Central Park. She was right; they did look happy and active. Most people, when in Central Park, *are* happy. I understood why Lauren loved it so much. The euphoric affect it had on your spirit was instantaneous. It has the same energy and pulse of the city that surrounds it but with the beauty of nature forcing you to appreciate life's most basic gifts. An oasis away from the insanity and worry intrinsic to the steel and cement that made up the rest of the city. I was hoping this would be the case for Rebecca and me. We both needed a little pick-me-up. The year had been extraordinary and full of change for all of my girls and me in one-way or another. And though we usually took it in stride (with the aid of an adult beverage and a good time), we were human. Now I was feeling every bit of my mortality with Gerand's heart stopping.

"You never know. You, just never know," said Rebecca, who must have been reading my mind.

"It's been some shit."

"You ain't never lied." Rebecca was back to basics. She was raw, and her bones were showing. "Life doesn't give a fuck who you are. It's still going to be life." There was no punctuation needed for that statement as the cab pulled into the park. "Actually, sir, we'll get out here," she said to the driver. "Do you mind if we walk?"

"I would love to walk." We stepped out into air that was fresher than before, with the smell of life emanating from the trees. This time Rebecca grabbed my hand and smiled as we passed the cyclists, the lovers, the horse-drawn carriages and the many children playing with no cares in the world. We laughed at the ginger-headed little boy about four years old who ran down a ball that was almost too big for him to manage. His mother and his nanny looked on in sheer amusement. Children that age can't help but make you recall the wonder of the world. Through their eyes, everything is new and splendid. There is no greediness except for those things that truly make a person happy. None of the foolishness we promote as adults. Rebecca produced a full and genuine smile this time. It was working.

"He's going to be alright. And the two of you are going to walk through this park together."

"I don't know about together. But I sure as hell want him to be alright."

Chapter Fifteen

The Gayest Winter Ever

Believe it or not, I had never attended a gay wedding or any of the festivities surrounding one. Not sure why I hadn't because I certainly had friends who were married, but not as many as I would expect since marriage equality had landed in New York and now, the entire country. For this and so many other reasons, I was excited to attend Anthony and Christopher's engagement party. I was overdue for something upbeat, I love a great party and, it was Lauren's first major event as a professional event planner. The party was at Pier 70 at Chelsea Piers on the Hudson River. I was sure the view of the river would be amazing, but I remained skeptical about the theme they'd selected — a winter wonderland — in September. The trail along the west side highway was bustling with Saturday bike riders, runners, and roller-bladers. It was a perfect afternoon for a day out, and had I not been so filled with anticipation, I would have begrudged having to dress up.

As I pulled up to Chelsea Piers in a black town car, I noticed the oversized Haddad's trailers, which let me know they were also filming something in the giant, multi-use complex. The *Law & Order* series filmed here so often that they'd named one of the entrances *Law & Order Way*. A tingle went through me as it always did when I saw people on a production set. A tingle followed by a longing. As much as I love a great party, I love being on set even more. I love creating new art. So I pressed my face against the window, trying to identify the name of the production on one of the trailers. There were at least ten lined up so it was a pretty substantial project. A sure budget identifier is the size and number of trailers and crew. It had been a very long time since I had been a part of a production, and seeing this one made me sad for a split second. I was using the full extent of my networks to get back in the game. It dawned on me that I had been so busy looking for work and a job that aside from the article for Vikki's magazine, I hadn't actually created anything new in a very long time.

We pulled into the circular driveway that was flanked by a cruise ship on one side and a collection of smaller yacht-sized boats on the other. I spotted Vikki waiting on the other side of the glass door. She was on the phone and didn't notice me among the other arriving guests also donned in all-white attire as the invitation had specifically requested. Though the all white party had been done to death, I was encouraged by what I knew Lauren was capable of creating, particularly with the spare-no-expense budget Anthony had thrown at her.

"You look wonderful!" Vikki did in her white, knee-length knit dress that was held up by two delicate silk straps revealing the fullness of her breasts in the most appropriately sexy way.

"Sweetie, did you expect anything less? Plus, it feels like ages since we've seen each other. I had to do it up. I know Christopher is at NBC. But why don't I know this Anthony? You should have seen the parade of people coming in here. I could easily have done something in the magazine for this on the guest list alone."

"Anthony don't play. He's like a younger David Geffen. Most people didn't even realize he was gay until the engagement announcement in the Times."

"What does he do?"

"He's produced everyone from Mary J. Blige to Bono. But on the low. Not really a flashy type. You wouldn't know him unless you were in music. Now he's formed a production company and management firm."

"We need to get you one of those."

"I know, right." As we passed down the hall, I began to see exactly what Vikki was talking about. The room was full of New York's well-to-do. I'd met Anthony some years back when I produced and directed a commercial for a juice company he owns. We'd instantly hit it off because we were perfectionists when it came down to work but knew how to have fun, too. He was definitely a stickler for detail. Totally no nonsense, but always with a smile. I was 100 percent excited about Lauren's first professional event. I knew she was going to soar, and when we reached the main hall, I was in awe.

Winter wonderland indeed! Vikki and I stopped in our tracks to consume every extravagant detail that had gone into transforming this blank canvas. An abundance of waiters and waitresses greeted us with well-bought smiles and our choice of frothy beverages — some kind of liquid ice or other trick. Other picture-perfect statues doubling as living decoration slid down a gigantic slide, and there was a small house made entirely of ice. A light dusting of snow floated around. An elf frolicked about in a miniature sleigh, and Mrs. Claus was serving chilled shots. An endless amount of food arrived perfectly synchronized as we stepped further inside. It was so over the top amazing that had Lauren described it to me beforehand, I would have cringed in the mistaken fear it would be gaudy. But no. Lauren had skated right to the edge, and it was exactly on pitch. Now we just had to find Ms. Perfection Planner so we could bestow our bravas.

"This is something else," I said to Vikki.

"Sweetie, this is otherworldly. I was worried about the theme, but Lauren did her thing."

"I still don't know why you haven't asked her to do your wedding."

"Because there is no wedding." Just as Vikki's words dropped, Lauren whisked up behind us.

"No wedding?" I asked.

"We'll talk about it later."

"What are you two talking about? Whose wedding?" asked Lauren.

"I was just saying that I can't wait to see what you're going to do for this wedding, sweetie. This is spectacular," said Vikki, deflecting the question.

"Oh, you think so? I was afraid it was too much. But it's what they wanted," said Lauren, taking in her work.

"No, it's right on the line, and it really is fabulous. I know Anthony and Christopher must be super excited," I said.

"They have been such a joy to work with. It's been more fun than anything."

"Because you're a natural." And just as I had told her in the Hamptons, I meant it. I had no doubt that Lauren would do an amazing job, and I was excited that she seemed happy with her work. Even if I never imagined saying *Lauren* and *work* in the same sentence, I was definitely digging this transition. It suited her well.

"I really don't know why I didn't do this before now." Lauren continued to assess the room as a slow smile of satisfaction came over her face. Accomplishment is a specific kind of joy drug that driven people feed off to keep going even when that drive has lain dormant for a while. Lauren had proven she was up to the challenge of redirecting her life. It was inspiring to see her make it work at such a high level.

"I have to run. We're presenting the fabulous couple in a few."

"Are Santa and Rudolph going to bring them in?" Vikki chuckled.

"Not quite. But not that far off." Lauren smiled. "I'll see you in a minute. Enjoy!" Confident and with her head up and shoulders back, she sashayed away as an assistant quickly stepped up out of nowhere in close tow. This day was under her control.

I waited until she was fully out of earshot before getting back to Vikki's earlier statement. I hope she didn't think I forgot. "What's this about no wedding?"

"I don't trust him. And I refuse to go through that again."

"What happened?"

"The same shit that always happens. When they think they've got you, all this secretive shit starts happening. Doors close on conversations. You walk in the room, and the computer screen is minimized." Someone on the mic said something about finding our seats. We made our way to our assigned table.

"So you think he's cheating on you?"

"I know the signs. Been there. Not going back."

"Couldn't you be misreading? Have you talked to him about it?"

"I'm meeting him for dinner and calling it off."

"Listen to him first, Viks. You might be..."

"Sweetie, I know you mean well, but I know what I'm talking about. Same script, different cast." The bubble created by Lauren's accomplishment deflated at yet another failed attempt at love by my sister-friend. Here I was, surrounded by the lavishness of love and commitment, all the while sitting next to crushed hopes. Vikki was being tough as nails, but I knew it was an act. She was pulled together with tight string in fear of what might be let go if she allowed herself to go there. A learned numbness she'd long acquired as armor for these moments.

Then the voice of Queen Bey started pulsating through the sound system. Two expertly constructed male dancers took the stage in the center of the room and commenced an electrically charged pas de deux to Beyoncé's song, "1+1." The skimpy white dance shorts popped from their muscular frames as they went from various stages of entanglement and futile attempts to disentangle, all the while remaining intertwined. It was a flawless execution of eloquent choreography about the commitment of marriage. I was proud to be sitting in this space celebrating Anthony and Christopher whom I knew deeply loved each other and wanted to be committed to one another. Because of the progress of the current times, they could be. Proud of them for the patience, understanding, and compromise I imagined it took for them to get to this moment. Proud of our society for, no matter what setbacks came, most of us were moving in the right direction. Proud of my sister-friend, Lauren, who found herself having to step out of her zone of comfort and do what had to be done. And proud of Vikki who, despite having repeatedly been dealt a tough set of cards, never completely lost hope.

As Mrs. Carter reached the highest altitudes of her ballad, the couple arrived, hand in hand, on the stage. A simple entrance that was the antithesis of the scene, but one that amplified the point — they were two people in love standing in a room full of their family and friends to declare it.

Then Anthony took the microphone and looked at Christopher. "Chris and I thank you all for coming to our engagement party. We know what you all are thinking. If this is the engagement party, what are these bitches going to do for the actual wedding? Well, stay tuned 'cause it's going to be epic." The crowd rolled with laughter because the thought had definitely crossed our collective mind. Anthony continued, "But it's not because we want to be the talk of the town."

"We're already that," joked Christopher, faintly off-microphone.

"It's because my love for this man is so big that our celebration had to try to equal it. I truly found my soul mate and best friend. And I am truly happy to share this moment with each of you. You were handpicked because you've loved us along the way. Now I'm going to hand this over to my soon-to-be husband and baby daddy." He paused. "Wow, I really like the sound of that." He passed Christopher the microphone.

"As you all know, Ant is the speaker in the family. I just wanted to say thank you as well for joining us. I also want to thank our event planner, who is beyond spectacular. Thank you, Lauren. We know dealing with two neurotic and persnickety queens ain't easy, but you do it with grace. Thanks to our family for supporting and loving us. Thank you! Now, let's get drunk! Cheers!" Anthony passed Christopher a glass, which they raised to the crowd, and we all toasted them on in celebration.

And, as they declared in their words, looks and toast-inspired kisses, I was renewed. It was a night about love. Plain and simple. I thought about being single in a way that gave me hope for the first time in years. Everybody wants somebody, and although I had denied it, I certainly did, too.

I took a peek at Vikki, who too had softened among all the warm and gushy. My hope was that she would not go straight into neck-rolling, finger-popping assumptions when she confronted Dax on her suspicions. Then I thought of one of my favorite quotes about love: 'We come to love not by finding the perfect person but by learning to see an imperfect person perfectly.' I owned that I might have poisoned Vikki's spirit with my earlier sentiments about Dax. I regretted doing that to them. Everybody is carrying around baggage. And it's especially hard to lose when the people that want the best for you carry those same suitcases.

After the ceremony, Lauren came and found us with a jubilant smile.

"You would not believe who I just met!"

"Try us," I said, surveying the room of power again.

"A publisher from PS Books!"

"They publish all our coffee table editions," added Vikki.

"Well, you know how these things go. And it's probably on name alone. But...." Lauren took a pregnant pause.

"Girl, spill it."

"Welll, their CEO has been to a couple of my Hamptons parties, and now they want to talk about me doing an event planning book!" Lauren started jumping and squealing until she realized she was in a room rafter-packed with elite guests. She continued in a close whisper, "If that weren't enough, Christopher wants to build a show around me. He's going to have me on the *This Day* show to give me a screen test of sorts. Can you believe that?"

I could. It's how things happened. Lauren had long been preparing for this moment, and now life had pushed her onto a collision course with opportunity. I was beyond smiles from the inside out. I was beyond the pom-poms and high kicks. I was so ecstatic for her that it propelled me into action. I used her charge of inspiration to power my own getting back to it. I wanted to be beyond smiles from the inside out for me. It was time to get back to creating my own future and not waiting around for a job handout. It was time to stop contemplating what my next move would be. It was time to propel myself toward that next opportunity.

◆ ◆ ◆

When inspiration rings, your spirit and you have the choice to answer the call or not. Most artists have learned that having too much control is a detriment to the art coming down like it's supposed to. When inspiration hits, you pull out a piece of paper, your phone...a napkin. Anything that will protect the thought from escaping you like an elusive butterfly. The entire taxi ride home I scribbled nearly illegible thoughts about a new script I was going to write. How had I missed it? The life I was living at this moment was breathing art. It was the opportunity, and living it had prepared me to create it. The taxi driver must have thought I was drunk as I ferociously scribbled on the stack of napkins I had grabbed when I abruptly cut the evening short. I made sure to say goodbye to the handsome couple and my event planner extraordinaire sister-friend. I also practically threw Vikki into a taxi without much reverence to what she was about to unleash on Dax. I felt only a stitch of guilt because the thing that pulsed through my veins made me not give a damn. I was being unapologetically selfish, and I had to get out everything that had boiled up in me like a good New Orleans gumbo. All of the ingredients contributed to this need, a deep need to retreat to my very own form of therapy. Until the wee hours of the next morning that's exactly what I did.

At some point around three a.m. I realized I had not taken a breath or break for over five hours. The ideas and words were gushing out like a popped fire hydrant in the hood during hundred-degree temperatures. There were many moments where I felt a simple inhale or even a sip of water might have been required. Those sensations were ignored because what was pouring out of me had not been uncorked in so very long, and I delighted in all of it. I couldn't tell if anything I was transferring from my collection of napkins and now banging out on my laptop was good or not. I didn't care because at least it was coming. Tomorrow or the next day would tell that story. For now, it was all about what I had to get out of my spirit. The thing I had to share with the white paper. The thing that even if no one ever read that now black and white paper, was on its way to making me feel connected to me again. That in of itself was good. Maybe not the art, but the feeling of creating it made the rush of blood noticeable. Palpable. I could see the life pulsing through my veins again. And it too was good.

Chapter Sixteen

Movin' Out

The pungent smell of curry and cumin floated out of the plastic bags I carried up to Krissy's apartment. It wasn't until I met the anxious delivery guy in the lobby and he'd handed me the bags that it dawned on me that the entire day had passed and all I had eaten was the white parts of two hard-boiled eggs, two strips of uncured turkey bacon, and a protein shake. That would have been a great start to a day of dieting, but I wasn't on a diet. I was just consumed. For the past three weeks, it had been me and my script. When I got up, I wrote. Until I passed out (usually on top of the laptop), I wrote. The computer accompanied me on trips to the bathroom. Even when I'd decided to get some fresh air by actually going to a nearby restaurant, I barely put my MacBook on sleep and was bothered by the disturbance and necessity of actually ordering food. Krissy's call to come over for dinner was my first and welcome legitimate break. With a garbage full of empty cartons, crumpled foil, and old pizza boxes, Krissy's promise of a home-cooked meal was a significant draw.

"What's this?" I asked with thinly veiled disappointment as I raised the bag to Krissy when she opened the door.

"What do you mean? Tandoori Kitchen. You love that place."

"Do you know how many times I've had Tandoori Kitchen in the last three weeks?"

"That's my fault because...? And hi to you, too."

"My bad. Hi. I was just looking forward to a home-cooked meal."

"I'm sorry, boo. The only thing I could make today was a phone call. Hell, I didn't even do that. I used Seamless." Well, another night of chicken masala and palak paneer wasn't going to kill me, and I'd needed to get out of the house anyway. Just as I was trying to check my sulky attitude and coat at the door, I noticed the living room full of brown cardboard, Styrofoam, grayish wrapping paper, and rolls of those now-annoying air-filled bubbles that I loved popping as a kid. As an adult, it all signified only one thing — moving. Singularly, I despised no activity more. Moving was my own bona fide Guantanamo, part of the reason why I had been in the same apartment for over a decade. My friends knew the rule: You don't ask me to help you move, and I won't ask you. I glanced at the kitchen and saw pots on the stove ready for boxes. This was a damn setup!

"What's this?" I asked.

"Don't play dumb, boo. You know I'm moving."

"Don't you play dumb, boo. You know I don't do that."

"Ain't nobody asked you to do anything. So calm your ass down. I just wanted some company."

"Where's Justin?"

"Chile, who knows? Somewhere doing some business stuff as usual."

"You can't be mad at that."

"It's 9 p.m. on a Friday night. If I'm not working, then he sure as hell could be here to help."

"I feel you, but cut him some slack. This is your apartment, not his." Thankfully, all that was thrown my way was a long and heartfelt roll of the eyes. I went to the kitchen for some plates, all the while relieved she didn't expect me to actually do anything but talk. After three weeks of no real human interaction except for various waiters, order takers, and delivery folks, it could do me some good, too. It would also be great to share the concept for the script I was writing with Krissy, who always gave good, honest feedback.

Yelling from the kitchen, "You have movers, don't you?"

"We are not in the hood, we don't have to yell through the damn house." Krissy came up behind me, taking over plate and utensil retrieval duty. "Yes, I have movers, but some of my stuff has to go to storage since we bought new furniture. There's also his stuff. It all won't fit. I have to decide what goes to the new place and what goes to storage. Plus, I don't trust motherfuckers with all my shit. You know, a bitch doesn't buy cheap."

"Are you excited?"

"I hate moving."

"Not about that. About moving in with Justin."

"I hate moving." The look on Krissy's face indicated that this was more than just about moving. As she plated our meal, I made us two cocktails at the bar. Not a lot of packing was going to be done this day, but undoubtedly there'd be some unpacking of the emotional kind. I was prepared to handle yet another case of the chilly feet from one of my sister-friends.

"Wassup?" I asked as we sat down on the pillows around her coffee table. Very fitting for the cuisine we were about to enjoy and the mood that I'd encountered. Let the session begin.

"You know I been feeling some kind a way for a minute. There are little things here and there."

"Like what?"

"Inconsistencies in stuff he says. The fact that all of his money is tied up in his business. I mean, he paid for half of the cost to move in, but other stuff has been all me."

"Well, he is doing a startup. It takes a lot of capital."

"I get it, which is why I'm not completely trippin'. It's so damn fast, too. I can't shake that."

"Girl, you're just getting cold feet. I agree it has happened quickly, but I have seen people get married faster than this. It be's like that some times."

"I just don't want to fuck up."

"You're one of the smartest people I know, you'll know what to do. I think it's a case of the wedding jitters minus the wedding."

"But, a lease is business. You know I don't play with my coins, chile. It took me too much to get them."

"Case in point! Let me tell you what just happened with Vikki. She was all ready to break it off with Dax because she thought he was cheating on her. She called off the wedding and everything."

"What? I didn't know that."

"'Cause it didn't last long. Turns out all of his secretiveness was because he was planning a surprise engagement party for her and all of the friends that can't make Jamaica. She'd misread things as signs that he was cheating."

"I know she felt bad."

"As hell. She's all excited again. She won't stop talking about this damn dress. By the way, did you get your tickets to Jamaica yet?"

"Not yet. I'll have my assistant book something. Can you send me your flight info so we can be on the same flight?"

"Sure. Back to my point. You're acting just like Vikki was. Much ado about nothing syndrome."

"Yeah, you're probably right about the jitters. This shit is brand-new. There's no manual for moving in with your boyfriend. At this age."

"Change ain't easy."

"Shaking my lawyer brain is hard, too, but I need to learn how to separate my work mind from personal. Everybody's not a criminal."

"Exactly. Lighten up a bit. Live in the moment and enjoy yourself. 'Cause if you do end up married, there'll be plenty of time for stress."

"We ain't getting married no time soon. That's for damn sure." Krissy finished plating the food passing me a fork and napkin. "What about you?"

"Me?"

"Yeah, I'm thirty-three, you're not. When are you going to find you a new boo?"

"Geesh, not you, too. I have too much going on right now to even be thinking about finding a boo. Plus, it's not the same."

"Why not?"

"Because I don't have a clock that's ticking, remember. As far as I know my biology will be functioning for a very long time. Even if I need to take a little blue pill."

"Aight, I give you that. But you don't want to be some old-ass man alone with cats."

"Your metaphors are off. I'm definitely not in contention to be an old maid."

"Whatever. Old maid, old man. Who wants to be alone for the rest of their life?"

"I never said that. Actually, I've been thinking about dating and love and all that shit more lately than I have in a very long time. First things first. I gotta get this career back on track."

"Chile, I know you can multitask."

"I know you're not talking, Ms. Super Lawyer. We both know what you focus on expands, and I need for my bank account to expand before I start jumping back into dating. It takes so much, especially here."

"You ain't never lied. So, you're waiting until L.A. to find you a new cutie, huh?"

"You're out of control. No, I am not waiting to find a new cutie any- where. I'm focused on work. The good news is that my creative juices are flowing again."

"Oh, right. Now, what's this script that has you all excited?"

I had skillfully changed the subject. "I don't know Kris, it started flow- ing out all of sudden. I was at the engagement party that Lauren planned for my friends, feeling sorry for myself because everyone seems to be getting married, moving in, successful careers, and I feel like I'm stalled. Then it clicked while I was there and in the taxi home. Why not write a movie about what I know best?"

"What?"

"Y'all crazy asses."

"Please don't make me call my lawyer. Wait, I am the lawyer. Please don't make me sue you. Friends or not: don't be puttin' my business in the damn street."

"Hush, it's not exactly about y'all. It's inspired by you. Us. Our rela- tionships. It's completely fictionalized though. A roman à clef. But I don't know why it's taken so long to write a movie about women."

"Your first chick flick. Seems spot-on because you do have a lot of girlfriends."

"And y'all do have a lot of problems." Another roll of the eyes, but this time playful and loving. One of my favorite composition professors at Northwestern said that the best thing you can share with the world is that with which you are intimate and passionate about. My relationships with my sister-friends certainly fit the bill and what was coming out on the page were some of the best words I had ever written. Each woman in the movie was an amalgam of the women I had encountered, infused with a major injection of my imagination. While I was writing, smoke erupted from my fingertips because I was typing so fast and hard. I felt for the first time the madness and virtuoso of a sex-addicted, juvenile Mozart or a manic, earless Beethoven. I had no intentions of losing my mind, though. I was quite happy, hopefully walking up to the ledge of genius while maintaining a firm footing on the ground of sanity. But again, how anyone else perceived the work was of the least consequence to me, which was far different than the scripts and shows I had written before. It was the mere exercise of writing and the love for it that had returned after so many dormant years.

"Well, what's the premise?"

"One of the women dies at the beginning, bringing the other ladies together to help her husband and kids deal with her death. It causes all of the women to examine their own lives and the choices they've made. A lot of juicy shit."

"Sounds like it. A lot of sex, too?"

"But of course. It sells."

"Nice. Are we talking *Madame Bovary* or *50 Shades*?"

"Haven't read *50 Shades*, but I would imagine somewhere in-between. It's definitely an R-rated movie."

"Wait, have any of your films been R?"

"Nope, which is why this is so exciting to me. I get to unleash a side I didn't know was there."

"Chile, you knew it was there, you closet freak." I couldn't argue. In my twenties, I was as far from prudish as you could get. My mid-thirties brought about a fear of everything that, upon reflection, had made me a bit boring. I was afraid of sex. I was afraid of a relationship. I was afraid of intimacy. Fear is a powerful force. I knew better. I'd read Marianne

Williamson and all the other self-help gurus, and still I had fallen victim to a deep, repressive fear of the very thing I spoke about the most — love. The script was tapping into something (as art creation often does) that had lain asleep for years. I was feeling the pulse of my existence and purpose again, and it felt awesome.

"Excited for you. I love what you write. Can I read it?"

"Sure, when I get through a couple more drafts."

"I can't wait! Now, let's finish eating so I can get back to packing and you can get back to this Oscar-winning screenplay."

"For now, I'll take box office-winning."

"Fuck it, do both!" We high-fived. "Actually, do all three — movie, money, and a man."

"Girl, hush!"

Chapter Seventeen

All For You

When Vikki walked into the Amsale showroom, it was clear that this was a woman in love. She glided effortlessly across the floor as if the tiles were as soft as clouds. Even among all of the beautiful dresses — the billows of tulle, silk, and satin — her joy reigned sublime.

"I'm so sorry I'm late," Vikki said, pulling off her silver aviators.

"No worries. They have Champagne," I said, giving her a hug. I was excited, too; her energy was contagious. It was such a contrast from the last time I'd seen her one-on-one with all her suspicions about Dax. Even though the surprise had been foiled, the engagement party was exceptional by all accounts. I had missed it because I was in L.A. again discussing my new script and beginning the apartment hunting process. We walked together to the receptionist who had been waiting to take us back to the fitting room. The showroom was impeccable and perched atop my favorite New York Street, Madison Avenue. I snuck a peek out of the window and saw New Yorkers busying in the perfection of a summery fall day in the Big Apple.

As the receptionist closed the door to the softly appointed dressing room filled with mirrors and a small square stage in the center, I turned to my friend and gave her another tight-gripped hug. Clearly, I was infected and happy to share in the joy. She deserved it. Had earned it.

"You're more excited than I am," she joked.

"How could I not be excited? You're getting married!"

"This isn't the first time," she replied with her trademark cynical wit. "Someone's made a one-eighty. "

"I admit definitely a change of heart. But when I dropped my own stuff and just looked at it, this time feels like a right thing for you." True, I'd seen her walk down the aisle before, but neither of those moments felt like this. And although I didn't express it at that time, I knew her second marriage was doomed from the start. Mistakenly, I thought I was doing a good thing by keeping my feelings to myself. I believed my job was just to be there when and if the pieces needed to be picked up and not to butt into her business uninvited.

For the years following her divorce from Paul, that's exactly what I'd been helping Vikki do — pick up the pieces. Standing there amongst all this beauty was my friend-reward for the 3 a.m. therapy sessions over pancakes and pastrami sandwiches. I don't know how she or my waistline survived it all. But they did! And here we were for her final fitting of the "perfect white dress" she'd been raving about since she called the wedding back on. No one had seen it except Vikki and the pitch-perfectly trained saleswomen at Amsale. She was right, I was very excited – for the wedding and to see the dress. Now I was certainly sure that Dax truly did love her with all of the back-and-forth she'd put him through.

"Can you believe this is the first time I've ever been to a bridal store," I asked as I realized, at that moment, another truth.

"I knew you weren't really gay. First gay wedding. First bridal store. What gives? I'll be happy when you come out of the closet as a straight guy," she joked.

"I can't even argue. What kind of self-respecting gay man am I? No gay weddings and no trips to a wedding boutique. That's all changed now, and my gay card is safe."

Vikki laughed and grabbed a glass of Champagne from the receptionist who had returned with a tray of bite-sized cookies, a triangle of Brie, water crackers, and some grapes. We toasted through our laughter, and then I plopped on the sofa to catch another peek of my favorite street in my favorite city.

As I looked down, I couldn't help wonder if all of those ant-sized humans were in love, had experienced the love I witnessed in my friend, or would ever. I said a prayer wishing everyone the joy that Vikki had the privilege to know and wished it for myself, too.

Just in the nick of time, the just-enough tanned sales associate entered the room and saved me from my sappy, sentimental conundrum. The saleswoman, Jackie, was a sophisticated bubbly. Calmer than the valley, but more energy than our East Side location would usually suggest. I immediately liked her. I could tell Vikki did too because they embraced when she came into the room.

"Jackie, I'm nervous!"

"All brides are nervous, but you're marrying a wonderful man. At least from the stories you've told me," Jackie comforted.

"I can assure you, he's wonderful! I was skeptical at first, but I'm sold and a believer. Hallelu!" I stood up to shake Jackie's hand and perform the double-cheek air kiss required in these settings.

Vikki corrected us. "No, I'm not nervous about the wedding. I'm nervous about fitting the dress!"

"Girl, you're snatched. What are you worried about?" I asked, throwing back the last gulp of Champagne. 'Ahh, Domaine Ott Rosé,' I thought. Another favorite. Refill.

"That's the point. I think I got carried away and lost too much damn weight!"

"Oh, what a burden!"

"Shut it. It *is* a burden. I can't have the dress refitted again. And as much as this dress costs, it had better fit like skin. Shit, as much as this dress costs, it should *be* skin."

"Well, eat a donut or something. I don't know why you had to lose weight in the first place. You looked great before."

"Because I refuse to wear a couture gown as a size ten. You're gonna see all of these curves when I walk down the aisle."

"Don't worry, Vikki, even if we need one more alteration, we'll make it happen. You've been a great customer, and we want your day to be flawless," said Jackie. The fact that Vikki was the publisher and editor of a major fashion magazine was probably not lost on her, either.

"Before I show you, I know it's white and this is the third time. But it feels like a fresh start," said Vikki, standing in front of a mirror.

"Girl, you wore white your first time, and you weren't a virgin. That's for damn sure. Who cares? Your wedding. Your rules. Now, let me see the damn dress," I demanded.

Then Jackie slid one of the mirrors to the side to reveal a hidden closet. Hanging on an expensive looking white silk, padded hanger was the most gorgeous wedding dress I'd ever seen. A strapless form-fitting dress that moved from a tight bodice into a structured bottom that opened up like a trumpet. Flowers constructed of the same white faille caressed the left hip and lower waistline. It was divinity on a hanger. All of Amsale's dresses have names. Hers was Taryn.

I gasped. Vikki turned to me, smiled, and said, "Yeah, me too!" In a flash, she disrobed to her notably sexy undies and almost lunged for the dress. Without pause, Jackie jumped in to help Vikki into the dress. As she stepped into the folds of fabric, I heard a slight giggle. The giggle you do when you're over-the-top happy and can't believe something is happening to you. It's a good-feeling giggle whether you're feeling it or just seeing your friend feel it.

When she stepped up to the small, grey stage in the center of the room and stood fully in the mirror, I gasped again.

"Yeah, me too," she whispered in wonderment, lightly brushing her hands down the form of the angelic dress. She looked completely amazing. The glow she had walked in with was at full blast, and she turned around to face me. And then, it happened.

Two tears dripped down my cheeks, almost hitting the Champagne. I couldn't believe I was being such a weakling. Man up! I couldn't be crying all over the place at the wedding. I had done that at Lauren's wedding. During the couple's first dance. Standing on the dance floor. Drunk. Certainly, my reputation couldn't survive another incident like that, so I had to get it together right then and there.

But, it was useless. Vikki, the showroom, the rosé — it all proved to be too powerful an intersection of those things that make you feel love.

Remember love. Hope for love. And celebrate love. I was certainly reassuring Vikki I was gay now. And I mean the original definition — happy!

"Do you like it?"

"Like it? Girl, you look like a picture from your magazine! Dax is going to bust his shit when he sees you in that dress. And the kids are going to go IN hunty," I exclaimed, digging deep to channel my inner queen. I jumped up and began to walk around her slowly to take in the full moment and because I was a bit tipsy after finishing my second glass of the Ott.

"It's just enough. Actually, it's my favorite dress this season," added Jackie. I shot her a look. "I promise, it's not because I'm paid to say that. I love this dress. And Vikki, you're the prettiest bride I've seen in it. Hands down," said Jackie as she made some adjustments around the bodice of the dress. "How does it feel?"

Vikki turned back to face herself in the mirror and said, "Like triumph!"

Then, her phone began to sing, "I.N.D.E.P.E.N.D.E.N.T — do you know what I mean." As sophisticated as Vikki could be, she was still hood from time to time and a little out of date with that ringtone, even though it fit her perfectly.

She slowly stepped down from the stage and reached for her purse. As she peered at the screen, the energy in the room shifted. Don't nobody bring me no bad news! Favorite street, favorite city, Domaines-Ott, sublime sister-friend, and now...Taryn. This was a moment I wanted to last, damn it. From the look on Vikki's face, I knew it had quickly become a memory, at least for now.

"What happened?" I cautiously questioned. I really didn't want to know. I wanted to go back to all of those happy things. I was hoping it was something like her brother forgot to get fitted for his tux or the confectioner ran out of strawberry frosting. Something that was fixable. Something that didn't interrupt our moment for too long. By then, I had claimed the moment as mine, too.

To my surprise and relief, Vikki shook off whatever it was and sent the call to voicemail. I think she was determined not to let anything ruin this moment either. She stepped back up on the platform for one last look at the dress. That smile returned. And the energy that had filled the room before quickly did, too. I breathed another sigh of relief knowing I'd get the scoop since we were lunching at Fred's. But for now, our moment was preserved. Refill.

◆ ◆ ◆

As we walked into Fred's at Barneys, Vikki and I both were obliged to do a round of hellos. Fred's is one of those places. Filled to the brim with rich, Upper East Side overdressed and over done socialites spending their husbands' (or ex-husbands') money. The ladies who lunch.

Even with its pretense, Vikki and I both loved the restaurant for its food and its view of my favorite street in my favorite city. It was a "treat lunch" for me, though, because the prices verged on ridiculous. So unless you had an expense account, trust fund, or your man's black card, this was a lunch saved for the most special occasions. And this occasion was most certainly special.

As we sat at our table looking over the menu, I couldn't help but think of the phone call Vikki had received during the fitting. Although I was apprehensive of spoiling the Amsale moment, I was now dying to know. I wasn't, however, going to pry. I knew she would tell me if and when she was ready.

A tall, handsome waiter with flawless caramel skin and pearly teeth approached the table to take our order. The way he greeted us and refreshed our water was in harmony with the atmosphere of the day. The service at Fred's was almost as good as the view and the gossip you could hear buzzing around the room.

The waiter smiled at Vikki, "What will the lady be having?"

"Two Grey Goose gimlets. Stat! And I'll start with the lobster bisque and then, uhhhh...I really want the lobster salad, too. But that's too much lobster, right," Vikki asked hoping for approval.

"You can never have too much lobster. Plus, the lobster in the salad today is deliciously fresh," said the also perfectly trained waiter. "And for you, sir?"

"I'll have the lobster bisque as well and the club salad."

"Excellent! I'll be back with your two Goose gimlets momentarily. Please let me know if there is anything else you need."

As the waiter whisked away, Vikki looked around the room at the other ladies lunching. "I'm so glad this isn't me anymore. Most of these women are miserable. They hate their husbands. They hate each other. And money is all they have."

"It's easy to get caught up in this scene when you first arrive on the island. It's nice to come play, but you gotta take it for what it's worth, which isn't much," I replied as our overflowing gimlet martinis arrived with an unusual quickness. The waiter placed them on the table and then breezily disappeared without comment because I'm sure he could tell we were in the middle of a conversation.

"It was Paul," Vikki said as a matter of fact.

I was confused and quizzed her with a, "Huh?"

"It was Paul calling when we were at Amsale. I sent it to voicemail and listened to it in the bathroom," Vikki said with a slight sadness. "He wished me congratulations on the wedding and asked if we could meet for lunch. He said that he'd been through a lot over the past year and realized how awful he was to me. Wants to apologize in person."

"Are you going to see him?"

"Hell, no! After what that man put me through, it'll be too soon if I ever see him again. Chapter closed. He can kiss my ass," Vikki spewed this with the venom that I knew she felt in her heart toward husband number two. She took a sip of her gimlet and threw her hair back. It was very dramatic and *Dynasty*-like, and I appreciated the theatrics. But I also knew from where it came — a deep, deep place of hurt.

"Maybe he has changed. I think about how much I've changed since my last relationship. And there are plenty of things I look back on that I'm now sorry for."

"That asshole has not changed. He's still a grown-ass spoiled rich kid who thinks the world revolves around him and his penis. I have zero desire to grant him absolution for all that shit he did just because he's feeling some kind of epiphanic moment all of a sudden. And how ironic is the timing? I haven't spoken to Paul directly in over two years, and he calls me a couple of months before I'm getting married to 'talk'? Please! He's up to something, and I don't want that energy anywhere near me or this wedding. We've had enough issues."

Vikki had every right to feel like this about Paul. Paul came from a family of old school money and had the stereotypical rich, arrogant jerk thing down to a science. It didn't hurt that he was also model-gorgeous with the body of a young Tom Cruise. Actually, he looked like Tom Cruise and Keanu Reeves's love child, if you can imagine. Plenty of women did more than imagine during Vikki's marriage.

"Maybe meeting with him before the wedding is exactly what you need."

"What does one have to do with the other?" she retorted.

"You need to forgive him before you get married. It's not for him, it's for you. You can't enter this marriage with that negative stuff still occupying space in your spirit.

"Despite all your Deepak Chopra mumbo jumbo, I'm definitely not bringing anything from my marriage with Paul to my relationship with Dax. Two separate things."

And there were two choices here. Keep my thoughts to myself and nod in loving agreement. Or tell her what I really thought like I had on the beach in St. Barth's and run the risk of ruining our lunch. Damn, I was looking forward to that lobster bisque. Oh well! "I disagree. You consistently let your baggage with Paul affect your relationship with Dax," I said bravely and braced myself for her reply.

With the same Dominique Deveraux flair, she exclaimed, "Absolutely not true!"

"Look, Viks. You know I just want the best for you. I know that sometimes my advice comes from my own shit, but I really believe that this is something that would be good for you and Dax. From your reaction to Paul's request, I know you're still harboring some bad blood. And, mumbo jumbo or not, it affects you."

"Name one time that it has!"

"Just last month when you thought he was cheating and he was actually planning the surprise engagement party for you. You had called off the wedding before you even spoke to him about it." I then gave her a look questioning whether I should continue. Because I could. She and I both knew that she'd taken Dax through the back-and-forth ringer because of the insecurities her relationships with Paul and Mark had created.

"Paul sent me on vacation and then locked me out of our home with a note attached to our prenup on the fucking door. Who wouldn't be insecure?"

"I know."

"Then he and his lawyers painted me to be some gold-digging tramp during our divorce. And you expect me to forgive that?" Vikki said with tinges of the hurt and embarrassment she had felt over the last seven years. It had been her undeniable hell.

I knew in that instant that forgiving him was the only option she had. "I know you're not all touchy-feely, but it really is simple physics. Two things can't occupy the same space at the same time. That hate you have for Paul is preventing your heart from being completely filled with love. You don't want that evil energy taking up residence any longer."

"What he did to me was fucked up. I didn't do anything to him but love him and try to be a good wife. The entire time he was screwing around on me. The asshole gave me gonorrhea. You just don't forgive shit like that easily."

"Everyone makes mistakes, gorgeous. Some bigger than others. But we all make them. My mom always says, 'The forgiveness you refuse will be the forgiveness you seek.'"

"I won't be seeking his forgiveness for a damn thing."

"Maybe not from Paul, but from someone."

"I don't know if I can stomach seeing him, let alone making nice."

"You owe it to yourself to at least hear him out and then figure out a way to forgive him."

The lobster bisque arrived like the sound of the bell in a one-sided sparring match. Vikki sat quietly processing it all. At that moment, I felt bad for her; this was supposed to be a time of celebration. She shouldn't have had to deal with Paul today. Nor should we be at odds over something like this. But wasn't that the ironic timing of life? All out of wisdom from my self-help library, I did what I knew best to do next —ordered two more gimlets and two Patron shots. Patron makes everything better.

You're probably right. I have to think about it, though. I don't want to catch a case before my wedding."

The waiter set the drinks in front of us. "Y'all are trying to have a good afternoon," referencing the Patron shots, smiling hard at us both. "I wish I could join you."

I started to say something smart-ass, but Vikki interrupted holding her shot glass, "Cheers to great friends who celebrate us through our triumphs and our trials!" We toasted as the caramel waiter continued to smile.

"Sounds like great friends," he said.

"The best," I proclaimed as we downed our shots and gave the satisfying grimace only a shot of chilled Patron can birth! Afternoon saved by tequila's entrance. Back to glowing and favorite things.

Chapter Eighteen

Castles Into Caverns

Living in New York City can be like taking a great lover for granted. Before you had him, you appreciated everything about him and the passage of time made it easy for you to forget why you fell in love in the first place. New Yorkers take so much of what the city has to offer for granted. The pace and grind of it all can eat you up and leave you too empty to appreciate its magnificence. But there's no place like New York and that's probably a good thing because it takes a very special person to survive here, let alone thrive.

It is why when Lauren suggested we meet for a walk at the Central Park Zoo, I didn't think it odd. I hadn't been to the park since my lunch with Rebecca. Lauren and I, however, often swapped our typical afternoon cocktail rendezvous for something more natural. Walks along the Hudson, a trip on the Staten Island Ferry. It was great balance for me because as much as I love my gimlets, I also love being connected to creation. Lauren was the one who got me to try meditation for the first time, a practice I had previously misunderstood.

Solemnly, Lauren sat on a bench in front of the entrance to the zoo with a pair of glasses almost identical to the ones Rebecca wore that afternoon in the Hamptons. Not a good sign then or now. As I approached, I could tell that she was deep in thought because she didn't notice me and my bright yellow polo shirt, even when I was close enough to touch her. "Hey pretty lady, this bench taken?" I joked, startling her out of her daze. She turned her head slowly. A stark contrast to the woman who was riding high off her accomplishment a little over a month ago.

"Can we walk?" she asked with a determined quietness.

"Sure, honey. Whatever you want to do." And so, we walked. In silence. From 65th up to 110th and back down Central Park West to the Great Lawn. In complete and utter silence. Silence so loud that I didn't hear the constant cries of the city. As we climbed the steep hills of the park, cyclists blew passed us and the trees bristled in the slight wind. And although the grade of the hill was taxing for both of us, we remained silent save the occasional deep breath for more energy. A workout for sure, but not just of the body as I knew whatever she was processing was heavy and inevitably had something to do with Josh. She needed this exercise. And she needed me to be there. Not to say anything, but just to be there. My presence was purely to make sure she didn't completely lose herself in whatever emotions she was feeling. I was reality's anchor.

As we approached the sunbathers, the soccer players, the artists and dreamers sprawled across the Great Lawn, I followed Lauren as she went to the far east side of it before sitting down on the lush green grass. Then she took off her glasses to reveal, to my horror, a severely blackened eye. I couldn't hold my tongue any longer, "What the fuck happened, Lauren? Did that motherfucker hit you?"

"Not quite."

"I will kill him!"

"If he doesn't kill himself first. He didn't hit me. Thankfully, I guess, he's not violent. He showed up at the house wasted out of his mind and was making a mess of the kitchen and himself. When I walked into the kitchen, he looked at me and fell to the floor pulling everything on the counter down with him. I tried to help him up, and I couldn't support us both, so we fell. Hit my eye against the counter. I just left him there. Right there in the middle of the damn floor. Got some ice for my eye. Went back to sleep. He was still there when I got up the next day."

"My God, Lauren! How are the kids?"

"They're fine. I sent them to my mother's for the week. Of course, he promised to go back to rehab, but I can't afford to believe empty promises anymore." She took a deep and long breath. "About a week go, I was driving and the thought crossed my mind to…"

"To what?" I said in a panic

The silence returned.

"For a split second, I just wanted it to be over. To end."

"Lauren, that's not…"

"The answer, I know. But in that moment. It's what I felt." She stopped speaking, but with the intention of continuing. "I've never been more grateful for my children." Uncomfortable pause again. "They saved my life. Because they don't deserve two selfish parents. And so, here I am. The apartment is packed up and I'm leaving. I love him, but I absolutely can't do this anymore. I'm filing for divorce."

"But, that's your apartment. And divorce?"

"I need to start fresh. There's no hope left."

Five months can change many things in a dynamic life. Five months ago, my sister-friend, Lauren sat crying in her closet. Five months ago, my biggest concern was for her sanity. Five months ago, she was married. Five months later, the closet was empty, she had launched a successful career she hadn't even considered, and she seemed clearer than she had been in a long time. Five months later, she was preparing to file for divorce. And with perfect karma, she'd received an unsolicited offer on her apartment that she couldn't refuse.

"Do you mind coming with me as I finish up?"

"Of course."

"You don't have to do anything. Well, maybe a little thing. I know you hate moving."

"None of that matters right now."

"I just don't want to be in that house alone. It's such a cavern empty."

My head hung as we walked toward the exit of the park in silence once again. The ground was not as interesting as the sky, that's for sure, but my head was heavy, reflecting the weight of my heart, causing me to gaze downward at the pavement. In spite of all that had happened, I hadn't lost the hope and belief that Josh would pull it together and return to his former self. Throughout it all, Lauren hadn't either until now. If I was a huge Josh cheerleader, Lauren was the president of his fan club, and so her losing hope was certainly the sign the end had come.

"You know why I love Central Park?"

"I can think of a thousand reasons. It's gorgeous. Nature. But you tell me," I said.

"It's normal." We continued to walk as I tried to understand what she meant. "So much of my life has been comparatively abnormal. I'm aware of that. The kind of life I've lived is only seen by such a rare few. The portion of the one percent that most people don't even know to hate. In their lives we don't even exist, and vice versa. But the park is something we all can relate to. When I was little I would come here with one of the nannies, and I wasn't Lauren from the rich family or any of that. I was just the little girl on the swing next to another kid on a swing, having fun. I was normal like I've always wanted to be."

As we continued to walk, I chose not to respond, but to process. We are all searching for something outside of ourselves, no matter who we are or what we have. The little girl with her grandmother from north of the park in Harlem swinging next to Lauren, wanting to be something else, too. I couldn't remember when that thought of being something else entered my own mind. Certainly, I knew from my observations of very young children that it wasn't present in them. Was it the time when we learned of princes and princesses in castles in faraway places living lives far different than our own that we developed this yearning? I wasn't sure. I was clear that it was universal, and it universally created turmoil across the board.

When we arrived at Lauren's apartment, I was shocked to see it so bare. She'd mentioned that she had moved rather quickly, but I was not expecting it to be the cavern she'd described. In just five days, the movers had cleared out all three levels of Lauren and Josh's triplex home. Ironically, all that was left was some artwork that was to be auctioned at Sotheby's and Lauren's favorite family portrait that she wanted to take with her and not have packed away. As I walked around the shell of their once warm and beautiful home, a sadness overcame my spirit as I remembered the life I'd shared with them over so many years a life that was chronicled in the sole family portrait that clung desperately to the wall.

Lauren came down the spiral stairs into the living room, now resolved and seemingly unaffected by the task at hand. Determined instead to get it done and move on to the next chapter. It was I who was drenched in sentimentality. Probably the many years of holding on and trying to make it work had taken its final toll, and she couldn't afford to get lost in what wasn't any longer. I understood, and I didn't want to upset her, but the feeling was overwhelming. What I had anticipated to be a day in the park with a friend on the rise turned into a moving day, and well, I hate those.

"I remember when Demarchelier took this picture of you all, Jordan wouldn't sit still for more than two shots at a time," I said as I looked at the family portrait taken by the famed photographer.

"What I remember most is how serious you took it, as if it were a shoot for *Vogue*. You suggested I hire a stylist, makeup artist, and set designer," she laughed, recalling my obsessive perfectionism over any project.

"You were shooting with one of the best photographers in the world. You very well could've taken my suggestions," I retorted, continuing the banter. Yet, in true Lauren form, she'd opted to do the photo shoot au natural — no makeup, her own clothes, the entire family barefoot in, of course, the park. She was right; the photo was exquisite. It captured exactly who they were in that moment. A naturally happy family. The feeling of sadness began to creep back inside my spirit.

Looking at that family on the wall that would be no more, the hope of enduring love was difficult to believe in. True, Lauren and Josh would always be connected because of the children, but they'd no longer be "Lauren and Josh." And I adored Lauren and Josh — everyone did. In retrospect, I guess they hadn't been "Lauren and Josh" for quite some time because the Josh we once knew wasn't there anymore, and that was the point of why we were here.

Lauren moved about the multiple rooms as I continued to stare at the picture. I started to feel guilty. I needed to be there for her rather than wallowing in my own sadness. So I snapped myself out of it just as Lauren came up and hugged me fiercely from behind. Certainly, it shouldn't be the other way around. As I began to snap out of it, she came and hugged me from behind.

"It's going to be fine. This is what's best, and I'm OK with it," she said, embarrassing me with her intuitiveness.

"You do seem to be remarkably Zen about it all."

"I've spent too many moments lamenting on what was and what could've been. It is what it is. No, I don't like it in the least. Yes, I prayed for different. But, like you say, I have to live in the now, and this is my reality. If he's selfish enough to refuse to get help and really try to get better, then I have to be selfish enough to save myself and my children."

"I'm sorry. I feel silly getting caught up when you're so sensible about it. I'm gonna shake it off."

"Have your moment. I caught you off guard. Just don't start crying. This house has seen way too many tears." She took the picture down and began walking toward the door. "Now help me bring down these boxes for the Goodwill."

"You said no moving!"

"Shut it and lift!" Lauren and I laughed as she pointed to what looked like the heaviest box in the room. Of course it was. This damn divorce was already interfering with my happiness, and not one piece of paper had been filed. I sucked it up and lifted just as I had been ordered to do. I wasn't messing with her today as I also headed toward the door. In true Greek tragedy form, it swung open as we approached. Josh stood there, deflated, semi-sober.

Startled, I almost dropped the heavy box of charity. An epic pause followed in which none of us could breathe. On the way over, Lauren had said the deal was that Josh would stay away while she packed up the house and the kids. He'd designated what he wanted to keep, which had been sent to his parent's Hamptons home on the very first day. The brokers were scheduled to be there within the hour for a walk-through along with the Sotheby's representatives. Once again, I selfishly thought of my inability to fully cope with confronting the shell of a man whose strength and spirit I'd once admired. I loved Lauren first. Most. But I loved Josh, too.

"Please," crackled between Josh's lips. Helpless and broken, but as genuine a plea as I'd heard. It came again, "Please Lauren, please don't..." As he struggled to complete the sentence, several plump droplets fell from his eyes to the marble floor. Each one full of the pain, the memories, the lost dignity, and now, the hope that the love of his life would reconsider their life together.

Lauren just stood there staring at him. Emotionless. My knees began to buckle, but I was firmly planted, feet inward, awkwardly trying to hold it up. Lauren stepped around him, disappearing into the hallway, leaving me face to face, and holding a box full of his lost life. He sunk even further into his knees. The tears stopped as he slumped to the floor, no longer able to support his own weight. I succumbed as well and put the heavy box down to give him a hug.

"You'll make it through this, Josh. You're stronger than this. Stand up and fight. Be the man she and the kids need you to be." He looked up at me, but all of the glimmer was gone from his eyes. No hope. I knew I couldn't save him, and I wasn't there to save him. He would have to do that on his own. And I silently prayed he would. For now, I had to leave him and be there for my friend who couldn't possibly be still standing tall, either.

As the elevator slowly opened to the lobby, Lauren was sitting on a bench with her head in her hands, her glasses pulled up on her head. No tears. The silence of the morning returned as I set the box down again and lowered myself beside her. This time, I couldn't just sit there. "You'll be fine."

"I know. I just hope he will be, too." She lifted her head revealing the shiner, which reminded me that no matter what I felt for Josh, my sister-friend was doing the best thing.

"That's up to him, love."

"I wish I could help." She pulled her glasses back down and stood up, lightly brushing off her clothes and the scene. "You ready? Let's go."

And just like that we did. We picked up the box and the portrait leaving the life she'd known for so long so that she could continue living.

Chapter Nineteen

Revelations

There are certain staples of the New York social calendar that I look forward to like a child on Christmas Eve. The Alvin Ailey American Dance Theater Gala is one of those nights. I'd fallen in love with the world's premier African-American dance (and modern dance) company in my teens when the virtuosos Desmond Richardson and Desiree Vlad were in the company and in their full glory. From the first moment I saw the Ailey company step onstage and glide across it, a collection of multihued gazelles, I was hooked. Never before had I seen such athleticism enveloped in the elegance of grace. And at the end was the singularly most spiritual moment I have experienced in the theater — the first time I saw Mr. Ailey's tour de force, "Revelations." I'm not sure I took a breath during the entire performance.

Every November, a star-studded black tie gala kicks off the company's season at the City Center in New York. It's always one of the hottest tickets in town for New York's elite. Once, when the company was on the brink of financial disaster, the legendary Judith Jamison not only carried on the Ailey legacy but also ushered the company into seasons of unprecedented financial success and recognition worldwide. With the help of many Wall Street titans, she made "the Ailey" the most fiscally successful modern dance company in the world and also very fashionable to support. Although she'd moved into emeritus status, Ms. Jamison's legacy of both artistic and financial excellence was still most evident at the gala.

As I stood outside the City Center in my black Armani tuxedo with black satin accents, my excitement for one of my beloved New York evenings was overtaken by my anxiety that Krissy was late. Pre-performance was one of the top moments of the evening and a parade of fashion dos and don'ts. The don'ts are far more fun than the dos because there is nothing like a rich woman with heinous taste. I got more anxious as the trail of politicians, celebrities, and other assorted well-to-doers passed by me in the brisk November air. Normally, I would have simply left her tickets at the box office. However, she'd specifically requested that I wait. Against my better judgment, I had agreed to do so. Now she wasn't answering her phone or responding to my text messages. I decided to take a breath and put it all in perspective. This would be my eleventh gala and, although I remained excited, missing moments of it would not be the end of the world. Still, I hoped she showed up soon. These tickets were not cheap.

I paced in front, all the while taking deep breaths because I needed to greet her not with anxiety but with love. Just as I was truly becoming settled in the fact that we might miss the pre-performance rodeo, I was blasted with the sight of Ruby. A large gulp accumulated in my throat and a pit hit my stomach. We hadn't seen each other since the "break-up" and I'd heard a string of awful things that she'd been saying about me, all untrue. She even said that I had pushed her, which was absolutely ridiculous and borderline slander. I would never touch anyone, especially a woman. She'd clearly lost her damn mind. It was all to justify her obvious mistreatment and calculated dismissal of me. The gossip didn't bother me as much as the gossiper. Or the accusation that I had physically touched her. Thankfully, most people dismissed Ruby's wild statements just as easily as they dismissed her. It also helped that both of our reputations spoke for themselves, and mine was light years ahead of hers. Still, it was a new experience for me with one of my sister-friends, former or not. Imagining the moment we did finally come face-to-face again, and I knew we would (New York for some is a small town), various scenarios had played out in my mind. The more common was a good ole' fashioned cuss out like Krissy wanted to do for me. Then I would contemplate my better self and just respond with a gentleman's hello. Most of my other sister-friends advised the former. Thankfully, my spirit opted for the latter.

"Hello Ruby, you look wonderful (even though she didn't)," I said politely through a pliers-forced smile. It was obvious that she had been contemplating this moment, too, but was clearly startled and uncomfortable. Usually happens when you know you've acted despicably behind someone's back and you're confronted with yourself and your actions upon seeing them. We both knew what had happened. We both knew the truth. I could see it all over her face. Remorseful, but with a resolve that she'd done what she had to do to get what she wanted. The Holy Grail, Steve, was finally in her clutches, and I sadly knew that she felt the casualty was worth it. Ironically, she was alone this night. Hope she got used to it because if the gossip was true about him, she was going to be spending many nights alone in that castle on the hill.

"You, too. Enjoy the evening," she said as she grabbed her overly dramatic ball-gown and flew nervously up the stairs. I could feel the eyeballs on us from the many familiar faces that knew the story and were waiting to witness the interaction. I felt good. Her nervous energy reassured me that she knew she was wrong whether she admitted it or not. In the same moment, I felt sorry for her, considering how desperate she must be. It was the only way she could stay in the position she'd grown to believe was genuinely who she was and what her life was about. It was quite sad.

A tap on my shoulder shook me out of my sympathetic lament for a lost friendship and soul. "Chile, I'm so sorry, I know you must be furious." I turned to see Krissy, resplendent in the form-fitting green satin Dolce & Gabbana gown she'd showed me a couple of weeks ago. The hanger had not done it justice because in person it kissed the floor in front and emptied into a slight train in back. Its tightly corseted bodice gave Krissy a knockout 1940s pin-up girl figure. The dress alone made up for the wait. She looked spectacular, and I'd long grown accustomed to forgiving my sister-friends who were tardy but arrived stunning.

"No worries, dear, it's just great to see you." I couldn't haven't meant that more. I needed a hug and went in with a tight grip. She responded with a tight grip as well. Apparently, we both needed one. "Girl, you look amazing. Worth it. Where's Justin?"

"I'll tell you about that later. He's not coming, which is why I'm late."

"Really? Does he know how much these tickets cost?"

"No, and obviously doesn't care. Considering he didn't pay for it, why should he? Seriously, I just want to go in and grab a drink or two before we have to go to our seats."

"No rush, you know they do thirty minutes of speeches. We have time to get some libations. Lord, I need one, too. I have a feeling this might be a long night."

"We are going to have fun. Whatever happened before this moment is in the past, and that's where it's gonna stay."

"You sound like me."

"I listen to you. Most of the time." As we stepped further under the light, I saw that her eyes were puffy underneath an exceptional amount of makeup even for Krissy. There was definitely more to Justin's no-show, and she clearly wanted to leave it alone for now, and so I would too. Luckily, there was no one waiting at the bar, and we made a beeline for it.

The bells alerting us that the performance was to begin soon started chiming just as I ordered "Two vodkas on the rocks with a splash of water." I looked at Krissy who approved with a nod. Good thing because I hadn't bothered to ask her what she wanted. Didn't need to — the selection was not relevant just as long as it was cold and it stung.

"Every time I see you, you have a drink in your hand." I knew the voice, and speaking of stinging, the midget scorpion king was standing behind us. I started not to turn around, but the asshole in me bubbled up, and I jumped on the opportunity.

"Duh, it's because you only see me at parties, Victor. That's the point." Krissy burst into laughter in his face and I followed suit. I'd channeled my inner high school mean girl and had responded with something I knew I would feel bad about later. Maybe. With Victor it was preemptive because he was surely seconds away from saying something despicable himself. I only beat him to the punch.

"How's your new film?" he asked, knowing or believing I didn't have one. I knew it wouldn't be long before he vindicated me for being a jerk myself.

"You mean, the one with Halle Berry? It's going great. I am flying out to L.A. tomorrow."

"Halle Be…"

"Sorry, boo, they're ringing the bells. Buh-bye," said Krissy as she grabbed my arm and headed toward the theater. It was wrong, but so right. We downed our drinks before heading inside where the usher directed us to Aisle J in the center. The seats were awesome, and we only had to crawl over four people to get to them. The rush of the alcohol and the moment with Victor made me a little loopy as we sat down.

"We were bad," I said. Krissy adjusted herself in the seat.

"No, we weren't. He's a pompous prick who I was not feeling tonight. The years we've put up with him going on about this famous person or that one, he better be glad that was all we said."

"You know he probably knows Halle Berry."

"Who gives a fuck? At this point, he can go screw himself. Who cares?" Krissy was really feeling it, and it became clear that the drink we had just had was not her first of the night. I giggled at her just as the lights in the house dimmed and the spotlight for the speeches was brightened. Elegantly dressed people followed, and it was show time.

◆ ◆ ◆

The performance was every bit as remarkable as I'd expected. "Revelations" capping off the vast range of choreography — from ballet to hip-hop to modern — it was an evening of exquisite dance. To boot, the gala performance of "Revelations" is always performed to live music — exceptional dancers twirling to a collection of exceptionally sung spirituals. Grace personified on stage via these divinely inspired performers. The drama at the evening's start was quickly replaced by the joy that dance brings to my spirit.

After numerous standing ovations and encores, a caravan of well-dressed people flowed out of the City Center onto the New York Streets for the short walk to the Hilton, which was the site of the actual Gala dinner and dance. Although it was nearby, they still provided shuttles for those more seasoned attendees and people who didn't feel like walking. I loved the walk because it was always interesting to see the tourists' faces as this glittering caravan passed. Surely, they weren't used to such sights in Middle America or in most places for that matter. The Ailey had long become a multicultural company drawing a diverse audience, yet the Gala remained primarily an African-American event. To see that many black folks dressed to the nines was not only a treat, but also a rarity.

Krissy and I walked in silence as we left the theater. We'd done this stroll many times and besides our smiles to familiar faces, we were both on autopilot. For me, I was still reeling from the performance. I could tell something else was on her mind. So we walked into the brisk night, both of us collecting our thoughts.

As we arrived at the hotel, her energy shifted. Somber during the walk, she was now turning it on, a quality I always admired about Krissy. I slipped my hand in hers and gave it a little squeeze. "You alright, girl?"

"Gonna be. But this motherfucker obviously has gotten it twisted. I'll tell you what's going on when we get to our seats."

"OK!" It was show time, and we expertly worked the room over Grey Goose gimlets. It was a particularly star-studded year. Diehards like Cicely Tyson, Jesse Jackson and, of course, Judith Jamison were no surprise. However, Iman, André Leon Talley, Audra MacDonald, John Legend, Mo'Nique, and even Oprah were shockers. Always a high-level, big-ticket event, the addition of these names stepped it up even more. The atmosphere was festive, and the crowd was ready for a great time. Two gimlets in, I certainly was. While waiting for the introduction of the company, the customary signal to the start of the dinner, we continued to mingle.

"Did you see Ruby?" asked Krissy, catching me off balance. I hadn't thought about Ruby since we walked into the performance. But, she was right; we should have seen her by now. The ballroom wasn't that big.

"Yes, before you got to the theater. Why?"

"I was just wondering if she would show up after the word on the street."

"What word?"

"Chile, Steve done got one of his new artists knocked up. That's why he proposed to Ruby in the first place."

"Well, damn. Where'd you hear that?"

"My girl Tasha that works at the label told me about it yesterday. I've had a lot going on so I didn't get a chance to call you."

"For two seconds I started to feel sorry for her. But fuck Ruby! She deserves that shit."

"Well, alrighty then. You know I agree. Fuck her!" We both began to laugh at our brash and crude honesty.

"And fuck Justin," she added, causing me to wobble a bit again. It probably wasn't going to wait until we got to our seats. "If that's even his name."

"What?"

"I went through his wallet and found an ID with a completely different name. Instead of Justin Heard, it was Justin Langley. So, I Googled Justin Langley, and a lot of the same stuff he's told me came up — except the part about a wife and securities fraud."

"Get the hell outta here!"

"Now, you know my ass had already done research, and this brother is even better than you can imagine. I had no clue."

"What made you go through his stuff? Besides the obvious."

"This mug asked me to borrow fifty thousand dollars."

"Whaaat?"

"Yes, chile. It sent me on a mission. I went through everything, which is when I found the other ID."

"I'm completely blown away. What did he say?"

"What could he say? He started stuttering and trying that reverse psychology bullshit that doesn't work with me. I was already late so I told him to give me my keys and get the hell out. The security at my building has been alerted and the locks are being changed as we speak."

"So he's a con artist, you think?"

"I don't know what the fuck he is. But I knew something wasn't right."

"Damn. I guess I got it wrong again. I obviously need to mind my own damn business."

"Not your fault. Who the hell knew this was going to turn into a *Dateline* episode?"

"What are you going to do? About moving and all that."

"That's the least of my worries. I can handle that or someone at my firm can. I signed the lease based on fraudulent representations. Yadda yadda. Just glad that I found this shit out before it went too far."

"Are you OK?"

Krissy took a seat at a table without regard to whether it was ours or not. I sat down next to her as the rest of the party continued on without regard to us. "I want say I'm good, but I'm not. I really wanted this to work out. Hell, I went against everything in me. No lie. The shit hurts. I know I play the hard bitch role, but I hurt, too."

"I know, love. We all do. You'd be a robot if you didn't feel something."

"I knew better. Damn!"

"This is not your fault. You did all that you could do."

"I don't know about that. Guys like Justin don't want girls like me. Or at least guys like I thought he was. I got caught up in some Star Jones shit."

"Baby, we've all been caught up one way or another." I grabbed Krissy around the shoulders and brought her in for a hug. "The good news is you found out what was real before it was too late or you had loaned him fifty thousand dollars."

"Now, you know that was never going to happen." We laughed as Krissy's eyes began to tear as they seemingly had earlier. She wiped them away while looking around to make sure no one saw her. "They say everything happens for a reason." She was correct, but I really hoped this would not force her to retreat to her old ways of shutting all men out. Couldn't really blame her if she did, though. However, it seemed that even with being pissed, she was resolved, which encouraged me. Still, I couldn't believe the story. It was one of those that happened to other people. On television. Or in books. Not in real life. And not to women like Krissy. I guess that's what the relatives and friends on *Dateline* all say. Not to my friend. But it had.

"Krissy," rang from a voice over the band coming from behind us. We both pivoted to catch the guy from Daniel's party fast approaching with a schoolyard smile on his face, clearly excited to see my sister-friend. God's timing is the stuff that makes truth stranger than fiction.

"Hey, Mike! What are you doing here?"

"I subcontracted with the main event planner, David. You never mentioned you were going to be here tonight," he said to Krissy, almost completely ignoring my presence.

"Oh, you guys talk I see," I said, more trying to make my presence known than anything.

"I'm sorry, Mike, this is my best friend. He's the one that invited me to Daniel's party that day."

"Ahhh, nice to meet you, man." He gave a firm, exuberant handshake that reeked of genuineness. "Are you all enjoying yourselves?"

"Yes, nice to meet you, too."

"Same here. Let me get you guys some drinks. You paid too much money to be empty-handed."

"That's sweet. But you don't have to do that," blushed Krissy.

"I insist. Plus, it's part of my job." He winked at Krissy, enchanting her to blush even more. "Are you a gimlet guy like the pretty lady?"

"Yessir."

"Got it. Two Goose gimlets stat." He hurriedly turned toward the bar before stopping in his tracks and regarding Krissy again. "It's so great to see you here." And in an instant, he redirected back to the bar.

"Hmmm, he knows your drink, Missy?"

"Don't start."

"No wonder you're not completely upset. You've been up to something."

"Cut it. Not like that. He's just a lot of fun. And yes, you can keep your damn advice this time. I got it from here."

"Dang, so harsh. I guess you told me," I joked. Again, she was right, and my batting average didn't give any basis to argue with her.

"Let's just have a great time and dance until our feet hurt. Deal?"

"Deal."

Chapter Twenty

Out of the Dog House

Seventy-eight floors above the city, I looked out of the floor-to-ceiling windows onto the pillows of green trees that made up Central Park. Although I had been in Rebecca and Gerand's Time Warner Center condo many times, the view never failed to take my breath away. Add the bustle of the city below and the expanse and mix of historic and new high-rises that made up Columbus Circle, and it was easily worth every ridiculous penny that they'd spent. High-rise living was not my thing, but this was one address I would gladly take as my own. In fact, the Time Warner Center and all its various residences was the only high-rise in which I aspired to live.

Excited, I jumped into the center of her ring shaped, taupe-colored suede sofa to be enveloped by mounds of plush crème, beige, and burnt yellow pillows on Rebecca's surprisingly comfortable albeit oddly shaped sofa! It was nice to be back in her lavish Time Warner Center apartment and not on the island of exile in the comparatively tiny Village apartment to which she'd previously been banished. It had nothing to do with the actual apartment; rather, what sitting here waiting for her to return with cocktails meant. While Krissy was moving on (well, back into her place) and Lauren had moved out, Rebecca was definitely moving back in and, for that, I had to smile as I rolled around on the massive donut that I had originally protested when she bought it. "Who has a round sofa?" I had questioned.

Suddenly, I realized something looming over me, witnessing my frolic, and I bashfully snapped out of it. Rebecca's throwaway chuckle confirmed that she didn't mind and applauded the carefree way that I played amongst her handpicked, handmade pillows and sofa. She was happy to be back where she belonged. Gerand was well enough to take moments alone with his closest friends. Although he wasn't supposed to be working, Rebecca knew he was sneaking in some work time out in the park and not just "enjoying nature." She also knew he needed that to keep going and keep fighting beyond the happenstance that had laid him down. But he was banned from actually going into the office by his doctors, his colleagues, and, most importantly, Rebecca. It was probably a good thing for the people worked for him as well because he had mellowed out; half by order and half because of his new perspective. Rebecca said the shouting at the phone and computer screen had been replaced by trips to yoga and afternoon meditation. The old dog was learning new tricks. No one knew how long it would last, but Rebecca didn't care, as she knew he would never return to the same person he was before the heart attack. Neither would she.

She sat down on the other, more traditional sofa across from me while I lay stretched out on my side, propped up on my elbow, my head in my hand. We both smiled as we let out deep breaths. It was once again the irony of life and the unexpected cards that you are consistently dealt. She exuded a warmth that made the apartment feel like a home and not a beautiful cage. That was definitely a first for me in one of their homes.

"You know, I never understood why you bought this place...until now."

"The view, of course."

"You have beautiful views in all your apartments."

"That's true, but to be honest, I knew we would grow into this space. Gerand didn't want to buy it, either. 'Who has three apartments in the same city?' he said. He was right, but something told me that one day we'd grow to appreciate this place and the park and the neighborhood."

"Nature, darling."

"Yes, nature for the gawds!"

"Someone's been watching a little too much Bravo."

"Way too much. I am so happy to be out of that damn hospital. I couldn't read another book. Watch another awful reality or competition show. How do those real housewives do it?

"Technically, you're a housewife," I joked.

"Oh no, I am nobody's housewife. Never have been. Never will be."

"True, true."

Rebecca looked over her shoulder and out the window down to the trees in the park. "I almost fucked this up, didn't I?"

"In some ways, yeah. But, it's different when you're in it. Monday night quarterbacking is so easy, especially from the sidelines or worse...the sofa."

"Yeah, but he wasn't even cheating on me."

"Hope there isn't, but if there is a next time, just ask." It was as simple as that because she and I both knew that the vision of the truth that she had created in her head had led her down a miserable path. And avoiding it was as simple as a question.

"Never woulda happened."

"But it did. I'm not a sadist, but I think you're both better for it," I said.

"Think you're right." In the blink of an eye, a black hole that had been building for a very long time spiraled out of control and caught them at its epicenter. Climbing out was a journey they made hand-in-hand. The harder the climb, the stronger their grip became. Having to save her husband made Rebecca know that she needed him.

Then she said, "Why do you have to be on the verge of destruction to get to redemption?"

Damn, that was deep, I thought. I didn't answer because I didn't have one better than "Because."

"What's going on with you? You said you had some news to share."

"Right! So, you know I have been working on this script like a maniac."

"Yes, but what's it about again?"

"Four women and their crazy love lives."

"Haha, sounds familiar. Anyone I know?"

"Um, there might be some real-life inspiration, but it's definitely fiction."

"A roman à clef of sorts," she said.

"Exactly."

"I already know I'm going to love it."

"Maybe sooner than you think. I had a meeting last week with one of my friends from Northwestern who is a big-time banker, and he is looking to break into the movie business."

"Really?"

"It's all preliminary, but he can put up the capital I need to make the film without having to go the studio route. I might even direct it."

"That's awesome. So how much do you need?"

"I think the movie can be done excellently for eight to ten million."

"I'll give you some money, too. Whatever he doesn't, I'll cover the rest."

"Oh no, you don't have to do that, Rebecca. But that's sweet."

"Excuse me. This isn't about friendship. This is about me making some money. I believe in you. We can talk details when I'm back from my trip. Cool?"

"Wow! Yeah, very cool. Thank you."

"No problem, love. I got it, so why not? I don't know why you've never asked me before."

"I technically didn't ask you this time. That kind of thing is very sensitive, and I didn't want anything to interfere with our friendship. Business and friends can be sticky."

"Not with us. Plus, we'll have contracts in place. So I'm not worried. Just promise to do your best. Will you shoot it in Los Angeles?"

"Actually, no. The story takes place in New York. We'd probably shoot the exteriors here and the rest in Canada."

"You mean, I get to keep you here? That's money well spent."

"Ha! At least for the duration of the shoot. Two months or so."

"I'll take it. Anyway, I gotta get dressed and ready. Like I said, we can settle all of this when I get back. I mean it, too," she said, quickly exiting to the back of the apartment.

As I waited on Rebecca to get ready, a sense of joy came over me again. It had been seven months since our lunch at Josie's, and it was an intense hell. Then Gerand had a heart attack and wound up on his back in Mt. Sinai. Health is certainly a great equalizer. No matter how powerful or how rich, when your health fails you, it's a wrap. Gerand had the best doctors in the world to attend to him, but he was no more or less than any man whose heart had decided to stop. The universe has a way of humbling us when we least expect it and often when we most need it.

It forced them to spend far more time together than they had in years, doing things they'd never done — like reading a book together. It's cliché, but near-death experiences have an ironic way of making you appreciate your life. True for the person experiencing it as well as for those around. Hate to say it, but I was glad he had almost died. It had given them a second chance.

"I can't believe I'm late. I was supposed to be down in the car twenty minutes ago, Gerand is probably popping a gasket," shouted Rebecca as she emerged from the back. "Probably not a good analogy, but you know what I mean."

"I'm sure he's fine. You're flying private; they'll wait for you. Plus, he's mellowed a lot since the surgery."

"You're right. I guess I'm just so excited. We've never been on a month long vacation. Now, do you have all of the instructions on how everything works in here and the other places?"

"Ad nauseam, my dear."

"You know, you can stay here as much or as little as you want before you leave and when you get back from Jamaica. Just come check on things from time to time. The staff will do the rest. I just don't want it to feel cold when we return."

"Girl, would you hush! You just focus on getting to Cabo. I got this!" Rebecca smiled at me as she gathered her purse from the coffee table and came over to where I was standing.

"Thank you so much for being there for me. You've gone beyond the call of duty in one of the roughest times in my life. Wouldn't have made it without you."

"Rain makes the flowers grow, my dear."

"Darling, I was in a thunderstorm," she joked as she laughed. "OK, so we're set, I'm going to run. Love you to pieces. Don't have too much fun with your other women." She gave me a tight squeeze and headed for the door. As she opened the door, she stopped and turned around and said, "And when I get back, you're going with because Gerand and I are getting a dog."

Chapter Twenty-One

Don't Stop 'Til You Get Enough

The steps leading down to the basement of Katra, one of New York's most selective lounges, are treacherous and almost cost me an embarrassing wipeout. How the armies of Choos, Louboutins, Zanottis, and other expensive-sounding foreign-named shoes make it down the stairs is a mystery to me. Actually, women's obsession with high heels is a mystery to me. Sexy to look at, until you've spent the entire night hearing how much her feet hurt and she's ready to go home. I've spent many of those nights, unfortunately.

Michael Jackson urged me not to stop until I'd made my way in past the third set of bounces. Clubs in this city constantly remind you that you're always seconds away from the sidewalk if you say the wrong name, thing, or made the mistake of wearing last year's Prada. Or these days, wearing Prada at all. Just saying. Of course, unless you know someone (or everyone knows you). I tend to go only where I know someone. Tonight, it was Vikki. Her last hoorah as a single woman. Take three.

Once I had made it downstairs, I was immediately greeted by Vikki dropping it like it was on fire at the edge of the small dance floor. Remember, Katra is exclusive, which when translated means small. Sorry, "intimate" according to the "reviews," which when translated can mean a publicity intern's online reiteration of the press release. Vikki's fire, however, immediately chilled my cynicism about the NYC nightlife, forcing me to run over to drop it like it was hot alongside. Let the geriatric twerking commence!

Since the "King of Pop's" death, you can always count on several of his crowd- unifying tunes being played at any party in the NYC. Leads me to the thought of, maybe if he felt that much love during the last years of his life, we might not have to celebrate his passing so hard. Reminds me to love my loves while they're here to receive it. And speaking of love, Vikki was wearing 7-inch purple stone-crusted heels. Art for the feet.

"How are you getting down in those shoes?"

"Sweetie, I feel no pain," she said as she threw up her hands to a chorus of 'heys' and 'get it, girls' from her girlfriends who were serving as her personal hype team for the night. "You likey? They're Barbara Bui. She made them just for me. 'Cause I'm getting married!!!"

"Heyyyyy!" I joined the chorus and jumped firmly in the middle of all of that gorgeousness. Vikki draped her arms around my neck, and we went into a combination of two-step and air-grind. Then they started playing Michael's sister, Janet – "The Pleasure Principle," which sent us all into a nostalgic fit and a survey of all the ole-school dances from "The Wop" to "The Cabbage Patch." We were so loud that some of the people who had been chilling on the sofas and chairs got up to join the fun. I was definitely ready for the turn-up after taking a much-required disco nap before getting ready. Plus, I hadn't seen Vikki since our day at Amsale and Fred's.

"Where's the waitress?" Vikki screamed. "I told her to keep the shots coming."

"We are on the dance floor, girl."

"What does that have to do anything? I want shots!" shouted Vikki in the direction of the bar like a three year-old crying for her toy.

She incited the rest of the bachelorette crowd to yell in rhythm, "Shots! Shots! Shots! Shots!" Like magic, two waitresses appeared with two trays full of chilled Patron shots. Vikki was definitely Queen of the Night, and I guess everyone was on notice. It was so pure that the atmosphere was fueled by her energy and happiness. Vikki and her other friends grabbed a shot each, but I had some catching up to do so I grabbed two.

"Cheers! To my best friend in the whole wide world getting married. They say three's a charm," I yelled as a toast.

"Hell, yeah! It better fucking be. Drink!" We happily obeyed, then continued to get our groove on to the various hits on Vikki's playlist. It was my kind of party, and as more shots were delivered, it got even better.

After thirty minutes of hot dropping, it was time to sit. All of Vikki's girls had joined by then. It wasn't as apparent on the dance floor with all of the other folks alongside, and although I was used to it, I still hated being the only guy in our group. It's how it is, though, at these "girls only" events. Half honored to be the only man included, half side-eyed at being the only one included. Maybe one-third side-eyed because girls are much more fun without their guys around. They do things they wouldn't do in front of men. Well, except for me. It makes me feel special. I knew we were going to continue to have a long night of fun. Good thing I had nothing planned until tomorrow evening because the recovery time almost triples each year I get closer to forty.

"I met Paul for a drink," Vikki leaned and slurred in my ear.

I turned in shock because I didn't know what was coming next. "So, what happened?"

"By the end, he was wearing the damn drink. That's what happened."

"Oh my. I'm so sorry. I shouldn't have pushed you to…"

Then the little devil started laughing. "I'm just kidding. You were actually right. I didn't realize it, but I needed to see him. Best believe I let his ass have it, though. He took that shit like a man, which I 'preciate. I hate to say it. We had a good time.

"So, do you think you were able to forgive him?"

"I dunno 'bout all that. But he seemed sorry. So who knows? I'm glad I did it. You know, you smart some times and shit."

Tipsy or not, it was hard to believe I was hearing this story. Two weeks ago, she wanted Paul's balls served on a platter, and now she'd had a "good time" with him.

"Thanks!" She started waving the subject away, "'Nuff of that. More shots!!!"

"You ain't said nothing but a word," I proclaimed, picking up one of the Patron shots from the fresh batch on the table as we all toasted my gorgeously happy sister-friend. All that she'd been through seemed worth it and justified by her arrival to this place here. Drunk in love!

Chapter Twenty-Two

Love Wins

Traveling out of the country sounds glamorous, and it is, except having to go through customs. Particularly when you first arrive at your intended destination. The last thing you want to do is wait in line to begin your excursion while some customs agent asks you the most banal, routine questions, gives you the once-over, and finally stamps your passport. It's even worse when arriving in someplace tropical that isn't so developed. Outside is paradise, inside the airport is a torturous, hot mess.

Thankfully, the several drinks on the plane plus Krissy and Lauren's company made this entry into Jamaica's Montego Bay at the very least tolerable. A bit tipsy, we joked the entire time about everything that had happened, including the Js — Justin and Josh. They were neither completely sad nor completely happy. Instead, both were in a state of acceptance, which was fine by me considering the screaming roller coaster we'd all been on for the past ten months. All that mattered was this moment. And we were together heading toward Vikki's wedding.

Passing through customs this time was actually not as onerous as the experiences I'd had in the past. It was probably the sugary cocktails and the good conversation, but when we walked out into the Jamaican sun, the slightest bit of burden disappeared. We immediately began to look for the driver from Half Moon Bay, the luxury resort that Vikki had taken over for her nuptials to Dax. It didn't take long for a well-uniformed gentleman to spot us as he held up a sign with our names on it. Reminded me of those red carpet moments when the photographers have a booklet with your name, picture, and claim to fame in it so they know who to take pictures of and who, well, not to bother with.

The man greeted us with a 1000-watt smile while running up, heading straight for the ladies' luggage. Out of nowhere another well-uniformed man dashed from the passenger's side of the small SUV to the other side, heading straight for my bags. Nothing like being pampered with exceptional service. I knew this was going to be a fantastical trip.

The first driver dropped Krissy and Lauren's bags at the side of the SUV and, turning, enthusiastically said, "On behalf of the Half Moon Bay resort, we'd like to welcome you to Montego Bay." He then opened the back of the expansive SUV and said, "Please" while motioning for us to climb inside. I could tell there were two other passengers already seated in the very back, but I couldn't make them out until I was in my seat and had turned around.

"Alex!" I exclaimed, surprised to see Ruby's ex-husband sitting there next to a stunning, much younger woman. "Wow, you were the last person on earth I expected to see here. Not to be rude, of course."

"Of course," Alex said sarcastically. "Small world. Meet my fiancée, Tricia." He presented her proudly.

"Nice to meet you, Tricia. Alex you know Lauren, of course."

"Indeed, always a pleasure, beautiful," Alex said with every bit of the slimy, faux charm for which he was famous.

"Alex, it's been too long," said Lauren.

"And this is Krissy, a dear friend of mine and Vikki's." Everyone gave very polite smiles and head nods. The shock of the moment left me speechless. I had been completely honest when I said that Alex was the last person on earth that I had expected to see in the back of that SUV. Maybe fantastical was not the right word for what this trip was going to be. Awkward was what it was at the moment.

"How do you know Vikki and Dax?" asked the stunning Tricia with a demeanor that seemed too sweet and good for Alex.

"I've known Vikki for an embarrassingly long time. I just met Dax several months ago. And you?"

"Dax is my oldest brother," she responded and sat back in her seat, smiling as the two gentlemen from the resort hopped in the front.

"All set for the time of your life?" the driver asked. Already an under-statement. My mind was naughtily focused on the math of the situation. Alex was at least twelve years older than Ruby who I knew to be just shy of forty. And, I also knew that Dax had a younger brother who was 5 years younger than him, making the other brother 28 or 29. He'd discussed a "baby" sister who he didn't grow up with much because he was a teen-ager by the time she was born. Sensing (or feeling) the wheels turning in my head, Krissy wing-manned.

"So, Tricia, what is it that you do?" she questioned with an undetect-able inquisitive shade.

"I'm finishing up my last year at Pepperdine, but I've taken a bit of time off to travel Europe with Alex. So it'll take me the summer and one more semester." Mind calculator computing with rapid speed. The dar-ling little sister couldn't be any more than twenty-one years old. In most circumstances, I would've frowned upon the age disparity, but she was stunning, and I couldn't wait until Ruby found out. Wrong, I know, but she was definitely going to find out. If I had anything to do with it. And I would definitely have something to do with it. New York may be a Big Apple, but its certainly a small town when it comes to gossip of this stature within our circles.

Delighted, I sat back in the comfort of my black leather seat in the SUV driving me to paradise. My inner Regina George had kicked in, but of all people, Ruby deserved this. Krissy looked at me and smirked while Lauren gave my knee a quick squeeze. It caused us all to laugh one good-bellied laugh. I was scared to turn back around to see if Alex or Tricia had noticed any of it.

As we pulled up to the resort, my thoughts switched back to the purpose of the trip. There they were, the cake-top couple, Vikki and Dax standing at the front to greet us, flanked by staff from the resort. It was a scene from a postcard with them perfectly placed between the trees that seemed to wave at us slightly with the tropical wind. As we descended from the SUV, I felt better than I had in recent memory. I felt bad about the previous musings that swirled through my head. But only for a moment. I was still going to make sure Ruby found out. I don't deny being human.

"So happy you made it safely. You all are the last bunch to arrive," gushed Vikki, who immediately embraced me. Dax shook my hand from her side.

"I see you've met my little sister, I hope she didn't talk your head off," said Dax as he kissed Tricia on her forehead and embraced her warmly. "Alex, glad you could make it," was the lukewarm greeting that followed, minus the handshake. I could tell I wasn't the only mathematician in the bunch.

"I absolutely protest. You two can't come in here looking better than the bride. Incosiderate heffas," Vikki scooped up both Krissy and Lauren in an affectionate group hug. "I'm so excited. YAY!! I hope you're hungry because they've prepared a beachfront dinner for us all that's beginning in thirty minutes. Just enough time for you to freshen up a bit and then come back here to the main building. It'll be just right on the other side of the lobby."

"These two gentlemen will take your luggage to your villas, but here are your two golf carts for the week. We've checked everyone in so you're good to go," Dax said like a man in control. "Lauren, I hope you don't mind that you're sharing a villa with my cousin. I think you two will get along famously. She's a producer for *Good Morning New York*. I've told her all about you."

"Yes, sure, no problem. I look forward to meeting her."

"Well alrighty then, I guess we'll see you all in thirty," I said, as excited as a twelve-year-old to hop in the golf cart. Krissy jumped into the passenger seat, and we took off, forgetting that we had no idea where we were going. Forced to turn around in slight embarrassment, Dax stood there holding out the map of the grounds with a grin on his face.

"This might help," he chuckled.

Half Moon is a breathtaking piece of property. Quite the contrast from the impoverished city we drove through from the airport here. The dichotomy between "the haves and have-nots" is one of the reasons why

I'm conflicted about Jamaica (besides the fact that they openly kill gay people). My social conflicts or not, it was awesome to be there. Riding in a cart alongside one of my best sister-friends in paradise can't be beat.

When we arrived at our villa, we were floored by the sheer size. Another welcoming staff member stood outside, joined by a woman who was equally inviting in her pressed threads. Conflicts gone.

"Welcome to your home while here at Half Moon. I'm Desmond, and I will be your butler."

"And I am Cassie. I will be your maid."

"Anything you need, please do not hesitate to contact us. We are here to make your stay happy and carefree. We have placed your bags in the master suite for your convenience. Will there be anything you and the Mrs. require, sir at this moment? Turn-down service?" asked Desmond.

Krissy and I looked at each other and smiled. Remembering that we still were in Jamaica, we silently opted not to correct him. Proud and liberated, I choose my battles, and this was an unnecessary one, and he meant no harm.

"No, we'll be fine," I replied as we tried to pass them both twenty-dollar bills, which they refused. The wattage in their smiles increased when Krissy put both bills in Desmond's pocket. Some rules were meant to be broken, especially harmless ones that involved dollar bills. Rainbow flags may not be welcome, but green is a universal color that, with arms open, will always be.

"Very well, please do let us know if we may be of assistance. Thank you," said Desmond as he walked down the lane leading to the parking bay, followed by the still smiling Cassie. Krissy and I walked into our villa. It was absolutely magnificent. Clearly, it was intended for more than two people, but I guess that's how Vikki and Dax were going to roll. I certainly was not complaining. In the center was a grand living room flanked with various rooms that circled its majesty on two sides. In front of us was a full-sized pool that sat just past a wall of French doors and a terrace. The furniture was island chic perfection. Comfortable enough that you were relaxed. Luxurious enough that you felt your money was well spent.

"Can you believe this place? This is wonderful," I whispered, in awe.

"Forget the villa, can you believe that grandpa-romper room situation on the way over here?" exclaimed Krissy with a gossipy disbelief.

"Oh, you noticed that?"

"Notice it? It's the only thing I could think of? Wait until "Miss Thang" finds out!"

"I'm so glad I'm not the only one. I was starting to feel bad for even thinking like that."

"Chile, please. If you don't make sure she finds out, I will." We laughed a laugh that only good gossip and a bit of revenge can evoke. Ruby might have moved on, but I personally knew that if Alex asked her to come back, she would. Unbelievably, she actually loved him and not just his money or status.

"In the meantime, let's get ready so we're not late to dinner. Shall we jolly up to our master suite, Missus?" I joked, imitating Desmond's presumptions and accent.

As we drove back up to the main building, more smiling staff greeted us and directed us to the dinner. Among the rich and famous it is gauche to discuss money, but they sure do think about it. Seeing I was neither rich nor famous, I couldn't help but think how much money it had cost to shut the entire resort down. Krissy and I were on the same page again as she said, "Now what kind of Internet company did Dax sell? Google?" We giggled as we strolled through the lush lobby.

The setup on the beach was ridiculous. I wanted to pull out my phone and take a picture and post it to Instagram. Again, postcard perfect. All the guests were mingling on the Tikki lamp-lit beach surrounding an obscenely long table. Each place setting was immaculate with flowers everywhere in the wedding colors of sand and salmon.

I looked around for Oprah and Colin Cowrie because surely they had something to do with this. Yet, it wasn't about the apparent expense. It was the feeling. A warmth that exuded romance.

"Sweeties, you're here," screamed Vikki from down the beach. "We can get started." Out of nowhere, Dax rolled up behind us with two more tropical cocktails that looked yummy, and potent.

"I think you'll need these. Your places are marked by number on the seating charts. I hope you don't mind, but Vikki and I have split everyone up. You sir, are next to my friend Brent. I've been dying for you to meet. He's moving to New York in a month, and I think you two might hit it off. Krissy, you're next to my friend from MIT, Dillon."

"Dillon!" Krissy and I said in unison, looking at Dax.

"I know. Pure coincidence. These gentlemen have the seating charts, if you'll just grab one."

Lauren came up behind us as we were looking for our seats. "OK, I have to admit I was put out that they didn't ask me to do the wedding, but this is exceptional. Look at the centerpieces. Do you know how much all of those hydrangeas cost? And they're spray-colored too. And their initials are so discreetly on everything."

"Everything?" Krissy asked as she spotted her seat.

Lauren picked up one of the knives from Krissy's place setting and turned it on its side revealing a faint "V&D" in script on the tip. "Everything!"

"Who's the event planner?" I asked."

"A native woman from Negril. She's amazing. I have to go speak to her some more before we get started. This is unreal." Lauren whisked away as Krissy took her seat.

"I'll catch you after," said Krissy, greeting Dillon with her eyes as he approached the table.

As I continued to follow the seating chart along the massive table, I came upon a very handsome man of indescribable but definitely mixed heritage who was equally engaged in the act of finding his seat. The most notable thing about him, beyond his undeniable good looks, was the fact that his linen shirt was unbuttoned down to just above his navel. Yet it wasn't vulgar. It worked. Admittedly, I was checking him out until we both stumbled upon our seats, next to each other. "You must be Brent," I said, trying to fight back the schoolboy smile burning inside.

"And, you must be…"

"Everyone please have a seat. We promise to let you get back to getting to know each other, but we must do this first," yelled Dax from the head of the table. Brent and I continued to smile at each other as we took our seats.

"Vikki and I are so happy that all of our closest family and friends have traveled so far to celebrate this occasion with us. It wouldn't be the same without all of you. We want you to have a blast, and we hope that some of what we feel for each other will rub off on you. Truly, this woman right here is my dream come true," said Dax. He took a long pause, clearly fighting back a tear. "I never thought I'd find a woman so perfect for me, but God delivered her, and I'm just so honored that she's agreed to be my wife. Finally!"

He wiped away the one tear that he couldn't fight from falling. "Now, let's just hope she goes through with it tomorrow. 'Cause if not, that would be really fucked up!" Everyone laughed as the ever-charming Dax sucked up his sappiness and raised a glass. "To great family. Great friends," then he looked at Vikki, "and to love!"

"And I just want to say thank you as well. You all mean so much to me. But I have to say a very special thank you to my best friend right there." Catching me off guard, Vikki motioned to me with her glass. "You gave me the best advice I ever got, and it led me here. Never give up on love because it won't give up on you."

With the entire party looking in my direction with applause, Brent leaned in so close that his cheek brushed mine. I didn't mind. And said, "You know my name. I don't know yours. Not fair."

"Patric...it's Patric. Nice to meet you, Brent."

"Nice to meet you, too. So you're the one Dax has been telling me about. I don't know if he mentioned it, but I'm moving to New York in a month. Too bad you're moving away so soon."

"Well, Brent, one thing I have learned over this past year is that you never really know what life has in store. I've resolved to just roll with it and enjoy the amazing ride."

"Nicely said. Cheers to Vikki and Dax," said Brent.

"Cheers to love!"

Acknowledgments

God is AWESOME! That is all and enough!

Some mothers just give birth to their children, do the job of raising them and the heavy lifting is done. Marcia "Momma J" Williams you never stopped. In fact, you go above and beyond by helping me give birth to my dreams – my babies. Even as a storyteller, I don't have the words adequate enough to thank you for the blessings you bestow on me daily by encouraging me…by supporting me…by educating me and, by just being you. I will be eternally in your debt and in awe of your greatness. You are the BEST Mommy in the world. Love, Pook aka Duke Duke Johnson aka Nate the Great the Skate.

I have the best family in the world and although I can't name you all know that you all are in my heart. Special shout to: Granny & Big Daddy; my kindred spirit, the fabulous Auntie Gayle; my brother/cousin, André Christopher; Uncles – Gerald ("Uncle Fats"), Darryl, André; Jorie; Cousins – Dominique, Courtney, Chloé, Darryl James, Charlotte, Ashley, Sherry, Wendy, Matt, Jason, Shawn, Lisa, Gwen and it's so many of y'all and these black letters cost money. I love y'all.

Behind every (great) man are his fabulous lifelong best friends, Andrea (Madame CEO), Antonious & Danielle. Not many people can claim that they've had the same friends their entire lives, but I am blessed to be one of them. Calling you all friends is like a demotion to what you really are and that's family. I would never be able to do any of this without your counsel, your support, your encouragement, your coins (LOL), etc. I love you from the core of my being. Thank you! To Christopher (my "Notorious B-I-L") & Darwin, thanks for embracing me from day one.

To the best friend "Trinity," Dorian & La – you both are the lyrics to my songs. But, I love you beyond words. I'll see you in the "Hampton." You are amazing lights of powerful energy and I stand in humble existence in your presence.

My brothers and sisters in love, the "Babes" – Qwynn, Hal & Linzey. My "Dancing Dolls" – Brandi & Rocky. The "RD" – Phillip Bloch ("sloppy never messy"). "Big Bro" – Sean (& Steeve). The "Voice" – Shannon. The "Crew" – Bobby Duron, Corey, Brent & Jabbar. The "Dinner Club" – Michelle, Derrick & Tracy. The "Virtuoso" – Lenaé. The "Chef" - Rodney "Love" Jones. You guys rock my world beyond comprehension. Thank you. Tell QRR, Hattie Mae, OMG Zella, Louise, Raquelita, P, Chardonnay, Sheila, Sheneathe, Odessa, 'Rine, Marge, Jabs, Lovies times Sushi, "Where's My Checks," Skank, Lil' Man, & Tawny - I said I love them too.

To the best editor this side of Saturn, Cherise Davis Fisher of The Scribes Window (www.thescribeswindow.com). You are a blessing in the truest sense of the word. Without you none of this would have been possible. I hope I didn't wear you out on the first one because there's like fifty more coming. Smile. Thank you!

To my wonderful "Girl Friday," Qiana Hair Brown. You keep the wheels turning at iN-Hale Entertainment. You always thank me for believing in you. No, thank YOU for believing in me. The sky is just the beginning. To your wonderful family, Momma Scott & Prince, for lending you to me from time to time, thank you too!

My creative dream team of encouragement and support – (Carol Ann) SHINE, Jenifer Lewis & Julia Walker thank you for having my back in so many ways. I love you!

My adopted parents, you all have done so much to help me become NHW and I love you like my own. George & Barbara Smith, Bertella Warren, Linzey & Gloria Jones, Diane Kenner, Reverend Dennis Oglesby & Bonnie Porch (RIP).

To everyone who has been "Team Nathan" on this project and so many more, my superstars – Patrik-Ian Polk, Keith Boykin, the one & only - Flo Anthony, Copper Cunningham, Bevy Smith, Daphne Davalie, BJ Coleman, Vivica A. Fox, Somi, Shauna Thomas, Daisy Lewellyn, Lloyd Boston (the "Gentlemen of Style"), Charlie Lewis, Reggie Van Lee, D'Angelo Thompson, Shelley Wade, Russell Taylor, Vernard Gilmore, Dwayne Ashley, James Grooms, Tai Beauchamp, Charli Penn, Terra Winston, Tara Smith, Donna

Smith Bracey, Jason White, Rodney Chester, Marja Vongerichten (thanks for St. Barth's & all the fashion tips for the book), Patrick Riley, Anthony Harper, ButtaFlySoul, Gary Linnen, Charles Ingram, Lloyd Williams, Dwight Allen O'Neal, Dion Summers, William Thompson, Arielle Berry, Roderic Montrece, Derrick Thompson, Elijah Ahmad Lewis, Kiwan "Twin" Anderson, Emil Wilbekin, Frenchie Davis, Terrell Mullin, Kyra Kyles, Toni Long, Joshua Leach, Marlin Davis, Tamika Covington, Em Corece, Markovist Wells, Ricky Day, Bryan Slotkin, Paul Zahn, Smoke, David Dolphin & the Dolphin Family, Troy Leonard, RéShaun Frear, Tammy Ford, Richard Pelzer, Chris Jackson, DeMarco Majors, Priya Scroggins, Derek Fleming, Maurice Jamal, Christalyn Wright, Scott Tepper, Desmond Richardson, Abdul Latif, Brie Miranda Bryant, Markel Smith, Lodric Collins, Robin Mark, MK Knight, Linda Belle, Tanya Harris, Gena Miller, Brandy Garris, Anahi Angeleone, Lace Halton, Duane Cramer, Kijana Wright, Mark-Anthony Edwards & B.Michael, Rahsaan Gandy, Fleur Lee, Ashlee Neal, Aisha & Danielle Moodie-Mills, Rashad Robinson….please know this is not in any order of importance – my brain is almost 40 and I am riding up to the deadline. LOVE YOU ALLLLLLLL! Thank you!

Sharon Gold, my copyeditor, you are the bomb. You elevated the book to the next level. Many more projects to come.

My Native family, we have shared so many laughs, cocktails, tears and a great bond of love, y'all the ones. Ary Tolerico, Michelle Milton, Turiya Minter, Brian Holiday, Belinda Munro & Nakia Hicks. Cheers!

To D.S.C.C. of Alpha Nu Chapter of Delta Sigma Theta Sorority, Inc., you already know. Point 5 in the house.

There are just too many people that have shaped my life and have helped me to realize this dream. If I have forgotten anyone please charge it to my credit card because it probably won't go through anyway. Thank you!

Finally, I would also like to also dedicate this book to my dear-friend, Nathan "Seven" Scott. You may be amongst the angels now, but your spirit lives on and you were the inspiration behind me having the courage to do this. Fly on silver bird! You have your wings now.

Gimlets and Patron shots for everybody!!!!!

Made in the USA
Charleston, SC
06 October 2015